Alex J. Cavanaugh

DANCING LEMUR PRESS, L.L.C.
Pikeville, North Carolina
www.dancinglemurpress.com

Copyright 2022 by Alex J. Cavanaugh

Published by Dancing Lemur Press, L.L.C.
P.O. Box 383, Pikeville, North Carolina, 27863-0383
www.dancinglemurpress.com

ISBN: 9781939844842

Printed in the United States of America

All rights reserved. No part of this publication may be reproduced, transmitted, or stored in a retrieval system in any form – either mechanically, electronically, photocopy, recording, or other – except for short quotations in printed reviews, without the permission of the publisher.

This book is a work of fiction. Any resemblance to actual events or persons, living or dead, is coincidental.

Cover design by C.R.W.

Publisher's Cataloging-in-Publication data: pending

To my wife and her endless patience while I'm off on this writing adventure.

Also by Alex J. Cavanaugh:

CassaStar

To pilot the fleet's finest ship...

Print ISBN 9780981621067

EBook ISBN 9780982713938

CassaFire

CassaStar was just the beginning...

Print ISBN 9780982713945

eBook ISBN 9780982713969

CassaStorm

A storm gathers across the galaxy...

Print ISBN 9781939844002

eBook ISBN 9781939844019

Dragon of the Stars

The ship of legends...

Print ISBN 9781939844064

EBook ISBN 9781939844057

"...calls to mind the youthful focus of Robert Heinlein's early military sf, as well as the excitement of space opera epitomized by the many Star Wars novels. Fast-paced military action and a youthful protagonist make this a good choice for both young adult and adult fans of space wars."

- Library Journal

PROLOGUE: CassaFate

CassaFate first appeared in Heroes of Phenomena, a collaboration of authors and musicians produced by Audiomachine.

A message from Drent!

Bassan scanned the note, eager to hear from his fellow Kintal friend. In five months, Drent would complete training on the planet Cassa. He could come home. The last line stopped Bassan cold.

'No guarantee I'll return to Tgren though.'

Damn.

His mother's voice rang in his head. *Time to eat!*

I'm coming, Bassan thought, replying in kind with his telepathic mind.

Bassan joined his parents. His father offered a nod as formal as the uniform he wore. His mother's smile offset the tone, and Bassan dove into his breakfast.

His father scooped a chunk of the thick Tgren dish in front of him. "Your counsel session is tomorrow?"

Bassan swallowed and reached for his drink. "Yes, sir."

"I understand you're in the top ten percent?"

"Cassan standards." Bassan shrugged off the accomplishment. "Top one percent Tgren though."

His mother smiled and Bassan sat up straighter.

"What matters are your Cassan scores," his father said. "Those determine acceptance to the Academy."

Bassan bristled and stared at his father. Eyes as grey as the hair on the man's head greeted him. The commander of the Cassan base presided now, leaving no room for argument.

But I can't leave Tgren. I'm linked forever with the

Kintal ship. It represents me, knows me. I can't lose the connection.

His father scooped another bite. "Your work here on Tgren's Kintal ship will definitely help."

Drent's message flashed in Bassan's mind.

No guarantee I'll return.

"I'm not going to Cassa."

The words dropped with an audible crash in the room.

"Not going to Cassa?" his father demanded. "Why would you pass up such an opportunity?"

"Because," Bassan said, mustering his courage, "I can attend the Tgren school here and complete my training faster."

His father rested his fist on the table. "The Cassan program may take longer, but you'll be accredited to work across the galaxy. The Tgren schooling is only accepted here. Don't narrow your opportunities."

"But I want to remain here." His chest tight, Bassan struggled to prevent his mental voice from projecting. Or his raging emotions.

"Bassan." His mother stretched her hand across the table. "I know you don't want to leave, but it's an enormous honor."

"I know," Bassan said, slumping in his chair. "But I can't leave the Tgren ship."

His father shoved his plate forward and arose. "We'll discuss it later."

Those words haunted Bassan all day.

Nobody understands me.

Even the prospect of his final class of the day didn't elicit joy. He rode his cycle to the Kintal ship in a daze. The glittering blue haze of ancient metal greeted him as he rounded the last corner. The sight of the ship, exposed and inviting, did little to lift his spirits.

Bassan located his instructor in the control room. Translating the once-lost language held scarce challenge for him. Not when his mix of Cassan and Tgren blood assisted him with his Kintal ancestors' language. But the class placed Bassan on the ship, and that pleased him.

He became aware of someone behind him. As he spun

around, the wide eyes of the senior science officer greeted him.

"I didn't mean to startle you," Officer Mevine said, holding up his thin hands.

"Sir!" Bassan straightened his posture. Drent's father deserved his respect. No one outside of the Kintal community knew more about this ship than Senior Officer Mevine.

"Your instructor said I could borrow you," Mevine said.

"Yes, sir. Of course."

Curious, Bassan followed. They traversed the glow of the corridor. The rings of blue light were the same in every hallway, but their route struck a chord. Even the ramp carried familiarity. He'd been here before.

The control room over the pods!

Excitement grew with each step. He'd not entered this area in ten years. Not since he'd touched a forbidden console, downloading a special code into his mind. Drent had warned him...

Bassan! Mevine thought, a patient smile coloring his lips. *You saved all eleven races because you held the code. I'm glad you touched that console.*

Why am I so bad at shielding my mind?

They entered the room and Bassan glanced to his left. That particular console sat in an alcove, its panel alive now with data. They strode past to a station at the end of the room. A curved screen dominated the wall, shimmering with light.

Mevine's hand waved over the console. "This system recorded the journey of your mother's ancestors to Tgren, including the period when the people disembarked. Would you like to see it?"

Bassan snapped to attention. The moment the Tgrens awoke from their long sleep and left their pods to begin a new life here? "Yes, please!"

Mevine ran his fingers across the crystal surface, tapping a sequence. He gestured to the metallic orb at the base. Nerves tingling, Bassan placed his hand over the cold ball.

The screen sparked to life. It grew dark and Bassan

leaned forward, excited to catch the first image. Streaks of green appeared, forming a pattern that trailed into the distance. The pods!

Dark forms moved, their thin bodies outlined against the green capsules. One passed across the sensor. The body's gentle curves glistened with moisture. A Tgren woman!

Bassan grinned. So realistic. He lifted his free hand to grasp the top of the console. He missed and staggered forward.

Wait a minute!

He no longer watched on a screen. He stood in the pod room itself.

What's happening?

He searched for the woman. She continued walking, following the others toward a distant yellow glow.

Wait!

His left foot came forward. He fought to maintain balance and swung his right foot. It was difficult to see in the gloom. And yet the glowing, empty pods stung his eyes. Dampness permeated the air, humid and thick, but dryer air beckoned ahead. Cleaner air. What surrounded him now reeked of recycled air and perspiration.

On cue, sweat dripped from his brow and fell on his bare arms. It stung.

He raised his hands to his face. Globs of a yellow-green substance covered his palm. The slime slithered down his arm, and Bassan realized his whole body was covered. His breath quickened.

"Bassan?"

The room faded. Bassan grasped for the nearest empty pod. He needed to reach that yellow glow. He had to get out.

"Bassan!"

Something wrapped around his wrist, severing the connection. He gasped and pulled his arm free. Bassan's eyes adjusted. He stood in the control room. Mevine leaned against the console, hands raised in warning. Bassan caught his breath and gasped.

"What happened?" Mevine said.

Bassan glanced at his hands. They glistened with sweat, but the slime was gone.

"I was there," he said.

"Where?"

"When the Tgrens were leaving the ship."

"Bassan, that's impossible."

He lowered his hands and faced Officer Mevine. "Sir, I was there. It was hot. And humid. It even smelled damp. It was dark, and yet my eyes burned from the pod's light. And this yellow-green slime covered my body..."

Mevine's mouth opened. "How could you know that?"

Bassan clenched his fists. "Because I was there. I tell you, I'm connected to this ship. Ever since I touched that console, I've felt the bond. It remembers the first Kintal. It remembers me!"

The science officer's gaze shifted. Bassan spun around. The cold eyes of his father greeted him, and Bassan's enthusiasm wavered.

His father stepped closer and peered at the console. Placing his hands behind his back, the commander turned his attention to Bassan.

"Wait for me on the first level."

Father, please...

Now.

His father's mental voice left no room for argument. Bassan's heart tightened and he raced for the exit. He barreled down the ramp and didn't stop until he'd reached the pod room entrance. He grasped the edge of the door frame and sighed, clinging to his vision.

I was there. Among the Tgrens leaving this ship. Damn, if I'm forced to leave, I'll never have another opportunity.

Bassan stared at the empty room, lost in his cheerless thoughts. A touch on his mind caused him to jump. He turned and a steel gaze greeted him.

Father, he thought, dropping his chin. He didn't trust his voice yet.

You really witnessed Tgrens leaving this room?

The question startled him. Bassan met his father's eyes. For once, they didn't appear so unforgiving.

I saw them! he thought. Bassan pulled his fists to his

chest. *I was with the Tgrens as they left the pods. Father, the ship knew it was me. I believe it could show me more.*

Bassan...

His name shot through the fiber of his being. Bassan stepped closer and straightened his shoulders.

Father, you trusted me before. Please, let me stay on Tgren. Let me fulfill the role this ship has given me.

His father shook his head. Bassan steeled himself for disappointment.

"Bassan, I want the best for you," his father said. "And that means giving you the opportunity to pursue your own goals. I had to fight for my future and prove myself." He paused, his stoic expression softening. "You can attend the Tgren school."

Shock rippled through Bassan and his mouth fell open. *I can stay?*

Yes. This is where you belong.

Weight fell from his shoulders. Bassan stepped forward and hesitated. His father offered a wry grin. Bassan accepted the invitation and hugged his father.

If your mother asks, it was my idea, his father thought.

Bassan smiled. *I won't say a word.*

1

"We give him back to the desert. Say-vee!"

Bassan dug fingernails into his palms. Unable to look away, he focused on his uncle and mother holding the urn high. His mother closed her eyes and Bassan wished to do the same. Nausea welled up in his guts and he shifted his gaze to the urn.

Such ornate carvings. Fitting for a former prefect.

The urn tipped. The contents flew into the wind and away from those gathered. The ashes swirled in the breeze, spreading wider with each passing moment. The sight mesmerized him. Say-vee. Transformed. Changed. A life so full reduced to such tiny particles...

A gasp tore his attention from the ashes. Tears streamed down his mother's face. Seeing her resolve broken, Bassan's slipped. Great-uncle Orellan was truly gone. Unable to breathe, or even move, his body stiffened. Trapped in the moment, Bassan reached out with his mind.

Fingers curled around his and Bassan returned the grasp with gratitude. The delicate touch on his mind matched the hold on his hand. He closed his eyes. Sirella.

I am here, she thought.

Unwilling to show weakness in front of Sirella, he took a deep breath and opened his eyes. The urn now in place atop the pillar, his mother and uncle stood facing each other. His Uncle Istaner's expression remained guarded, but Bassan noted the quiver in his chin. He dared not look at his mother again though. Intent on the urn and the sandy-red hills behind it, Bassan held still.

"We pray you might receive and care for him until we meet again."

Emanating from the far right, the presiding cleric's

words landed with a dull thud in Bassan's heart. Until they met again? It would be a long, long time.

A soft moan escaped from his mother, and his father stepped forward. Uttering a sob, his mother fell into his arms. Bassan dropped his chin and fought against his own tears. Orellan might have been Istaner's father, but his mother regarded the man as her own father, and he'd acted as both great-uncle and grandfather toward Bassan.

So unfair. Why do people have to die so soon? Maybe our ancestors knew how to cheat death a few years.

A hand curled around his arm, pulling him close. Comfort poured from Sirella. Bassan let his head drop against hers. *And why does it have to hurt so much?*

It hurts because you loved him. There's no shame in that.

Sirella's thoughts filled him. Bassan clung to her gentle and caring support, grateful for her presence and the ability to communicate in private with their minds.

Still hard to watch it upset my mother so much.

She offered no response, only continued comfort. As she'd done for years. So much quiet strength in his girlfriend's tiny frame. Bassan needed to draw upon that.

He took a deep breath and gave her fingers a squeeze. *I need to be strong for my mother,* he thought, releasing her hand and stepping forward. *Thanks.*

Bassan approached his parents, determined to show a brave face. His mother moved away from his father, her tear-stained face turning to her son. With a sob, she wrapped her arms around his shoulders. Bassan held his mother close. Years of devotion and support flashed through his mind and he tried to convey those feelings to his mother. Her arms tightened.

You were always his favorite.

Stunned, Bassan didn't know how to respond. His mother didn't appear to need an answer, much to his relief. Sighing deeply, she released him and stepped back. Bassan's father pulled her close and she wiped away her tears. Resignation and acceptance flowed from his mother's thoughts and Bassan wished he felt the same. He didn't deal well with loss. Or change.

Sirella fell in beside him as the crowd retreated from the funeral shrine. Most of Ktren's population had turned out for the ceremony. A feast was planned afterwards to celebrate Orellan's life.

Not that I feel like celebrating.

Use the time to remember him, then.

He fumbled for her hand. *You always know what to say.*

She squeezed his fingers in response, the digits so petite in his hand. *My mother's family always spent time reflecting on the deceased afterward, sharing stories to uplift and adventures to honor. Your great-uncle was the prefect for many years. He touched countless lives. There will be much to share about him this evening.*

Is that a Kintal tradition?

I'm not sure. It could be Arellen.

Sharing stories. My great-uncle accomplished so much in his life. Will people have time to discuss even half the events?

That sent his thoughts down a new path.

I wonder what people would say about me? 'He was a quiet kid who saved the eleven races when he was ten'?

Bassan observed the throng of people around them, most of whom knew him for that single event fifteen years ago. And outside of him being the commander's son, they knew little else.

Yeah, that probably sums up my life.

* * *

"You're stepping down as commander?" Bassan said. He reached for the kitchen counter behind him, the news catching him by surprise. His father had commanded the Cassan base on Tgren for most of Bassan's life.

"Son, it's time," his father said, running fingers through grey hair. Bassan stared at his father's head, watching the pale strands fall into place.

When did that happen?

"I scaled back my duties years ago to spend more time with you and your mother. But it's time I step down and focus my energies on her. Neither of us is getting any younger. And I want my final years spent making your mother happy."

A force hit Bassan's chest. "Father, you're not...?"

His father waved his hand and shook his head. "No, I'm fine."

"Mother?"

"She's also fine. I want to give her everything I possibly can in our last years, though."

Bassan's arms dropped to his sides. Last years? His great-uncle's funeral the day before filled his mind.

I'm not ready to lose either of you.

His father smiled. Bassan gritted his teeth and brought up his shields. Too late, of course.

"We're not going anywhere for a good many years," his father said, his tone soothing. "But considering recent events, I need to give her more time. And that means resigning as commander."

Bassan's fists clenched but he nodded in acceptance. His father approached and grasped his shoulder. The lines around his eyes deepened with his wry smile.

"When you have a mate, you'll understand."

"Yeah," Bassan said, his thoughts straying to Sirella. A fellow Kintal, Piten's daughter loved him. Bassan cared immensely for the thin, pale girl. Her adoring eyes greeted him with affection the first time they met and never faltered in their admiration, even after fifteen years. They were not committed mates though.

His father nodded and turned away. Bassan's mind returned to the present.

"Will you stay here?" he said, his words tumbling out.

His father snapped to attention. "Of course. This is our home. I won't take your mother's heart away from Tgren. Or my own."

"Yours?"

Standing straighter, he crossed his arms. "Cassa was never my home. Tgren is where I belong. Despite its damn sand penetrating every crack and seal."

Bassan smiled. His father had long complained about the gritty dust that permeated life on Tgren. Came with living on a half-desert planet.

"Our family and friends are here. You are here," his

father said, placing extra emphasis on the word *you*. "With your special connection with the ancient Kintal ship, I know you're not going anywhere. Neither shall we."

"You know I'm not leaving Tgren."

That's a change I can't handle at all.

Bassan exited his parents' dwelling and paused. Desert winds caught his face. Heat curled around his cheeks, blowing the shaggy strands of hair from his sight. Parched sand burnt his nose. The glow of the late afternoon sun, vibrant in the clear, dry air, caused him to squint.

He ducked his head and strode to his desert rider. Hunkering over the vehicle, Bassan started the engines and blasted off when they attained the appropriate charge. He couldn't reach the sanctuary of his own home fast enough.

Not a chance I'm leaving Tgren! Not when the Kintal ship shows me so much. I wouldn't give up slipping into the past for anything. Viewing previous worlds through the eyes of our ancestors—that's the reason I stayed here for training rather than be shipped off to Cassa five years ago.

Bassan sailed past the Cassan base checkpoint. He careened through the streets of Tgren, mindful of pedestrians but determined to reach his destination in record time. Despite his frequent journeys down this path, he tried to increase his speed every time. The pale sand structures flashed by in a blur. The monotonous shapes and tone, causing one street to look like the others, might confuse some. Bassan knew the journey home all too well. After five years, nothing obscured the route.

He pulled up outside a two-story dwelling. Securing his desert bike in its alcove, he raced up the stairs to his flat. He hesitated at the door, his hand hovering over the press plate. All Tgren residences now boasted one, an electronic scanning device for entry, and his building received theirs recently. The merging of Cassan and Tgren culture now complete, the former manual locks represented the last vestige of Tgren customs. While Bassan appreciated the convenience, he wondered at its implication. What else would be lost of Tgren's history and culture?

Think how much we lost of the Kintal way of life.

He shoved his hand against the device and waited for the chime. His door slid aside, and he entered the cool room. Slapping his gloves on the counter, he then brushed his hair with vigorous strokes, freeing the loose sand.

Father's right, this stuff is everywhere.

Fighting the itch across his scalp, Bassan strode into his media and entertainment room. Tgrens called it the receiving room, designed for guests and socializing. Since he rarely entertained guests outside of Drent and Tarn, the focus of the room turned to multimedia and the center of all things visual and sound. With its windows, narrow though they might be, facing the mountain slope and open desert, Bassan found it the perfect place to relax.

Slumping onto the dark couch, a sharp contrast to the room's sandy orange walls, he dropped his head against the cushions. The softness comforted him, and he closed his eyes.

"Music! Playlist ninety-three."

A swelling chorus of music and vocals filled the room, its sound as alien as those who created it. Bassan drew strength from the rhythmic melody. His shoulders unknotted, and he smiled.

My first Kintal composition. And all from my memory.

His thoughts traveled back to that day. His unique connection with the old Kintal ship provided information in a manner no other could experience—a dreamlike state placing him in the body of one of his ancestors. In that moment, he gained full access to the person's surroundings. Bassan often reached back into Tgren history before the ancient ship brought his mother's people to the planet. Those moments, experiencing life as another race, thrilled him. It also revealed new data regarding the eleven races, which included his mixed-breed heritage, the Kintals. A blend of all races, people today knew little about them outside of the ten ancient ships. One such journey back placed him in the middle of a celebration. And on that fateful spring morning, he heard Kintal music for the first time.

His grin grew.

And I worried Mevine to death about replicating it.

After badgering everyone connected with the alien ship, including his father, Tgren musicians came in to listen to the music playing in his head. Replicating it required Cassan technology, and a Fesellan called in to add the final touches lifted the piece to perfection. His ancestors, his people, would be proud of the results.

But your music didn't last. You sacrificed it all to save the other ten races. You let your own culture crumble, the particles lost in the winds of space. Why? Was survival of the others more important than your own? What about those of us who are Kintal now? Who are we, really?

No answer came. Just the emptiness of always wondering.

A beep penetrated the swelling music. His eyes flew open. "Music off."

Bassan pried himself from the couch and located his tablet. He tapped the device, and Drent's grinning face filled the screen, quite the feat for those narrow cheeks.

"About time!" his friend said. "What are you doing tomorrow evening?"

Bassan blinked and composed his thoughts, the Kintal song continuing to haunt his mind. "Nothing."

"Great! You, me, and Tarn. Our bikes and the North Face. We're going to conquer that mountain."

"Are you serious?"

"Of course," Drent said, his forehead crinkling in disbelief. "It's about time we completed that trail. Didn't we traverse the entire length of Echo Canyon last week? It's time. Do or die."

"There's a reason we haven't conquered it yet," Bassan said, the narrow path and sheer drop-offs swirling in his head.

"Which means it's time. Come on, when's the last time you took a risk?"

"It's been a while..."

"Tarn's game. Let's do it."

Upon hearing of Tarn's commitment, Bassan knew he couldn't back down and agreed.

"You let me know when you're free. We'll meet at the

base and tackle the trail from there," said Drent.

"Will do."

Drent pointed a finger at Bassan and winked. The transmission ended, the black void a stark contrast to the energy filling the screen not a second earlier. Shaking his head, Bassan dropped his tablet onto the counter.

"You're going to meet your match one day, Drent."

Spoken out loud, that thought troubled him. He expected Tarn to take chances, but at twenty-seven and two years older than Bassan, Drent's wild lifestyle and penchant for risky behavior concerned him. He stared at his tablet for a moment, his fingers tracing the edge of the device. Taking a deep breath, he shook his head.

Is it the Kintal in you talking? The new or the old? Damn, with life in such a state of turmoil and change, I don't know anymore.

I don't even know me anymore.

* * *

The wind whipped his face despite the face guard and goggles. Grit from the trail pelted his skin, the sand tiny pinpricks of discomfort. It even rammed up his nose, threatening a sneeze. He ignored the irritations and focused on the bike in front of him.

Bassan found himself in the rear as they raced up the North Face. He gave up competing for the front spot early, letting Drent and Tarn battle it out. While this meant he choked on their dust, at least he wasn't responsible for leading the group. All he had to do was follow.

You always follow, dummy. One of these days, I need to be more assertive and get in front.

Enjoying the view? Drent thought.

Your ass? Not really.

Drent's mental laughter filled his mind. Bassan gripped the handles tighter, determined not to let his friend get to him. He never led the way. Not even when they were kids. Older and wiser, Drent always took control. Even Tarn challenged Drent more than Bassan, and Sirella's brother was younger than either of them.

Yeah, I definitely need to be more assertive.

They rounded a wide curve. Bassan focused on the

trail in front of his vehicle. The sun now sank behind the crest, casting deep shadows across the path. The final stretch lay before them. A narrow sweep with a tight banking curve. And at their current speed, a dangerous obstacle.

Tarn, slow down.

Piten's son glanced back. Resistance met Bassan's mind before compliance set in. Their headlong flight eased, and Tarn guided them safely through the curve. Bassan's gaze remained locked on Drent's back as they spun out onto the crest of North Face. The sunlight hit him full force and Bassan blinked.

Dead ahead. We did it. Tarn thought.

Damn right! Drent thought.

Still blinded by the sun, Bassan eased off the accelerator. His comrades would reach the top first anyway.

A jolt of panic from Tarn shot through Bassan's chest. Squinting against the bright light, he focused on the lead bike. Twisting at an unnatural angle, the bike and rider went down. They skidded along the trail, throwing up rocks and dust. Tarn clung tight, curled in a ball. He skidded to a stop in the middle of the path.

Drent!

Whether due to the setting sun or his inner exuberance, Drent failed to react in time. His bike faltered, teetering left and right in his approach to the fallen Tarn. Tossing his efforts to his left, Drent attempted to skirt Tarn's bike. His wheels spun, sliding him closer to the edge.

Bassan's breath caught in his throat. Drent's bike caught the edge of the cliff.

His friend yanked hard. The wheels kicked up, lifting Drent and bike from the ground. When they came down, the bike went into an incredible spin. Drent didn't so much as hang on as be tossed around by the rotations. Bike and rider flipped many times before skittering to the edge of the cliff.

Bassan jammed on his brakes and stared in horror. Tarn leapt to his feet and rushed forward.

Drent's bike teetered on the edge, his friend tangled in the wreckage. Tarn slid into the rocks and reached for

Drent.

"Bassan!" he said, grasping his friend's arm.

A chill shot through Bassan's body. It rooted him to the spot. He opened his mouth, but no sound emerged.

Drent's bike rocked, twisting his body. The vehicle tipped to the left and tumbled over the edge. Drent cried out and the bike pulled his body over the cliff.

"Bassan!"

The sight and Tarn's desperate plea shot through Bassan.

Move, dummy.

He launched himself onto Tarn's back and reached for Drent's arm. At that moment, his friend vanished.

"Drent!" Tarn's scream exploded in Bassan's head.

No!

Pulling himself forward, Bassan looked down. His stomach knotted. Drent's bike tumbled down the cliff, parts exploding off it with each impact. Mesmerized by the horrifying sight, Bassan could only watch it summersault its way to the bottom.

Tarn grasped his arm and pointed. "Drent."

He peered straight down. Their friend lay ten feet below them on a wide ledge. Drent's low cry welled deep from within, wavering like a wounded animal, and his upper body curled. A mental wave of excruciating pain burst forth. One leg remained still, already twisted in an unnatural position. Blood soaked his pants below the knee.

Drent's alive!

Relief, followed by a wave of nausea, hit Bassan. A chill rolled down his chest. Mouth open, he stared at his friend, at a loss.

"Don't move," called Tarn. He yanked off his goggles and turned to Bassan. "We need to call for help."

Call for help. Those words snapped Bassan out of his momentary shock. He reached out to the first person who came to mind.

Father!

The response came within a second. *Bassan, what's wrong?*

It's Drent. We were riding on the North Face and he wiped out. He fell off onto a ledge. He's injured. Bad.

I'll contact medical at once. Show me your location.

Bassan sat up and spun around, probably faster than needed. Slow enough for his father to pinpoint their location though.

Don't move. Help is on the way.

Without thinking, Bassan nodded. Tarn flashed a puzzled look.

"Medical is on its way," Bassan explained.

"Good." Tarn peered over the edge. "Drent!" he called, his mental voice as thunderous as his physical one. "Help is on the way. Don't move."

Pain radiated from Drent and he reached out one arm, fingers clawing at the ground. Bassan winced.

Please don't move, Drent.

Are you all right?

His father's question calmed Bassan. *Scraped and scared to death, but I'm all right. So's Tarn.*

Watch for the medical ship. They'll be there soon. I won't be far behind.

You're coming as well?

Of course.

That knowledge comforted him. Bassan's attention returned to Drent. Anguish still rolled from his friend's thoughts, pounding at Bassan's senses.

"Help will be here soon, Drent," Tarn called. He elbowed Bassan, his charcoal face scrunched tight. *Talk to him. Keep his mind occupied until medical gets here.*

Damn!

He shifted, easing the pressure of rocks pressing into his knees. Yanking his goggles off, Bassan peered down at Drent. His friend's face lay buried against the ground.

It's all right, Drent. I know it hurts. But it will be all right. My father is sending a medical ship. They'll take care of you.

Drent clawed at the loose gravel around him but didn't look up. *Damn, it burns worse than fire.*

I know. Think of something else.

A new wave of excruciating agony rolled from Drent.

CASSADARK

Hurts too bad.

The sight of his friend's bike tumbling down the mountain surfaced in Bassan's mind and he relayed the thought to Drent. *Bet your bike feels worse.*

Drent opened one eye—only for a moment—but Bassan knew his friend caught the implied humor.

"There they are."

Bassan followed Tarn's gaze. The medical transport raced toward them, resembling a soaring bird on the wind. The hold around his chest eased.

They're here, Drent. Not long now.

The ship rose over the edge of the cliff and hovered above them. The new design placed the thrusts around the edge of the craft, but dust still stirred in the air. Bassan squinted and ducked his head. He and Tarn moved out of the way, coughing fine sand. The warmth of the vessel grew closer, and a large hatch opened in her underbelly. Bassan and Tarn continued to shuffle farther away, and the vessel dropped even lower. The left side settled on edge of the cliff, blocking their view.

Bassan scooted back a smidgen more. Gravel crunched at his back and he slammed into something solid. He dropped to his knees.

They'll get him, Tarn thought, sinking beside him.

Bassan nodded, unable to speak. He grasped his knees tight.

Please save him...

The medical shuttle's door opened. A man stepped out onto the cliff and approached them at a trot, a small pack in his hands.

"Are you injured?"

Bassan found himself staring up at the senior emergency officer. He knew most Cassan officers on sight but had never met the man.

"Are you injured?" the man repeated, kneeling and grasping Bassan's arm.

"No," he said.

The officer's attention shifted to Tarn. "How about you?"

Tarn coughed, dust continuing to swirl in the air. "No,

sir. Just scraped up a bit."

"Then go wait by your bikes. A second ship is on the way."

The man returned to the ship and the hatch closed.

Come on, let's get out of their way.

Tarn pulled on his arm. Bassan scrambled to his feet, keeping his head down. Following his friend, he staggered toward their fallen bikes. Adrenaline ebbing, his feet shuffled and dragged across the rocky trail. Bassan reached his bike and attempted to lift it. Still shaking from the ordeal, he couldn't hold it steady. Giving up, he dropped to his knees beside it. Tarn followed suit.

They regained their breath, watching the medical ship with anticipation. Bassan didn't know how long it would take to retrieve Drent from the ledge.

Why didn't I move faster?

The vessel's engine whine shifted. They watched in silent fascination as the medical ship began to rise, its lower hatch sealed. Bassan then caught sight of another ship approaching, one splashed in Tgren reds.

"That must be our ride," Tarn said.

The second, larger vessel swung wide left and out of the medical ship's way. The engines blasted and the medical ship dropped over the edge and into the valley below. Despite a successful retrieval, Bassan's heart plummeted with the vessel.

Drent...

Bassan!

His father's voice rang loud in his head. *Yes, sir?*

We can't land here. You and Tarn will have to go back down the trail. About halfway to the bottom, there's a plateau. We'll pick you up there. Are your vehicles in working order?

I believe so. "We'll have to meet them farther down the trail," Bassan said to Tarn.

Piten's son yanked on his bike. Despite his small size, he righted it easily. Tarn studied the body and nodded. "No damage other than scratches. I can ride down."

I'm glad one of us can.

Bassan took a deep breath and grabbed the handles

and pulled. His arms shook, but he managed to right the vehicle. Swinging his leg over the seat, he dropped down hard, and the whole bike trembled from the force. He flexed his fingers.

"You all right?"

Bassan closed his eyes and nodded.

"You go first. I'll follow. Watch your speed," Tarn said.

With the push of a button, the engine came alive. Air blasted out around the thick wheels, gearing the vehicle up for motion. Pulling the goggles over his eyes, he leaned low and throttled the engine. The bike lurched forward.

Easy! Bassan swallowed the lump in his throat and reduced the vehicle to a slow pace. His arms shook and he trusted the bounce of the rough terrain hid the bike's wobble.

Fortunately, they didn't have far to go. They swung around an outcropping and the shuttle greeted them, engines roaring. The plateau provided enough room for the ramp. Bassan's father stood in the doorway and he gestured them forward.

Bassan eased up to the ramp and switched to hover. He leapt from the seat and pushed the vehicle forward, and his father grasped the handle and pulled. The ramp vibrated under his feet, spurring him to move faster.

"Secure it at the far end," his father said, twisting the handle to the left.

Bassan shut off the engine and angled the bike into the shuttle. Designed for cargo, this model boasted a large hold where he could secure the vehicle. With the last of his energy, Bassan pushed the bike to the far wall. Removing his goggles, he grabbed a strap and dropped to the floor to secure it. Tarn entered behind him and did the same.

His fingers fumbled with the last strap. The shuttle moved and the clasp pulled free. Bassan reached for it and his father appeared at his side. Together, they secured the bike.

They helped one another up. Bassan met his father's gaze, his chest heaving from exertion and apprehension. His father frowned before pulling Bassan in for a rough hug. Relief flowed from his mind and Bassan took comfort in his father's concern.

The shuttle shifted, pulling him away from his father.

"We need to take our seats," his father announced, one hand still grasping Bassan's shoulder.

They staggered forward to the two seats by the door. His father made sure they were secure before returning to the cockpit. The shuttle vibrated under his feet, shaking his already jarred nerves. Grasping the harness tight in his hands, Bassan leaned his head back and closed his eyes.

I hate flying.

He focused on the hum of the engine in hopes it would sooth his agitation. It partially succeeded. Bassan couldn't shake his surroundings though, no matter how hard he tried. The tight walls, the mechanical smell—it all reeked of flying.

No longer consumed by apprehension, his mind allowed other forces to creep in. A pounding sense of guilt rang through strongest. But not his own. Following the source, Bassan realized it emanated from Tarn.

He opened his eyes and rolled his head to the right. *You all right?*

Tarn gave him a quick glance, eyes darker than his complexion, and nodded.

Liar.

Tarn dropped his chin and rubbed his forehead. *Drent almost died today because of me.*

He didn't though.

Yeah, but if I hadn't lost control and gone down on the trail... Tarn's thought trailed off.

No, he almost died because of me.

Bassan grasped the harness tighter, searching for words. *He'll be all right.*

Tarn's chin dipped once but he continued to stare at the floor.

Crap, idiot. What would Drent say? It wasn't Tarn's fault. It was mine.

Bassan took a quick breath. *Drent's always complaining nothing challenges him anymore. Well today, you gave him a doozy of a challenge. And when he's better, we'll give him grief for flopping so badly.*

Tarn tilted his head, the barest trace of a smile on his lips. *You give him grief. Drent can still kick my ass.*

His observation brought a grin to Bassan's face. Adulthood had failed to add a lot of pounds to Tarn's thin frame. Too much Arellen in him while his Vindicarn heritage revealed itself in his dark skin rather than a bigger frame. Drent could indeed kick his friend's butt.

You have no reason to feel remorse. It was my inability to react that sent Drent over the cliff.

The shuttle landed and his father rejoined them in the main compartment.

"We're at the medical facility," he announced, opening the hatch. Light flooded the cabin. "You need to be cleared first."

Bassan's mouth opened in protest as he rose to his feet. The look in his father's eyes caused him to remain silent though.

"Someone will be here shortly to get a full account of the accident from you. Once you've been released, you can retrieve your bikes from the hangar. Check with the senior officer on duty. He'll know where they are stored."

"Yes, sir," Bassan and Tarn said in unison. Bassan followed Tarn, his steps less steady than when he boarded. His father's hand grasped his shoulder and Bassan paused at the door.

"Glad you're all right."

Bassan nodded. "Thanks. I hope Drent's all right."

Our medical staff is top notch. He'll be fine.

Bassan turned and trudged down the ramp.

Yeah, he better be. I don't know what I'll do if my best friend dies because I couldn't move my ass fast enough.

* * *

"You wanted to see me, sir?"

The senior science officer looked up from his work. He blinked and widened his eyes. "Yes, Bassan, I did. Come in."

Bassan slipped into the office between two desks, turning sideways to do so. If one could call it an office. Mevine's rank warranted him a separate room, but the man preferred to work in the lab with the rest of his crew. Surrounding himself with computers on every side gave the illusion of a private work area.

Mevine punched a couple more buttons and leaned back in his chair. The lines on his face and bags under his eyes were nothing new, but they appeared more pronounced today. Like Bassan's father, Mevine's dark, curly hair bore an equal amount of grey. Stress accounted for some of it because no one worked harder or longer hours than Mevine. One of the many reasons Bassan's father relied so much on the man.

Mevine rubbed his forehead and allowed the chair to swallow his wiry frame further. "I want to thank you again for saving Drent's life," he said.

Bassan shook his head. "Tarn's the one who reacted first. I just helped."

"It took the two of you. My son's alive thanks to you and Tarn. I appreciate that, more than you will ever know."

"Drent's my best friend," Bassan said. He figured that summed it all up. "I was going to visit him today, if you think he's up to it."

Mevine nodded and leaned forward. "He'd appreciate a visit. Mind you, he's still groggy from the medicine."

"I won't make him say or do anything he'll regret later."

The senior officer tendered a faint smile. Bassan might poke at his friend, but he'd never do anything mean. However, he entertained no doubts if the roles reversed, Drent wouldn't hesitate to make a fool of him.

"Was there anything else, sir?"

Officer Mevine sat up straighter. "Yes. Actually, that's not why I called you in. It's about the Tech 381 conference."

Bassan recalled seeing details about the conference several weeks ago. "The one on Procura Space Station in Charren territory?"

"Yes, that's the one. It begins in three days, and I was to give a lecture on accessing Kintal technology. I'm afraid I'm not going to be able to attend now."

"Because of Drent? I'm sorry, sir."

Mevine waved his hands in the air. "Now, Drent's a grown man and well beyond the fussing of parents. But the accident shook up my mate. I don't think it would be prudent for me to leave tomorrow."

"I'm sorry you'll miss the conference, sir."

"I've been to many conferences. It's the lecture that concerns me though. It was the first one to fill up. Everyone wants information on the Kintals and the best way to access data through their ship's computers."

"We've shared most of our findings though, haven't we, sir?"

"Yes, but scientists want access to firsthand knowledge and experience." Mevine paused and clasped his hands together in his lap. "So, I'm sending you in my place."

The room exploded, sending shards of panic into Bassan's skin. Every organ in his body sank toward the floor, threatening to pull him to his knees. Bassan grasped the edge of the desk.

"M-m-me, sir?"

Mevine's eyebrows came together, puzzlement drifting from his thoughts. "Yes, you. Bassan, almost everything we've learned about Kintal history is from your research. I've based my lecture on it, including your unique experiences. You could probably do the talk better than I could and provide the audience with genuine, firsthand involvement."

The floor continued to battle with Bassan's body even as Mevine's words scrambled his brain. Give a lecture? Him? And halfway across known space? It meant traveling on a ship. He hated flying...

A hand grasped his elbow and brought Bassan back. "Are you all right?" Mevine said.

"Sir, I... I'm honored you would ask me to take your place. But sending me to Procura Space Station—"

"Is the wise thing to do. You know the material and you'll have all my notes. You'll have plenty of time to study and prepare during the trip."

"The trip," Bassan began before fear cut his words short.

"You've been working so hard and deserve a break. You need some time off world. It will do you good."

"I've never been away from Tgren, though. Well, once.

But it wasn't fun."

"That's why this is a grand opportunity for you." Mevine cocked his head back, offering a crooked but genuine smile. "Best to get out there while you're young. I traveled to many planets before settling here. A little wandering might prepare you in the same way."

"I can go wander the desert instead."

The senior officer's smile faded a touch and he straightened in his seat. "Bassan, I need you to do this for me. I can't leave my mate alone after Drent was injured so badly. She needs me here."

The muscles in Bassan's body stiffened.

He's injured because me. Crap. I can't say no.

Innards sinking further, he nodded. "I'll go, sir."

Mevine clapped his hands together. "Excellent! I will send you all the files and my notes. And the full itinerary. You're one of the first speakers, so once you've completed your session, you'll have ample time to listen to the other talks. I'm sure you'll come back bursting with new ideas."

If I don't burst before I get there.

Bassan plodded his way to the medical center, his thoughts heavier than his boots, which dragged like lead across the ground. He sought Drent's room and paused outside the open door. He'd come to cheer up his friend. How was he going to manage that now?

And do I tell him he fell because of me?

He peered around the corner. Drent rested alone, his eyes closed. Loath to wake him, Bassan took a cautious step forward. The corners of his friend's lips twitched.

You couldn't sneak up on an argan lizard if it was dead.

A bark of laughter escaped Bassan. Those rotten, petite vermin who invaded every home? *Is that so? Are you saying you are beyond dead?*

Drent's smile deepened. *Ass!*

Bassan drew closer and his friend opened his eyes. Fresh scars cut across his face, and his leg lay wrapped tight. But considering his tumble and subsequent fall, it could be worse. Drent raised his free hand and Bassan gave it a gentle but firm shake.

How are you feeling?

Like a dead argan.

Well, you're not dead, so get over yourself.

Drent snorted. *Better than yesterday. I'll be here a couple more days though.*

Bassan shoved his hands in his pockets. *Just glad you're still with us.*

I have you and Tarn to thank.

The tip of a dagger poked at his heart. *Yeah, well, save your thanks for Tarn. It was his quick thinking.*

But it took both of you.

Guilt flushed through him and he shifted his stance. He considered telling Drent the truth but couldn't bring himself to utter the words.

I still should've reacted faster. Damn, I don't know what to do in a crisis.

Bassan clenched his teeth.

And here Mevine is about to send me across the galaxy…

Where are you going?

Bassan stared at Drent.

He heard? Damn my crappy shielding.

He cleared his throat. *Your father is sending me to the conference on Procura Space Station in his place. I leave tomorrow.*

About time you got away from Tgren.

About time? Bassan's eyes widened. *Need I remind you of my trip to Vindi and how I nearly died?*

You're going to a conference. Unless you do something stupid, how could you possibly die there?

I don't know.

Then stop worrying and go. Besides, you don't want that first trip of yours into space to be your sole claim to fame, do you?

Bassan dropped his gaze to the floor, annoyed by the accusation. The trip to the Vindicarn home world to deliver the code in his head sat many years in the past. That code saved the eleven races from annihilation by the probe. What had he done since then? He squeezed his hands tight, hoping his shield held back the thought.

You'll have a great time. What could be holding you

back? Sirella?

"Sirella?" Bassan snapped to attention. *No, I haven't even talked to her. I guess I should let her know I'm going.*

Yeah, you should. Bassan, come on. You two are practically mates.

What? No! We're not mates. Not even close.

Really?

Really!

Drent closed his eyes and chuckled. *You'll figure it out one day.*

Bassan suppressed the urge to pound his fists with impatience. What did Drent know? Well, usually more than he did.

His friend yawned. *Have a good trip. Sorry, I think the drugs are kicking in. I'll see you when you get back.*

All right. When I get back.

Bassan touched his friend's arm. Drent's fingers twitched as if reaching for something but grew motionless. Eyes closed, his head rolled to one side. Bassan slipped out of the room, still fighting feelings of guilt.

I should've told you...

* * *

"Bassan, it's such a wonderful opportunity."

Sirella's enthusiasm added weight to his burdens.

But I'm not grateful for it. I should be, but I'm not. What's wrong with me?

She embraced him in a fierce hug. *I'll miss you. So much. But I know you can't pass this up. It will mean so much for your career.*

Shame crushed him further. She always thought of him first.

And why am I not more grateful for you? I'm a double idiot, I guess.

Before Bassan could respond, she planted a firm kiss on his lips. His troubles took a back seat in a hurry.

She pulled away and stroked his cheek. *You just come back to me. Safely. And then you can tell me all about your adventures.*

I'll do my best.

You always do.

Sirella smiled, pride beaming from her thoughts and her eyes. Those big, beautiful Kintal eyes. Despite everything, Bassan could not suppress a grin. The girl lit up his world.

The night air crept inside his jacket during his walk home. Bassan gazed up at the sky, the stars hidden by the glow of the city lights. The black expanse loomed over him and his shoulders drooped.

Sirella's parting kiss lingered on his lips. Enticing.

Now I don't want to leave. Maybe Drent's right. We're closer than I want to admit.

He turned down a side street. The complex housing his quarters drew closer. He paused at the entrance, his gaze straying again to the sky. Over the crest of the mountain, Tgren's smallest moon greeted him. Such a familiar sight. The last time he'd witness her rising for a couple weeks. Bassan's stomach knotted.

Drent's probably right about Sirella. He's certainly right about my first trip. I doubt this one will shake anyone's world though.

Bassan slung his pack over his shoulder and exited what had been his tiny quarters for the past few days. Several people trotted past him, their rapid strides and smiles conveying anticipation. Taking a deep breath of recycled ship air, he settled his pack and straightened his shoulders. Bassan stepped forward and joined the crowd bound for the ship's exit. He kept his gaze forward, his mind replaying the material provided by Mevine. After five days of little else to do but recite his talk, Bassan figured he could recite it in his sleep.

If I talk slow enough, there won't be time for questions. Then I can get out of there without making an ass of myself.

Five minutes later, he strode down the ramp and into the receiving area. The guard scanned his badge and cleared Bassan to the next area. He entered the room, packed with bodies and information stations, and searched for an open unit. An Arellen on the far side cleared his screen and reached for his bag. Bassan scurried to secure the station before anyone noticed its availability.

He scanned his badge and entered a code. Details regarding the conference and its location filled the screen. He made note of the building, unsure how he'd get there, let alone find it on this massive space station. Before panic set in, Bassan noticed a message waiting for him.

'Welcome to Procura Space Station, Officer Bassan. We are pleased you have arrived. An escort from Tech 381 will be there shortly.'

"That's a relief," he mumbled. He cleared the screen and followed the signs pointing toward the exit.

Bassan walked what felt like the length of the Tgren base before he reached the exit. He marched through the open glass doors, overheated and grinding his teeth. His step faltered when he got his first look at the station.

The ceiling rose far above him, its light casting a sun-like glow. Most of the buildings towered over him, eclipsing every structure on Tgren, yet none blocked the strong light. Used to the sandy color adorning everything in Ktren, he thought the vibrant splash of colors shone with radiance. Each building reflected the illumination in a unique manner. The cascade of light and hues dazzled, comparable to the morning sun striking the sand of Tgren, each grain vying for attention with its sparkle. The memory of home rooted Bassan to the spot, open-mouthed, gazing at the spectacle.

A sharp jab to his elbow brought him back to the present. A mumbled apology reached his ears. Bassan caught sight of an older man striding with purpose into the crowd. His dark hair stood in sharp contrast to his pale, bluish complexion. The man paused, his head turned while slanted eyes scanned those passing the port exit. His lips curled into a sneer. The expression took Bassan back to the Vindicarn planet and his first experience with the race. But not Vindicarn. Bassan caught his breath.

You're a mixture of many races. You're a pure Kintal.

Bassan turned his attention to the surge of people wandering the streets of the space station. He knew the ten dominant races. After years of schooling, he knew their features by heart. The eleventh race wasn't so easy to detect. The blending of multiple races led to an unusual concoction of features. Few matched the exact Kintal qualities. More and more though, the purest form of the race made an appearance. Bassan noted several other Kintals with complete blends of the other races in their features. His people were in abundance here.

And I thought we had a lot of Kintals on Tgren.

"Science Officer Bassan from Tgren?"

Startled to hear his name, Bassan jumped. He whirled around, nearly knocking over the speaker. A man with fire-red skin stood in front of him. His eyelids blinked and the black pupils grew wider. Bassan guaranteed his eyes were equally wide. A Charren! A living, breathing Charren.

"Sir, are you Science Officer Bassan from Tgren?" the

man said, leaning back at an unusual angle.

Bassan's tongue caught in his throat. He swallowed and uttered a desperate cough.

Get it together, stupid.

"Yes, I am."

The man's torso twisted and he pulled his hands to his chest. "Welcome to Procura Space Station. I am here to escort you to your quarters during the conference."

"Thank you."

In one fluid motion, the man's limbs flowed into a single gesture. "This way to the transport."

Fingers locked tight around the strap of his pack, Bassan followed the man to a narrow vehicle resembling a bomb with portal windows. The man touched a panel and an opening appeared in the middle of the contraption. Bassan glanced inside before swinging into the single seat and dropping the pack at his feet. The door closed and the Charren entered the pilot's compartment.

Bassan caught himself.

Not a pilot. He's a driver. We're not in a spaceship. Not a proper one anyway.

The vehicle whirred to life, a gentle hum that tickled his ears, and lifted into the air. The milling crowd dropped below them and Bassan peered out the window. The masses grew smaller by the second. The vessel shifted, moving forward into the light stream of traffic high above street level.

Preferring not to watch the scenery flash by at an unnatural pace, he settled into the plush seat and studied his escort instead. The man focused on the airspace in front of them. His proper and professional manner intrigued Bassan.

"I didn't catch your name," Bassan said.

"I didn't give it, sir. I'm just here to collect you."

Bassan's body tensed. Had he crossed some Charren etiquette? They were a very orderly race. Every member held a place and such position could not be crossed. Ever.

This man is a driver. Will always be a driver. It's all he knows. All he will ever know. He'll fly one of these bomb ships forever.

That supposition sobered Bassan's thoughts and he spent the rest of the journey a bit less enchanted with Procura Space Station.

They landed on a platform outside a silvery building. The multiple spires reached for the sky, stretched narrow to reach the artificial light. They glistened in an ever-changing pattern that had nothing to do with the lighting. The crystal reflected a glow from within the structure instead. A living kaleidoscope. Bassan stared in wonder.

His escort spoke, breaking the spell. "This way, sir."

The Charren led Bassan inside, the escort's sinewy arms writhing, and instructed the host to take care of him.

Before the man departed, Bassan grabbed his shoulder. "I'd like to give you something in appreciation for the ride." He produced his tablet.

The man shook his head, his wispy fine yellow hair floating from his scalp with a life of its own. "Thank you, but I am paid to drive. No extra compensation necessary."

"No, not payment. I was going to show you something. Have you ever seen Tgren?"

A light flickered in those dark eyes and the man's shoulders jerked back. "I've seen a few pictures."

"I have something better than a picture." Bassan located the correct file. A view of Ktren and the Cassan base, taken from the far hills to include the entrance to the Kintal ship in the mountainside. A couple months old, but shot before the sun dipped too low, the video displayed his home in all her beauty.

"This is where I live, in the city of Ktren." He showed the screen to the Charren. The man leaned forward with interest. "To the left is the joint Cassan and Tgren base. And when it pans to the right, you'll see the entrance to our Kintal ship."

The Charren absorbed the scene before him in silence, but his wide eyes and twitching cheek muscles spoke louder than words. Most likely his first real view of Tgren. And it held his attention right until the scene faded.

Bassan turned off his tablet and waited. The man blinked a few times, his jaw working. He met Bassan's gaze. "That appears similar to where I grew up. I...I didn't realize Tgren and Charra appeared so similar."

I knew. I studied your planet when I was younger. Saw lots of videos as well.

"A lot of Tgren's climate is desert. Not all, but a large portion of where the people live is arid."

"I never knew." The man offered a half bow. "Thank you for enlightening me."

Maybe I've broadened your horizons a bit. Yeah, right. Look who's talking.

A scowl forming across his brows, Bassan watched the man leave. Born into a system, Charrens rarely ventured beyond their place in society. Such limitations bothered Bassan. They never took risks. Then again, knowing he never took risks troubled him more.

At least I'm here. Not willingly, but I took a chance.

The host showed Bassan to his quarters. A packet of information on the conference rested beside the computer. All the details and schedule resided on his tablet, but he preferred to hold something tangible. He settled in, sent a message to Mevine and Sirella to confirm his safe arrival, and then dug into the conference materials. It included information about the station in addition to the conference layout.

There I am. Tomorrow's morning session. Right there on the page. And they even had enough time to change the name. Great. I definitely can't get out of it now.

He slumped in his seat and closed his eyes.

Get through tomorrow. Survive the session. Then I can enjoy the rest of the conference.

* * *

Bassan scanned his notes for the millionth time. The rising murmur from the conference room swirled with the words on his tablet, and he comprehended neither his speech nor the voices. Frustrated, he dropped the tablet to his side. Despite the divider, a section of the room lay visible. From his vantage point, a body occupied every available seat. Not only couldn't he focus on what he needed to say, but a lot of people were going to witness his ineptness.

Why did I agree to this?

A message from that morning resurfaced in his head. 'It's comparable to instructing a class on the Kintal ship, just bigger.'

Mevine's note of encouragement sounded excellent at the time but it did nothing for Bassan's confidence now.

The coordinator appeared in his line of sight. "We're ready to go. I'll introduce you and then come back to field questions at the end."

Bassan's stomach muscles tightened. "Thank you."

His tongue fumbled with the words, longing for the water waiting for him at the presentation desk. He hoped one glass was enough. He examined the presentation area. One screen displayed his notes and the other monitor showed the image on the big screen.

The coordinator acquired the attention of those gathered and began his introduction.

I have my tablet just in case. And if I pass out, the desk is large enough to hide me.

A round of applause erupted from the room. Bassan held his breath and marched toward the desk. The coordinator nodded and backed away. Bassan set his tablet to the side and chanced a quick glance at the crowd. A sea of faces greeted him, stretching all the way to the back. Some even stood. At least a hundred people attended his session. Despite the size of the room, they filled it to the breaking point.

Bassan gripped the edge of the desk and focused on the screen with his notes.

Pretend you're talking to a small group of trainees.

"Thank you," he said, peering up. "Senior Science Officer Mevine apologizes he could not deliver this information in person. Hopefully, I can impart all the material to you today."

Eager eyes watched him from the crowd. Numerous open minds reflected expectancy. Focusing on those closest to the stage, he noticed a Cassan on the front row and an obvious Kintal beside him. His people.

You can do this.

Bassan launched into his notes. Only familiarity kept him from fumbling multiple times. After two such stumbles in the beginning, he found his stride. Focused on the words in front of him, he plowed through his talk. He paused to take a couple breaths and somehow managed to reach the end without a complete meltdown.

After delivering Mevine's well-written summary, he leaned back from the desk and gazed at the crowd. Silence met his ears, but only for a second. The room erupted with applause and many stood to their feet. A wave of mental excitement and appreciation flooded his senses.

I'm done! It's finally over.

He offered the crowd a polite nod. Before he could grab his tablet and run off stage, the coordinator approached.

"Thank you, Science Officer Bassan from Tgren," the man said, his words barely audible in the auditorium over the clapping. "We have time for a couple questions."

Damn, I forgot about questions. Please make them simple.

The first two questions were technical in nature. Despite their spontaneity, Bassan knew the answers. Confidence growing, he waited for the next one. The coordinator pointed to a Narcon in the second row.

"Much of what you've discovered has been a result of your direct connection to the Kintal ship," the man stated, his thick voice carrying across the crowded room. "Can you explain that connection, Science Officer Bassan?"

Bassan licked his dry lips and tightened his grip on the desk. Those on Tgren understood. But would a room full of strangers?

"I can access past events and information through the mainframe. It began with the transport system, but now I can access all the computers. It's not an exact science, I'm afraid. I must know what I seek and where to look. But through trial and error, not only can I access full Kintal history, but I can also lead others to the information."

"A process you shared today in your presentation, which is available to all for further study," the coordinator said. He nodded at Bassan. "I'd like to thank Science Officer Bassan for his time today—"

"How is it you are able to access that information?" the Narcon said.

"If you are referring to the process, the technical specs are included—" Bassan said.

"No, how is it you can access it?"

"Well, sir, I am a Kintal."

The man scowled and cut him off with the wave of his hand. "Kintals have accessed the other ships, but no one's experienced your results. What makes you different?"

Bassan's muscles tightened and he eyed the exit.

What makes me different?

Science Office Bassan? If you'd prefer to end the question session now, I'll close it, the coordinator thought.

Bassan toyed with his response. He wanted to run and be done with this whole experience. He'd fulfilled his duty. No need to answer the man. He nodded at the coordinator.

"I know why you're different."

Startled, Bassan's attention shifted to the speaker. A Narcon sitting next to the other one pointed a finger at him.

"You were the Tgren child who carried the code that stopped the probe on Vindi. Correct?"

A hushed breath rippled across the crowd, punctuated by a few exclamations. Bassan's mind caught the echoing wave of astonishment rolling his direction. The entire assembly stared at him. Heat crept up his neck, burning his ears.

The floor can swallow me up anytime now.

Science Office Bassan? the coordinator prompted.

He tightened his hold on the presentation desk and fought the nausea rising in the back of his throat. Swallowing hard, he forced a reply from his lips. "Yes."

Shock continued to swirl about the room. Unable to handle any more scrutiny, he grabbed his tablet. He offered a quick nod to the coordinator and retreated from the stage as fast as possible without appearing rude. Bassan darted into the alcove and pressed his back against the wall.

Why did I do that? Now that's all they'll remember. They met the kid who saved the galaxy from the probe.

Huffing in annoyance, Bassan pressed the door plate and beat a hasty retreat into the connecting corridor between the rooms. He strode toward the exit, hoping to escape before the occupants of his session filled the main hallway. Upon opening the door, he peeked to his right. A trickle of scientists filed from the conference room. Before it turned into a flood and someone recognized him, Bassan bolted to his left. He wove in around those drifting through the hallway. He wanted nothing more than to retreat to his quarters and hide for the rest of the day.

Damn, I want to hide for the rest of the week! What fascinating things did you learn at the conference? Nothing, because I was too terrified to leave my quarters.

That last thought annoyed him further.

Coward. Afraid to do anything. Afraid to stand before a crowd. Afraid to save your best friend's life.

That consideration brought him up short. If not for Tarn's quick thinking...

Why didn't I act? I just stood there. Drent's right. Downloading the code on Vindi will be the one worthwhile thing I do with my life.

What makes me different? Not much of anything.

The passageway brimmed with people. Concerned someone from his talk might recognize him, Bassan shuffled farther from his conference room.

He reached the end of the hallway and glanced at the open door on his left. Thermodynamics. Not his specialty but it might be interesting. Bassan slipped inside and chose a seat in the back on the far side. His head down, he composed a message to Mevine while waiting for the session to begin.

'Your talk was well received, and I covered each point almost word for word. You will probably receive a lot of comments and questions.'

Yeah, I'm sure you will get a lot of unexpected questions.

Bassan sent the message. Mevine wouldn't receive it for a while, but at least he'd know Bassan completed his task as instructed.

His mind drifted between the speaker and his lack of initiative. So, what if he could access the ancient Kintal ship in a way no one else could? He didn't need to be brave to accomplish that. Communicating with the ship provided comfort. A safe haven. Real life wasn't so comforting though. Like delivering the session today. And when it came to Sirella...

Applause broke out, and Bassan's focus returned to the speaker. The man fielded numerous questions before the session ended. And he remained on stage even when most people rose to leave, speaking with a small group in the front two rows.

I must've looked like an idiot running off.

He rose from his seat and turned to leave.

"Your talk earlier was excellent."

Startled, he realized the man in the last row behind him stood at attention, facing him. Bassan met his gaze and paused. Jet black eyes stared back. The ashen complexion contradicted his smooth skin and fair hair. A hint of blue highlighted his thin but athletic frame. Only one race possessed such unique traits. The man was a Kintal like Bassan.

"Thanks." He pulled his tablet closer to his chest.

"Your contributions to understanding Kintal technology are amazing."

"Our team has made huge progress."

The man smiled. "Mostly due to you, no doubt."

Bassan shifted his feet. "I'm just the conduit."

"Are you able to access all aspects of Kintal history? Navigation? Medicine? Weapons?"

"Yes," Bassan said, leery where the conversation was headed. Many aspects of the ships themselves remained classified.

"I'd enjoy hearing about it," the man said, his eyes wide in anticipation.

"I...I don't have time." Bassan sidestepped him and headed for the exit. The man followed, pressing close to his elbow.

"Please, I would appreciate a moment to speak with you, away from this crowd. Kintal to Kintal."

His observation caught Bassan's attention. He wanted away from this crowd as well. "I need to return to my quarters and get something to eat."

They stepped into the hallway. The man planted

himself firmly in Bassan's path. "How about we talk over a meal? Let it be my treat, then."

Bassan swayed. Could he handle a private interrogation?

What if you ask me another question I can't answer? Or worse, I answer inappropriately?

"Science Officer Bassan, please," the young man said, holding up a hand. "It's not often I get to hear about our history. Who we were as a race before the great migration? Despite our status, we are still a people without a past."

The words poked at Bassan's conscience. He knew all too well the Kintals' position in the shadow of the other ten races. His position on the Tgren science team afforded him a luxury many didn't enjoy. Despite his hesitation, he didn't want to deprive the man in front of him some Kintal legacy.

"I don't know my way around the station though."

"I do, and I know just the place to go." The young man's attention shifted and his smile faded. "And let's go before that Narcon catches you."

"Narcon?" Bassan peeked behind him. He spotted the man who outed him at his session moving through the crowd, homing in on their position. The scowl consuming his face broadcast like a warning beacon.

"He was annoyed you exited so quickly. Or frustrated by your responses. Either way, he's not one I think either of us wants to tangle with."

I need to get out of here!

The Narcon still in his sights, Bassan let the Kintal lead him away into the crowd. They found an exit at the end of the hall and wasted no time leaving the building. The man turned to the right, setting a fast pace. With no other option, Bassan trotted along at his side.

They blended into the masses moving throughout the station and continued at a brisk pace for several minutes. At the next split, the man veered to the left. Looking over his shoulder, Bassan watched the conference center vanish from view. Concern crept into his thoughts. At last, his companion's pace eased.

"I don't think he saw us," Bassan said.

The man offered a smirk. "Even if he did, he won't follow where we're going."

"Where are we going?"

"Down a level," he said, pointing to a teleporter pod up ahead, "where our kind is more welcome."

Several others entered the pod with them. Bassan hesitated inside the door. He spun around and faced the street. Bodies pressed past him, adding weight to his decision.

What if I can't find my way back?

"Wait."

The doors slid shut. Too late.

"Don't worry, I won't lose us down here," the young man said, slapping his shoulder.

Tablet pressed against his chest, Bassan shrank back into the group. He inhaled sharply and turned to his companion. "You didn't even tell me your name," he whispered.

The man cocked his head and held up his hands. "Where are my manners? I'm Zendar."

He swung his left hand out and offered it to Bassan. After a moment of fumbling, Bassan managed to offer the correct hand in return. Zendar's grip reminded him of Piten's handshake—firm but full of mischief.

They're both more Kintal than I am. Maybe it goes with the territory.

The teleporter's doors opened, spilling its contents into the passageway. Bassan stumbled forward and scanned around for Zendar. Tossing his head, the man indicated they move left. Bassan followed, determined not to lose his companion. His feet tripped again when their surroundings came into focus.

The false sky above no longer shone so bright. Despite their proximity to the ground, the lights cast an eerie twilight glow on the buildings and passageway below. Structures that glistened above reflected only the permeating gloom down here. Petite lights adorned the outer walls, their feeble glow attempting to break through the darkness. The brilliant colors were subdued by the lack of light. The reality they were aboard a space station sank fully into Bassan's brain.

The passageways of the Kintal ship are brighter than this.

A rap on his shoulder startled him. Zendar peered at him with streetwise eyes.

"This way."

At a loss, Bassan had no choice but to follow.

The darkness of their surroundings reflected in the masses gathered in this section of the space station. Bassan clutched his tablet tighter and contemplated stuffing it down his uniform. True to Zendar's claim, many were Kintal, and of a variety he'd never witnessed. Many sported the dark and ashen complexion of the Vindicarn or the yellowed husk of the Narcon. A touch of blue marked Arellen and Torbethian mixes. None possessed the qualities of either Cassan or Tgren though.

I am truly alone here.

"Come on, this place is worth it," Zendar said, prodding Bassan to move faster.

They rounded three more corners before the man turned and indicated with pride a squat building. Bassan gazed up at the sign, faded and dim even in the gloom. Whatever the language, he couldn't read the cryptic letters. For all he knew, it might be one of those twisted mental torture boutiques the Narcons so enjoyed.

"They serve food?" he said. "The kind you eat?"

Zendar laughed. "Of course. The best on this level. And something for everyone. Bassan, trust me."

I wish I did.

They stepped inside, pushing past heavy crimson curtains. A thousand odors wafted his direction, none of them unpleasant. And although the lighting matched the passageway, it shone upon a much cleaner atmosphere. Red dominated the decorations, punctuated by splashes of yellow. Warm and inviting. After the trek to reach this place, Bassan's spirits rose.

"Two?"

The deep voice startled Bassan. A short man stood in front of them and at attention. His portly appearance sat at odds with his pale blue-green skin.

I'm glad Sirella inherited her Arellen figure.

"Yes," Zendar said. "And please inform Master Witz that Zendar is here with a special guest."

The man's narrow eyebrows twitched, but he bowed and gestured for them to follow. He led them to a table in the back, away from most of the patrons. Bassan slid into his seat, nerves tingling.

"Our specialties today are diev soup from Narcon and ascape, a Kintal delicacy." He offered a quick bow. "I will notify Master Witz of your presence."

The man retreated through a door to their left.

Who was Master Witz? The chef or the owner? Bassan leaned back and turned to Zendar. His companion already flipped through the digital menu on the wall.

"Ascape might be a delicacy where you come from, but I want something more filling," Zendar said.

Distracted by the young man's comment, Bassan examined the entrées as they scrolled past in a blur. Nothing appeared familiar.

What am I going to order?

"What looks appealing to you?" Zendar said. "I'm going with Lorvendera prime. Never had one of their steaks."

"I...um," Bassan said. "Anything from Tgren?"

"I don't think so."

Zendar spun through the options again, slower this time. One item caught Bassan's eye. "Taccon! I'll have that."

"I think it's a Cassan dish."

"I've had it before. My mother used to cook it."

"She's Cassan?"

"No, she's Tgren. My father is Cassan."

"Fair enough. I'll order drinks and an appetizer for us. Something I think your Tgren-Cassan palate can handle."

Bassan realized he still clutched the tablet to his chest. With reluctance, he eased the device to his lap.

The host returned. Zendar rattled off their order and the man nodded at each request, his hands behind his back.

I wish I had that kind of memory.

When the host departed, Zendar leaned on the table,

his dark eyes full of expectancy. "So, tell me about our history."

Bassan racked his brain for information he could pass along without violating security. Kintal lifestyle before the great migration worked. Most of what he knew appeared in the records for mass consumption. But he could embellish upon a few items that might satisfy Zendar.

His companion soaked up his words. Buoyed by his rapt audience, Bassan continued to talk through their drinks and appetizer. The main course slowed his outpouring of historic data, though. And to the restaurant's credit, the taccon tasted as good as his mother's.

"You've accessed so much." Zendar wiped his mouth and tossed his napkin aside. "How are you able to retrieve so much from the Kintal ship? What enables you to connect when others can't?"

Bassan swallowed a mouthful of food. He'd talked so much, half his food remained on his plate. He reached for his drink, the second during the meal. The fruity bubbles tickled his nose. Unaccustomed to drinking, especially at this early hour, his thoughts and words flowed freer than he wanted. But with such a rapt audience, he couldn't help himself.

"I guess it's because I once carried the code that stopped the probe. Maybe the Kintal ship trusts me. Well, a machine can't really trust. But it provides me a connection and vision only I can see."

"What do you see?"

Bassan stared at his drink, contemplating his answer. The last of the bubbles floated to the top. "I see the past. I see what transpired as if I was there."

"You do?"

"Yeah, the first time it happened, I emerged from a pod after the ship's journey to Tgren. I was covered in embryonic liquid and staggering toward the exit. I felt it. All of it. The moment couldn't have been more real."

"You were Tgren?"

"Yes."

"Have you been any of the other races?"

"Most of them." Bassan finished his drink. "Usually,

my experiences are from the Kintals' point of view. They were—we are—an amazing race. The Tgrens might have created the probe that destroyed the other races, but the Kintals were actually the most advanced. That's why the ten races journeyed here on Kintal ships."

Zendar stroked the fine blond hairs jutting from his chin. "Their weapons were that powerful?"

"Everything about their ships held enormous power. If more Kintals realized..." Bassan gulped back his words and hiccupped as a result.

What are you doing? Shut up, idiot. Now you're jabbering about speculation.

His companion stared at him, motionless except for a twitch at the corner of his mouth. Zendar dropped his hand to the table and adjusted his position. "Were they more advanced in other areas? Medicine, perhaps?"

Relieved at the change of subject, Bassan smiled. "I don't believe many Kintals died of anything other than old age. Well, unless they were killed. Nothing cures death."

Zendar nodded but didn't speak. Bassan seized the lull in conversation and shoved another helping of food into his mouth. He needed some food to balance the bubbles inside his stomach. And his head.

After a moment, he glanced up from his meal. Zendar continued to watch him. Shoulders straight and hands grasping the table, the man's eagerness spilled from every pore in his body and radiated from his mind. Similar to a predator eyeing prey. Bassan reached for his napkin and eased back from his plate. He touched Zendar's mind but met resistance. Concerned, he opened his mouth to speak.

"Bassan," Zendar said, crossing his arms and leaning forward. "I'm going to cut right to the chase. I need your help."

Before Bassan could react, the host appeared with fresh drinks for them. Bassan waved it aside but Zendar tapped the table.

"No, I think you'll need it to hear my request." He nodded at the host who retreated at once from the table, leaving the two glasses. Zendar downed the last of his other drink and pulled the full glass closer.

"Bassan, my people are dying. Our medicine has proven ineffective. We need a miracle. We need access to Kintal medicine."

Access to Kintal medicine because they're dying? He's right. I'll need that drink.

Head swimming, Bassan grasped the glass and took a deep swallow. He set it down and closed his eyes. Inhaling deeply, he shook his head.

"I...I don't have access to everything."

"You're restricted?"

"No." He opened his eyes and blinked a couple times. "I mean I may not have access to what your people need."

"But through Kintal technology, you might be able to retrieve it?" Zendar said, his black eyes broadening.

"If I had access to a ship, maybe." Bassan burped and lost his train of thought.

Wait. A Kintal ship? If they have one, they can retrieve the information now.

"But if you have a ship...?" he prodded.

"We don't have a ship. But we have numerous components, including several Kintal consoles. They are operational but we can't find the information we need. We don't know where to look. But you do. You could help us."

Zendar's plea tugged at Bassan's conscience. If his people were dying, and he could help... But what did that entail? Where did his people reside that they didn't have access to Kintal knowledge?

"I don't know who you align under, but that race should provide the information you seek." Bassan sat up straighter, proud he'd delivered those words so clearly.

"They don't. We are virtually cut off. And soon we'll be extinct. Bassan, I came here seeking a miracle. You are that miracle. Please, will you help us locate a cure?"

Zendar's face blurred and Bassan rubbed his eyes. "I can look when I get back to Tgren."

"It might be too late for us."

"Well, if so many are dying, I can't go there."

"But if you locate the cure, it won't be a concern. Besides, it might not even affect you. Just those of us raised on the planet."

Bassan blinked, his eyelids remaining closed for more than a second. His thoughts swirled. "Can't go to your planet. Must go home after this."

"Your gift is so unique though. No one can do what you do. No one can see into the past. Please, we'll all die without your help."

Die... My great-uncle died.

Shoulders heavy, he leaned forward. The overpowering smell of his remaining food caused him to reel back. Bassan rested on his right elbow and his body rolled to the side. "I...can't..."

A weight clamped over his eyelids. Unable to fight it any longer, Bassan slumped forward.

I can't help anyone...

3

A light breeze tickled his nose. The motion brought him aware of other discomforts. His head hammered. Muscles ached from holding one position too long. A strange smell, both organic and dirty, entered his nostrils. Bassan attempted to open his eyes, and lights flashed before him. The world swirled and he curled into a tight ball.

It's the probe's code. It's returned.

"Bassan?"

Familiar yet distant, the voice roused him. He forced his eyes open. The glare from a small, uncovered window shone on his face. Something outside flashed, sending a strobe of pulsating light into the room. Again and again.

Not the code. A light. Nothing more than a light. I'm all right.

He moaned and rolled away from the glow. After its brilliance, everything else remained in shadowy darkness. He blinked, trying to make out the forms in front of him.

"Bassan."

He still couldn't see the room, but Bassan recognized Zendar's voice. He rubbed his eyes and rose on one elbow. The movement sent a new wave of discomfort through his brain. He gasped and froze.

"You shouldn't have drugged him," Zendar said. "We've wasted a lot of precious time already."

"We needed him. It was the fastest way."

The new voice resonated in Bassan's chest. Another Kintal? The man sounded more Torbethian.

"We'd begun to discuss his returning to Ugar with me. He might've said yes without your help."

"I wasn't taking any chances."

Return to where? Afraid to use his voice lest it rattle his head further, Bassan directed his thought toward the entire room.

"Bassan, are you awake now? Can you understand me?" Zendar said, voice growing closer.

Yes. But where am I?

"You're...in a secure location."

Secure? As in no one will find me, I'm sure.

He sat up, his movements slow and purposeful. His eyes began to adjust. No longer hindered by searing pain, he focused on the two men in the room with him. Zendar he recognized at once. The other man...sallow skin. Like a Narcon. But stockier, akin to a Torbethian. And what was with the wild, crimson hair?

Who are you? He directed his thoughts to the strange man.

"This is Witz."

Witz crossed his arms and leaned back against the wall. Jaw set, he gave the impression of a man not to be trifled with or crossed.

Zendar seems immune though. What does he hold over Witz?

"Why am I here?" Bassan said, braving his voice for the first time.

"Because you're going to help us, damn it."

"Witz!" Zendar tightened his fists and glared at the other man. He shook his head and dropped to his knee in front of Bassan. "We need your help. Desperately. Our people are dying on Ugar. We need you to access Kintal medicine and save us."

Bassan recalled the man's request before he passed out. Why did they need him? And why kidnap him?

"Your government should have that information."

"Our government..." began Zendar, emitting an exasperated huff. He returned to his seat. "They abandoned us years ago. We are cut off from the rest of the galaxy. Limited resources and no connections. We're desperate."

Desperate enough to kidnap a Tgren officer? Bassan thought, directing his question at Zendar.

That was Witz's idea. I wanted to convince you to help us without using force.

Crap, I've got to get out of here.

Bassan reached out with his mind, hoping to connect with someone, anyone, who knew him. His attempt slammed into a mental wall, preventing him from reaching beyond the room.

Sorry. Can't have that. Bassan, hear me out.

Exasperated, he rolled onto his back. Memories of his first meeting with Piten filled his head.

Why do I keep getting kidnapped by Kintals with Vindicarn heritages? The one race who can block my thoughts...

"My people need help," Zendar continued. "Our medicine has failed and we are dying. But we have access to several Kintal consoles. Somewhere in there lies our answer. We can't reach it though. But I bet you could."

"Even if I could reach it..." Bassan said, gesturing rapidly in frustration, "I'm no medical officer. I couldn't translate."

"We have medical personnel. You find the information and we'll translate."

Bassan moaned and lifted his head. He grabbed his knees and hauled his body to an upright position. The world swirled in front of him. Clenching his teeth tight, he projected with his mind.

You don't need me to access it. The information is out there. Hundreds of other scientists can locate what you seek. Put in a request. And if the local race's government interferes, you lodge a formal complaint with the Kintal alliance. You can't be denied medical aid. It violates the probe's code of protection. It would react in your defense.

A bark of laughter emanated from Zendar. The deep guffaw from Witz unnerved him more.

"The probe must know we exist first. And we are a deep, dark secret the Narcons will never let see the light of day."

With a groan, Bassan moved his aching head and faced the man. Zendar leaned forward on his stool, his hands clasped in a fist. Eyes even darker in the dim light, he focused on Bassan with an unnerving intensity. He meant what he said.

"Secret? What secret?" Bassan said.

A loud noise from Witz startled them. Zendar scowled at the man, and Witz beat his fist on the wall. Their gazes remained locked, sharing a conversation Bassan couldn't hear. With a glare, Witz pointed his finger at Zendar and slammed his hand against the door's panel.

The door slid open. In that moment, Bassan caught sight of a hallway and potential escape. Before he could force his body to react, Witz exited, and the door panel closed. Zendar uttered a growl and slammed one fist into his open palm.

"He's impatient and thinks we're wasting our time with you. If he understood..." He shook his head and sat up straight. The youthfulness present when they first met vanished. No longer a zealous young man, Zendar's desperation consumed him. Piten once exuded such despair.

"Hundreds of years ago," Zendar said, "a planet within the Narcon system was decreed habitable, but in the faintest sense of the word. The government decided it not worth the effort to colonize. They couldn't let it go to waste though. People could live there, even if their chance for survival was slim. And it was cheaper than maintaining prisons. So, they dumped all their captives onto the planet and let them fend for themselves."

A penal colony. Bassan wrapped his arms tighter around his legs. A deplorable practice but not unheard of, even in his time.

"They still dump prisoners, but now generations have grown up on the surface. Descendants who never committed a crime are resigned to spend their lives trapped on the planet. Except for a small handful who can steal a ride from the garbage ships. But you have to be strong to secure a line and climb it before the ship's hatches close."

Bassan snapped to attention. "You escaped that planet?"

Zendar nodded, rocking in his seat. "Yes, and I escaped with a purpose. Right now, my tribe is dying. A disease has swept our settlement, attacking those closest to pure Kintals, which is most of the population. We need a cure and we need it fast."

"That's terrible, but what does it have to do with me?"

"We believe the disease is old. Probably carried on the Kintal ships that brought us to this section of the galaxy. They most likely possessed a cure. We need to access it. You can access it by going back in time."

"I could look for the cure when I returned to Tgren—"

"There's no time." Zendar leaned forward, his eyes threatening to pop out of their sockets. "By the time you return to your planet, we might all be dead. You must accompany me to the planet's surface."

"What?" Bassan released his legs and slapped his hands on the floor. "I can't go with you to that planet. I'd be a captive like you. And no closer to a Kintal ship or database."

"You'd be closer than you think."

"To what? Dying?"

"No, to a Kintal ship's database."

Bassan froze, his mouth open. He'd mentioned Kintal information, but... Impossible! The Kintal ships all landed on the ten races' home worlds. Unless the Kintals themselves came on a separate ship, one that escaped the records and archives, it simply couldn't be true. Through his unique connection with Tgren's ship, Bassan witnessed the ten ships leaving, searching for new homes. He'd seen all ten races emerge after landing, watched them stagger toward the exit and a new life...

"You're lying."

"No, I'm not." Zendar sat up straight in his chair. "And I can show you."

The barrier around Bassan's mind eased. He reached out in earnest, seizing the open channel. Instead of venturing beyond the room, he found himself in Zendar's mind. He fought for a moment. But the image before him froze Bassan to the spot.

Two Kintal ship consoles sat side by side. Their displays glowed with configurations and symbols. The sight drew Bassan closer. A thousand times he'd connected with such consoles, letting them impart information. Only he could access their depths and see into the past. The Kintal ships knew him. Trusted him. And they connected with him in a way no one else ever could.

Mesmerized by the image, he lost track of all else. When the consoles shrunk to less than half their size, he realized the view now encompassed more. Instead of the bright lights and cleanliness of a Kintal ship, a dingy grey room surrounded the consoles. Dozens of power cords snaked out from under the devices. Away from their ship, the Kintal units were more out of place than a Vindicarn on Tgren.

"But how?" Bassan moaned, fearful of the answer.

The image faded and Zendar came into view. He clasped his hands together and sighed.

"Because Narcons value little beyond themselves. They obviously didn't see the importance of their Kintal ship and dismantled it. Those consoles were dumped with a load of garbage on my planet. Through a sheer miracle, we restored their power and brought them back online."

They tore apart the ship? The one gift the Kintals left to every race and they all but destroyed it? Bassan's lips curled in disgust.

"Their loss is our gain though. Through those databases, we can find a cure." Zendar leaned closer, his lips pressed together. *You can reach back, find a cure.*

The bottom dropped out and Bassan slumped.

I can't go to his planet. I'd be in so much trouble. And what if I couldn't return?

"You have Kintal control panels. Those could come from any of the ten ships. But are your people, for real, dying?"

The barrier around Zendar's mind eased again. Bassan reached out and a new image filled his vision. He stood at the entrance of a long, narrow building. Light dappled in from the patchwork roof. Beds lined either side, their blankets a similar myriad of colors. Not one sat empty. Stretching the entire length sat bed after bed filled with bodies. In the closest bed on his left, an older man rolled over and threw up on the floor. A vile stench slammed into him. Suppressing the bile rising in his throat, Bassan pulled out in haste.

All those people. He estimated the building held at least a hundred. Maybe more.

You're asking a lot, he thought, fumbling for an appropriate response.

I know. It was my plan to entice you to make the decision freely. We're desperate, though. I can't go to the authorities. I'm an escapee from a prisoner planet. They won't listen, they'll just send me back.

They might listen to me. If I can get word back to Tgren...

And then what? Zendar tossed up his hands. *Wait for the Tgren government to act? Then trust the Narcons even acknowledge we exist? No one will be left on the planet by then.*

Bassan rubbed his head. Zendar spoke the truth. It would take weeks. Probably months. If the situation were so truly dire, those people wouldn't stand a chance.

But why me? Why did you pick me?

I arrived two days ago and made contact with Witz. He told me about the convention, and we decided that was our best chance to find someone who could decipher the Kintal databases and find a cure. He saw your name on the list, which is why I attended your session. After I heard you speak, I knew you could help us.

"What's Witz's connection?"

"His brother is on the surface. He's the one who gave me a contact here."

"He's one of the criminals dumped there?"

Zendar's features grew rigid. He crossed his arms and tilted back in his chair. "Yes, he's one of the criminals. Along with thousands of us born there. Like my mother and father. And my sister, who was quite ill when I left and could very well be dead now."

Unable to maintain eye contact, Bassan dropped his chin. The prospect of death hit home. A thief of all that mattered.

I hate death. It took great-uncle Orellan. It almost took Drent. I couldn't help him, but I can help Zendar's people. Maybe this is my chance for redemption? Or my chance to do something else worthwhile?

He raised his gaze to Zendar. *What if I can't find*

the cure? I worked a miracle once before, but there's no guarantee I'll do it again. There's no code in my head. What happens to me if I fail? I have family back home as well.

"You do everything possible, and no matter what, I will get you off the planet. You are young and strong like me. We can scale the ropes and reach the containment ship before it departs. You just have to move quick."

Move quick. Right. I'm not exactly good at moving fast. Ask Drent. Or Sirella. She'll say I don't move at all.

Isn't this what you wanted though? A chance to prove yourself? But if I fail...

I know what you did to save all the races years ago. Your unique connection saved everyone then, and I know you can save my people now. Bassan, please. We are desperate. And dying.

Pins of guilt poked his skin. "Can I least let someone know where I'm going?"

Zendar arched his eyebrows. "You send a message that you're going to the Narcons' prisoner planet and security will be searching for you in no time. And monitoring the very ship we need to get down to the surface. It would ruin our only chance to return."

"I won't say where I'm going then. Just something's come up and I'll be out of contact for a while," Bassan said, desperate not to worry those on Tgren.

Although I'll certainly be in an enormous amount of trouble when I get back. If I come back.

Zendar slapped his knees and rose. "Right before we leave."

"Fair enough," Bassan said with a sigh.

Zendar extended his hand and hauled Bassan to his feet. Bassan groaned, his head adjusting to the sudden movement. Eyes closed, he focused on maintaining his balance. A clap on his arm jarred him.

"Thanks for helping us."

Bassan opened his eyes. Zendar stared at him, a genuine smile spread across his face. Despite the mental barrier, gratitude drifted from his mind as well. Along with a tinge of hope.

"Thank me when I find the cure. So, what now?"

"Right now, we need to find you some new digs, something that fits better. Those fine clothes won't work on Ugar."

Super, because these fine clothes aren't comfortable here either.

* * *

Bassan crouched behind a pallet of goods in the landing bay, dressed in sand-colored garments with official Narcon yellow garb covering them. The floor trembled under his feet. He tightened his body before he moved, peering between the boxes. Loading continued. The roar of the massive vessel pounded at his senses and he knelt, his eyes closed tight. He needed to muffle his hearing, but at this point asking for headphones was pointless. If he could shield sound, it would be a blessing.

What am I doing here? This is crazy.

Witz dropped from his observation point and crouched beside Bassan and Zendar. *Two more loads. Ten minutes tops. We move out in seven minutes.*

Bassan turned to Zendar. The man nodded and thought, *You have six minutes. And I will be reading.*

Tablet out, Bassan pulled up messages. He knew what he wanted to say. The past hour he'd spent rehearsing those words. But the recipient? Should he send to his supervisor, Officer Mevine? His father deserved to know though. Logic told him to select either, but his heart held his hand steady.

They'll both be mad. I'm doomed.

Bassan typed his message, letting his fingers guide the words while his mind continued to tussle with the recipient.

I should send it to my mother. But why? I'm an adult. There's no reason to contact my mother. It'll look suspicious anyway.

He finished composing his message and regarded Zendar. The young man took a moment to scan the screen before nodding his acceptance. Bassan's finger hovered over the recipient's section.

I should tell my superior officer. I am here on official business.

Bassan fought with his choice. Clamped his teeth together. In the end, he punched in the name and sent the message. His shoulders sagged with relief.

At least Sirella would know.

Is she your mate? thought Zendar.

Bassan turned off his tablet and shook his head. *She should be, but I haven't asked yet.*

A hand thumped his back. *Take care of that when you get back.*

If I get back.

Bassan tucked away his tablet and resigned himself to waiting.

A moment later, Witz pointed. He began to move and Bassan fell in behind the man. They crept to the end of the pallets. The three of them gathered and grasped the garbage cart. Zendar swung his pack atop the heap of tangled metal and wires.

Three attendants might seem odd, but with this cart loaded to overflowing, hopefully no one notices, Zendar thought. *We're going to have to hustle though. Those garbage rigs move fast. Get on board the ship and head for the entry door. Anyone stops us, show them your badge.*

If it gets weird, I'm prepared to take action, Witz thought, patting his left hip.

Witz was carrying. Bassan dropped his gaze to the hangar floor.

Please don't let it get weird...

Go!

The cart lurched forward and Bassan stumbled to catch up. Witz and Zendar moved with a purpose across the hangar floor, aiming for the ramp. Bassan pumped his legs in earnest to keep up. Every nerve tingled. He cast a sideways glance at the big rigs loading into the ship. The last one lurched toward the ramp, threatening to fill the width of it. If they didn't reach it first...

Move! Witz thought.

They picked up the pace. His feet threatened to tangle from the sudden inertia. The cart hit the ramp and Bassan pushed with every ounce of strength in his body. Each step carried them closer to their ticket to Ugar. Bile rose in his throat. Their goal was so close. And yet it spelled his doom.

What am I doing?

Bassan continued forward, clinging to the car. His chin dipped and he got a decent look at the rig rising up the ramp behind them. Rising fast. Much faster than their current speed.

We're about to be crushed, he thought, ramming his chest into the cart's handle.

Go, go, go, go! thought Witz, throwing his weight against the cart.

Bassan pumped his legs harder, spurred by mortal fear. The rumble of the rig behind them grew closer. The grinding of its gears filled the air. The sight of Drent's bike tumbling toward the cliff's edge filled Bassan's mind. He couldn't stop it. Nor could he stop the garbage rig from overtaking them.

The cart's front wheels went airborne. Momentum took them forward before the cart slammed against the floor. The very flat floor. They'd reached the interior of the ship.

Ditch the cart, thought Zendar, seizing his bag.

All too happy to rid himself of their load, Bassan released the handle and dove toward the right. His fists pumped the air, and he ran for his life. Not until the roar of the rig passed behind him did Bassan slow his headlong flight.

Zendar and Witz remained hot on his heels. Unsure of their direction in the giant maze of garbage, Bassan reduced his pace. The three collided, struggling to remain upright. Witz exclaimed and grabbed Bassan's shoulder.

This way! he thought, shoving Bassan to the left.

Feet still tangled, he almost collided with a massive, twisted piece of machinery. Momentum carried him past the relic and he focused on regaining his footing. Zendar sprinted out into the lead. Witz remained with him though, still pushing Bassan forward.

Watch yourselves.

Zendar's warning came as Bassan's boot connected with something. Prepared to take a hard tumble, he glanced at the ground. A rusty can skittered off to the side. His respite flashed for only a second though. Small piles of dark rubbish covered the walkway. Most of it comprised of metal but not all. A vile stench reached his nostrils, a mixture of rotting food and flesh. Nausea churned his stomach. His foot struck something more solid than a can and he stumbled.

Witz hauled him forward, placing Bassan in the middle again. *Don't trip, fool!*

Spurred on by the man's order—more of a threat—Bassan focused on the ground in front of him. He leapt over one pile. His feet danced when he avoided the remains of a stairwell. A quick glance and he located Zendar. Just ahead. He continued fighting the obstacle course of putrid garbage and mechanic refuge. At last, he reached Zendar, who hovered over a closed door.

"Move," Witz said with a hiss, brushing past them. He pulled out a tiny device and knelt at the door.

His breath rapid, Zendar scanned the ramp behind them. *I don't think anyone saw us. We should have at least fifteen minutes before the ship takes off.*

And I don't want to be caught out here, Witz thought.

Bassan wiped sweat from his brow and caught Zendar's attention. *What does he mean?*

No need to waste precious air here. By the time the ship reaches Ugar, most of the oxygen in this storage area will be gone. That's why we must get into the control section.

You mean if he can't get the door open, we'll run out of air?

Yes.

All the moisture evaporated from Bassan's mouth. He glanced back. Was there time to make a run for it?

Got it.

Bassan turned around and sure enough, the door opened. They slipped through into a nondescript hallway. Bassan staggered to the far wall and pressed against it, ignoring the pressure of the pack against his back. Zendar secured the door and sealed them inside.

"Well done," he told Witz, slinging his bag over his shoulder. "Took me ten minutes to get the door open the first time."

"Told you my device was better. Now, which way?"

Zendar gestured with his head, taking them to the right. Witz fell in line behind him, obviously no longer concerned with Bassan. Where would he go, anyway? Pushing off from the wall, he trotted after them, inhaling the fresh, recycled air.

At least I can breathe without puking.

"This corridor provides access to key systems," Zendar announced, playing tour guide. He gestured toward the yellowish-white corridor with one hand. "It's called the control section, but there's no way to control the ship from here. Navigation is programmed in remotely. We don't want to change the navigation, so that's not an issue."

"No but forcing the ship to land would be better than jumping," Witz said.

Bassan's toe caught on an imaginary crack in the floor and he faltered.

We're jumping from this ship? No one said anything about jumping.

"If you can find access to that system in this maze." Zendar snickered. "And you're an expert in Narconian coding. So far no one dumped on Ugar who managed to escape on one of these garbage ships has excelled in those two areas."

"Shame!"

Bassan caught up to his companions and nudged Zendar. "We're not actually jumping, are we?"

"We brought a rope, so the leap won't be far."

"How far?"

The ship shuddered and Bassan's step faltered. Even Witz glanced around with wide eyes.

"They've closed the hatch," Zendar said. "We'll be taking off soon."

He cut a sharp right and down the single corridor. Up ahead, it ended in another closed door.

"That's it?" Witz said.

"That's it."

"What is it?" Bassan said. His lack of knowledge regarding this mission grated on his nerves.

I should've demanded more details.

"The airlock where they hold prisoners. They always load it first. We might have company, Witz."

The man unzipped his jumpsuit and retrieved his weapon. "Then we'll be ready for them. Let's get out of these blasted things first."

He shook his shoulders and pulled on the sleeves. Zendar nodded at Bassan and they stripped out of the yellow outfits as well.

"Should I save mine?" he asked. Zendar's eyebrows came together and he cocked his head. "You know, for the return trip."

His expression brightened and Zendar snapped his fingers. "Good thinking. Yes, you'll need it to slip off the ship."

Bassan rolled the suit tight and crammed it into what little space remained in his pack. He swung it to his back and secured the straps. That's when he noticed Zendar also held a weapon.

"Are you going to kill whoever is inside?"

Zendar shrugged. "If they're trouble. With any luck, we'll convince them they can escape when the ship returns and they'll willingly leave the airlock."

"Can they escape?"

"Not without this baby." Witz held his device up to the door.

"So, they'll be trapped in this corridor?" Bassan said.

That's not right. Those people will be caught when the ship returns.

Zendar pointed his gun at the door. "Unless they want to come with us." He elbowed Bassan. "You might want to get behind me."

Hidden behind Zendar, Bassan pressed against the wall and ducked his head. He held his breath, waiting for Witz to work his magic. Seconds later, the door slid aside. Witz whipped out his gun and aimed it inside the room. Bassan leaned away from the wall and peered into the containment area.

Crouched on the floor, three young people stared back, their hands up.

They're kids, Bassan thought.

"Hey there," Zendar said, his gun trained on the occupants of the room. "We're here to hitch a ride to Ugar. We don't want trouble, so you're welcome to stay or take your chances out here and escape when the ship returns to the space station."

The eldest boy rose and nudged the kid beside him with his knee. "Don't want to go to Ugar. We get out the way you came in?"

Zendar lowered his weapon and Bassan eased out from behind him. Witz still held at the ready though.

"Yeah," Zendar said, indicating the direction with a jerk of his head. "Take a left and stop at the fifth door on your right. Wait until the ship returns to open the door and enter the garbage bay or you'll have no air."

The boy dropped his hands and nudged the other kid with his knee. The two stood, the rags hanging in strips off their bodies. The blue tint in their faces marked them an Arellen mix of Kintal. The shortest one reached up to brush aside dark, matted hair, revealing soft eyes and high cheeks. A young girl.

The oldest boy motioned to his companions and stepped forward. He glanced at Witz, moving with care past the man, before nodding again at Zendar. The other two followed.

You said no one could open that door without a code buster, Bassan thought.

Zendar tucked his weapon away and pressed his lips together. *They can't.*

Then those kids have no chance when this ship returns to the station. They'll be trapped.

Zendar scowled. Bassan grabbed his shoulder. *You can't do that to them. One is a young girl. What do you think will happen when the guards open the door and find them?*

All right, fine. He opened his pack. "Wait!"

The three stopped, the younger two pressing close together. Zendar dug in his pack and produced a device similar to Witz's. Smaller, it appeared in danger of falling apart. He held it up and the eldest boy approached.

"Know how to use one of these?" Zendar said.

The boy took it cautiously from his hand and smiled. "Oh, yes."

"It will open the door into the storage area. Once the ship lands, open the door. Be prepared to slip out with the other workers after they dump their loads and return for more refuse."

Bassan scooped the discarded service coveralls from the floor. "And here. These will disguise two of you at least."

The boy accepted the clothing. Chin down, he cast a suspicious glance at them and retreated to where his companions waited. They scampered around the corner and out of sight.

"Not so much as a thank you," grumbled Witz.

Bassan stared after the kids, wishing he could join them. "They were scared."

"Well, let's get comfortable," Zendar said.

Resigned, Bassan followed him into the room. Witz straddled the doorframe and punched commands into the screen. He glanced back at his device and reached around the corner to the control panel, one thumb poised over his machine's screen. Witz brought it down and yanked the device from the panel. Before the door shut, he pulled his body into the room.

"Gentlemen," he said, storing the code buster in his bag, "we have committed."

Bassan examined the wall. Outside of the door's seam, the metal remained unbroken. No way out. His legs trembled. They were sealed in for the duration.

"Have a seat, Bassan," Zendar said, sliding to the floor on the right. Witz slumped to the floor on the left.

Bassan forced his legs to move and turned around. The ceiling sloped to the far wall and floor, forming a triangular room. The lights directly overhead cast strange shadows in the corner where the two surfaces met. Where the opening formed perhaps? Bassan elected to sit where he stood and slid to the floor. The moment his rear planted, the ship shook. He gulped and reached out to steady himself.

"Just the ship taking off," Zendar said.

One more reason to loathe flying. "What happens now?" Bassan said, fighting the quaver in his voice.

"We wait."

Bassan gawked at Zendar. "How long?"

Zendar opened his pack and rummaged inside. "Less than three hours. Ugar isn't far into Narcon territory."

"You said you had a rope?"

The words barely out of Bassan's mouth, Zendar produced a thin, brown cord from his bag. A hook at one end, knots at intervals in the rope. Hand holds for descent. Another question formed on Bassan's lips, but the thought of scaling down that thin cord caused his stomach to shake and he kept his mouth shut.

Zendar and Witz spoke during the trip, but Bassan remained silent. He continued to fight his decision in his head.

Why did I agree to do this? I could've said no. What were they going to do—knock me out and drag me on this ship? Crap, Witz probably would've done it. I wonder if I could discreetly send another message?

He adjusted the tablet under his jacket. Neither man watched him, but in the tiny room, no movement went unseen. Witz stared at him when he shifted his legs and bent his knees. He couldn't tap a message without looking down or drawing the tablet out more.

I'm screwed. Everyone back home will kill me. If I don't wind up dead on my own.

The hour late, his adrenaline began to ebb. He closed his eyes and attempted to sleep.

4

A change in the ship's hum jolted Bassan awake.

"We're here." Zendar adjusted his pack and slung it over his shoulders. He tendered the cord, grasping the hook.

Bassan scrambled to stand, his body stiff from sitting so long. He scanned the room for a place to tether the line, but the smooth walls provided no purchase.

"Where are you going to hook it?" he said, fear gnawing at his chest.

Zendar moved to the far right corner where the ceiling met the floor. "There's a rung right outside on the ship. When the floor starts to open, I'll lean out and secure the rope. I'll need you two to hold on to me so I don't fall out."

Great. I'm so good at hanging on to someone.

Zendar lay on his side, his head wedged into the corner. Witz grabbed his leg and pressed his hand against the ceiling. He scowled at Bassan. "Hang on to him!"

Bassan crouched and grasped Zendar's pants. His fist tightened around the loose fabric. Mimicking Witz, he placed his other hand on the ceiling.

The ship shimmied, and the engine's roar changed pitch again. The shaking hid Bassan's own tremors, which grew with each passing moment. The vibrations lessened, and every muscle in his body tightened.

"Not a hundred percent sure where they'll dump us," Zendar said. "At least it won't be in the middle of a sandstorm."

"Why's that?" Witz said.

"They don't want their ship damaged."

Small mercy.

All movement ceased. The sensation sent a jolt through Bassan and he tightened his grip on Zendar.

A mechanical whir filled the room. The floor shifted, and Bassan sucked air.

Hang on to me, Zendar thought.

The floor dropped. A blast of warm air filled the room. The floor and ceiling separated. Zendar wiggled forward until his head and shoulders hung outside the room.

Bassan squinted at the bright light.

There it is! Zendar thought.

Bassan's heart beat wildly in his chest. The wind rushed in at him as the opening grew. One hand still on the ceiling, he braced his feet. The soles of his boots gripped, but for how long?

Got it, Zendar thought. *Everyone, grab the rope.*

Where is it? Panic choked Bassan as his feet slid a few inches.

Here!

Witz flung something at him, and it smacked him in the face. Zendar's legs pulled away, dragging Bassan closer to the opening. In terror, he released Zendar and grabbed for the rope.

His whole body slid.

Head pressed against the ceiling and the floor giving way below him, Bassan wrapped both hands around the cord. With nothing else holding him in place, his body tumbled out. A terrified shout escaped him.

Hang on! Zendar thought.

His hands slipped and caught on the next knot. When his feet swung wide, he held his breath. He fought to get the rope between his legs. The cord ceased its wild movement and grew taut. Pressing his knees together, he finally secured his hold.

Now move, Zendar thought. *It's not far.*

The cord trembled below him as Witz shimmied down first. His breath ragged, Bassan released one hand and brought it down in front of him. Clinging to the knot, he let go with the other hand. His body dropped faster than expected. He seized the rope and pressed tight against it. His arms quivered and he closed his eyes.

Bassan, move! Something tapped his head. *We must reach the ground before the ship finishes its dump.*

He squinted upward. Zendar hovered above him. Bassan eased his body down. Releasing one hand, he tried again. Prepared this time, he didn't drop so fast. Desperate to reach solid ground, he continued to shimmy his way down.

The roar of crushing metal crowded his ears. Terrified, Bassan moved faster. The cascade of sound filled the air, more deafening than every squadron on Tgren's base taking off at once.

Almost there, Witz thought.

Bassan reached for the next knot below and misjudged his hold. A chill overtook his skin. He slid. Opening his mouth to yell, the sound died in Bassan's throat as his feet slammed into solid ground. The air left his body and he staggered.

Rough hands grabbed his pack and hauled him aside. He dropped to his knees and rolled onto his side. Sand kicked up from the ship and entered his mouth. He coughed and sat up, attempting to spit out the irritating grit. When someone seized his arm and yanked hard, his breath caught in his chest.

We have to get clear! Zendar thought.

Bassan let the momentum propel him and squared his legs under him. He rose to his feet, still fighting for breath, muscles trembling. Digging his heels into the sand, he attempted to keep pace with Zendar.

Over the howling wind, the clash of metal grew noisier. Bassan threw a glance over his shoulder. Debris rained down from the ship. The onslaught of metal colliding with the debris on the surface created a deafening symphony of destruction, one that drew closer with each passing second.

Bassan clenched his fists and pumped his legs harder. We'll be crushed.

Zendar sprinted into the lead. He cut a sharp right, arms out for balance. Witz and Bassan skidded in the loose gravel. Bassan's right knee hit the sand. Left arm flailed in a search for balance, right hand slammed against the ground. The force propelled him forward and upward. He regained his footing and bolted after Zendar and Witz.

The sand gave way to rocky ground. Zendar darted between the rocks and small boulders. Behind them, the rain of garbage pounded the ground without mercy. Lungs laboring in the swirling dust, Bassan fought for every breath.

I'm not going to make it!

The boulders grew larger. Zendar's form vanished as he navigated the terrain, leaving Bassan trailing at a dangerous distance. Terrified of losing his guide and his one chance for escaping this place, Bassan called out.

Zendar!

Don't stop. We're almost clear.

His legs were about to give out when Zendar and Witz came into view again. Zendar continued at a fast trot, glancing over his shoulder. Slapping a boulder in passing, he slowed and turned around. After a couple steps backward, he came to a halt.

We're in the clear, he thought.

With an audible gulp for air, Bassan staggered forward and leaned against a smooth boulder. Rolling to press his back against the rock, he looked for the shower of debris. A change in the ship's direction sent the stream of garbage curving away to their right. No longer directly behind them, it glided along, resembling a storm across the planet's surface. Bassan let his head drop back against the flat stone.

That was too close, Witz thought, his breathing raspy.

I knew it would be tight. Zendar straightened his back and wiped his brow. *They always circle left though. Narcons are predictable.*

Bassan leaned against the rock, unable to move. His legs trembled with a life all their own. The Narcon ship filled his field of vision, the garbage still pouring from its hull. No longer focused on running, he realized the grinding of metal had grown quieter. Death no longer threatened from above.

"Now where do we go?" Witz said, regaining his voice.

Zendar pulled a small device from his bag. "Let's see where they dumped us."

The gentle roar of metal hitting the surface ceased.

Bassan turned his attention to the ship. The bulbous vessel hovered in silence, no longer spewing debris across the planet. The bay doors at the bottom closed and it began to rise.

I'm committed now. And completely stuck.

A sizeable portion of the area closest to them lay covered in rubble. Some of the piles rose into the air, towers of glinting metal, reminding him of Procura Space Station. An ugly Procura, of course. Beyond that, desert stretched to the horizon, ending in a hazy mountain range. Bassan squinted at the light reflecting from metallic stacks and the pale desert.

"Well, the good news is they didn't drop us off on the wrong side of the planet," Zendar said.

"What's the bad news?" Witz said.

Zendar's shoulders sagged. "We have a long trek in front of us."

Witz jerked upright. "I thought your contacts would pick us up."

"When we get closer. I can't send a signal this far."

Witz cursed. Bassan's optimism sank even lower.

"As soon as we're in range, I'll notify them. Until then," Zendar said, shouldering his pack, "we walk."

Bassan peered back at the Narcon garbage ship. It shrank farther from view, now but a speck on the horizon. Resolve sank in his guts. Like it or not, he had no choice but to go forward.

"Let's get going, then," he said.

* * *

Dusk settled on the rocky landscape. Boulders bubbled from the ground, threatening to erupt from the surface. Their long shadows grew more alive with every step. The sand and stone blended into one shade of grey, washing the planet in a monotone color, further emphasizing the encroaching darkness. Despite the silence, the planet's surfaced pulsed with synthesized energy.

Bassan's legs protested the long walk, and he longed to curl into a ball and sleep. Zendar pressed forward.

"How much farther?" Witz said, not bothering to conceal his annoyance.

"We're on the edge of Lethan territory," Zendar said. He paused by a large boulder and glanced back at them. "We don't dare camp here. I want to get us a couple degrees farther north."

Bassan grasped the closest boulder and hauled himself forward. "Who are the Lethan?"

"A rogue colony. Mostly comprised of prisoners. They would show us no mercy."

"Even with a bribe of escape?" Witz said.

"No."

Escape? On one of those garbage ships?

Bassan closed his eyes for a moment before trudging forward.

Why did I agree to this? I'm trapped. With no way to contact anyone. If I'd taken Sirella as my mate, I could speak to her now.

Regret twisted his guts. All his excuses fell by the wayside.

You're always right, Drent. Damn you.

He followed the others, no longer caring about their mission.

Absorbed in his own thoughts, Bassan ran into Witz. He jerked upright.

Sorry.

Witz growled and shoved Bassan with force. *Run into me again and it'll be the last thing you ever do.*

"I think we can rest here," Zendar said, obviously unaware of their exchange. He ducked under a large boulder.

Witz followed, Bassan on his heels but not too close. Zendar held up his light, illuminating a small cave. "We're out of Lethan turf now. Plus, this will provide shelter."

Bassan staggered forward and sank to his knees. The bag across his back now weighed him to the floor. Neither it nor his aching legs would let him go any farther. Not even the unforgiving rock under his knees bothered him.

"We'll be safe here for the night," Zendar said, dropping his pack to the ground.

"How close are we to sending a signal?" Witz said.

Zendar pulled his pack closer and retrieved the device.

He punched the keys and frowned. "At least two more days. Maybe more. Depends how far we get tomorrow."

"Damn, how far away are we?"

"Far enough!"

Witz grumbled and dumped his pack.

"Hey, I picked the garbage ship dropping us as close as possible to the settlement. At least we aren't on the wrong side of the planet." Zendar jammed the device back into his bag. "We could've had an ocean to cross."

That word caught Bassan's attention. He eased the pack off his shoulders. "This place has oceans?"

Zendar pulled out a water canister and slumped against the back wall. "Of course. Doesn't Tgren?"

Witz produced a light, dispelling some of the growing darkness. Bassan stared at the gentle glow, his reply to Zendar's question fading from his thoughts. Despite the surroundings, the light provided him a sense of comfort.

"Eat and drink something. You'll feel better," Zendar said, tearing into a food pack. "Then get some sleep. We have a long day ahead of us."

With a soft moan, Bassan dragged his pack closer. When Witz chuckled, he looked up.

"I don't think our scientist is used to a hard day's work." Witz pointed a finger at him. "Better keep up with us, soft boy. I'm not carrying your sorry ass."

"I'll keep up."

Or I'll die from exhaustion. One of the two.

* * *

"We'll take a break up there by those twisted trees," Zendar said.

Bassan paused and surveyed their surroundings. Four desert plants, a bit taller than him, grew together in a shallow dip in the sandy ground. Rusty threads wove throughout the green branches, warping the trees' appearance. Buds grew between the long thorns, proving life still existed inside the nubby shrubs.

Amazing anything grows here. I imagine quite a bit dies, though. Just hopefully not us.

Zendar reached the spot first and kicked around the sand before sitting on a flat rock. Witz took the other small rock in the shade. Bassan paused, weighing his options. Desperate to get out of the sun, even for a few minutes, he knelt—or rather collapsed—at the base of two trees. His body no longer cooking from the heat, he closed his eyes.

"How much longer before we're past this blasted sand?" Witz said.

"At this pace? Less than two hours. We'll start hitting rocky terrain again then. Easier for walking."

I'll take easier.

Bassan reached for his water canteen.

"We'd get there faster if soft boy wasn't dragging in the rear."

Bassan cast a scowl Witz's direction. The gesture was lost since the man didn't look his direction. Shifting his position, Bassan took a swig of his water and tossed it down his throat with force.

Screw you, Witz.

Bassan capped the water and slid it back into its holster. Staring blankly ahead, he imagined a normal day on Tgren instead. Awaken early. Ride his bike to the ancient Kintal ship. Delve into the ship's database. And its past. So many trips into his ancestors' past.

I wish I could escape there now. Hear a Kintal music piece played thousands of years ago. Watch the Tgrens tame the desert and leap forward in technology. Say-vee! What a moment to savor.

He focused on the sand nestled around the base of the stunted trees. Nothing about it suggested life. And yet, here the vegetation grew. The Tgren faced those tiny grains on their own planet and conquered them. Then and now.

I need to visit the Kintals' home world next time. I've been so focused on their technology, I ignored all else. I need to see how they lived. Maybe they lived in paradise. I'm sure they didn't live in such wretched sand.

Almost on cue, the sand in front of him shifted. Bassan leaned back and blinked.

Am I seeing things?

The grains parted and a small head appeared. Burnt in the same red as the tree above, the reptilian head blinked all four eyes at him. Used to the desert creatures on Tgren,

Bassan smiled.

"We have a visitor," he said, his voice low so he wouldn't startle the creature.

A mental jolt of terror. A noisy shuffle from behind.

Chills raced up Bassan's spine. Every muscle tensed.

Don't move, Zendar thought.

Already poised to jump, Bassan shot back. *Why?*

It's a xert. One bite and you're likely a goner.

The head wiggled, exposing more of the creature's body. Numerous arms appeared, propelling the creature forward. Closer to Bassan.

What do I do? Panic beat at his chest. He locked eyes with the little beast while it coiled its long body onto the sand.

Move back. Very, very slowly.

His body, exhausted from heat and the long trek, refused to budge. Only his eyes cooperated. They bulged so hard, he worried they'd pop from his head. The creature pulled its full length from the sand and coiled into attack mode.

I'm dead.

The beast hissed. Adrenaline kicked up a notch and Bassan forced his body to react. Like a coiled spring, he exploded. Leaping backward, he stretched his frame out to its full length. A blast rang in his ears and he hit the ground.

A cry burst from his lips. Before he could move again, a hand came down on his arm.

"It's dead!" Zendar said.

Bassan eyeballed the young man and then the creature. Not much remained of it though. A few smoking entrails and a foot. He closed his eyes and sighed.

A sharp blow to the side of his head jolted Bassan into a defensive crouch. He sought the source and found Witz scowling at him.

"You idiot! What part of moving slowly did you not hear? You're damned lucky I'm an excellent shot. Nearly blew your damn foot right off."

Now that Bassan was no longer in mortal danger, Witz's words rankled him. "I'd like to see you hold still with a xert about to bite you."

Witz sneered. "I had a clean shot until you moved. Fool. Get a backbone."

Bassan's hands curled into fists. "Who are you calling a fool?"

"Enough!" Zendar said, sliding in between them. "The xert is dead. That's all that matters. Let's keep it together."

Emitting a bark of contempt, Witz holstered his gun and turned away. Bassan stared at the man, anger still boiling in his system. Zendar nudged his shoulder.

Forget about it.

He's an ass.

Yeah, but he's our best line of defense out here.

Bassan turned to Zendar.

The young man pressed his lips together tight. *For better or worse, we need him. We must get to Jaree. Hang on for another day, all right?*

Tongue held tight, Bassan offered a faint nod. Zendar resumed his position on the flat rock. Still clutching the sand, Bassan stared hard at Witz, wishing all manner of evil on him.

When we get off this planet, I hope we leave your ass here.

5

They approached the next hill, creeping toward the top.

Bassan's pack threatened to pull him backward. He grabbed the straps and shifted it on his back. The adjustment propelled him forward and he struggled to maintain his balance.

Oh, what I wouldn't give for a Tgren desert bike now. Even if I went off a cliff, it would be better than this.

He reached the summit, thankful Zendar and Witz had paused. Straightening his back, Bassan took in the scene before him. More rocky desert hills. And mountains. Much closer than the last time he'd looked, though. They'd made huge progress since yesterday.

"We need to start leaning toward the right," Zendar said. He pointed to the far side of the mountain range. "We'll go around there."

"Great," Bassan said. "Can we take a quick break?"

Witz cast him a skeptical eye, but Zendar nodded. Without waiting for Witz's approval, Bassan sank to his knees. Witz muttered something foul and leaned against a rock.

"This will take forever if we keep stopping for soft boy."

"Hey!" Bassan said, tired of Witz's jabs. "You suggested the last stop. Don't tell me I'm the one who's damned soft."

"Enough. You each need to get out more," Zendar said.

Witz took a draught from his water. "We didn't grow up on this damned planet. I've had my fair share of hard work but hiking for hours on end wasn't part of it."

"I've been a scout and on patrols since age fourteen," Zendar said, standing taller.

"Good for you. Now shut up."

Bassan retrieved his water. His cracked lips closed around the opening and water poured into his mouth.

Aware they needed to save water, he relished the liquid swirling over his tongue. After a couple swishes, he swallowed. His throat soaked it up faster than a sponge.

The wind whistled past. In the silence, broken by the water sloshing in their canisters, he swore he heard the rocks cooking under the sun's oppressive heat. Everything around them reeked of burn. Even his nose hairs tickled from the boiling air. The desert threatened to bake them alive.

"When will we be in range?" Witz said, his voice a low growl.

"By nightfall. If we don't take too many breaks."

Witz shook his head. "Let me see the map. I do better when I know where I'm going."

Zendar produced his mapping device and handed it to Witz. The man studied it, his brows pulled together.

"Where are we trying to get to?" he said.

Zendar pointed at the screen. "Here."

Curious, Bassan leaned over so he could see. The spot lay beyond the mountains. On the left side.

"Why are we going to the right then?" demanded Witz.

"Because that's Lethan territory. We're going around it."

"But if we go straight through it, we'll reach the spot much sooner."

"And we'll risk being seen by a scout party."

Witz shook his head, his crimson hair flailing with annoyance. "If we cut straight through, how long will that take us?"

"But we might be seen—"

"How long?" Witz said, his voice slicing the air.

Zendar paused, his expression blank. "Three hours or so."

"What?" Witz cried.

Bassan scanned the sky. Their day began at dawn. The sun continued to rise in the sky. If they went around and reached the target by nightfall, twice the amount of time they'd already spent would be devoted to hiking. Twice! Maybe more.

"I know it's a long trek around. But to cut through

Lethan-occupied land would be risky."

"What's the worst we'd encounter?"

"Border patrols. Usually five or more people."

Witz turned toward the mountains. "The land is rocky. Plenty of paths through the terrain. We could get through unseen."

Zendar snatched the mapping device from his hands. "And you don't know the Lethan. They are hardened criminals and the descendants of even worse. They catch us, we're as good as dead."

"And you think we'll reach that spot by dusk? Do you think he'll reach it?" Witz said, pointing at Bassan.

Zendar glanced at Bassan and shook his head. "We have to make it though."

"We're already low on water. Do you think we'll have enough to last until tomorrow morning?"

Bassan shook the water canteen in his hands. It sloshed, the sound echoing off the metallic interior. A third of its contents remained.

"So, you want to march as fools through Lethan turf?" Zendar said.

"You're a scout. Or so you say. You can get us through."

"I am a scout, but damn it, this is risky."

Witz turned to Bassan. "Well, soft boy. Want another full day of marching hard? Is the risk too great for you?"

Bassan turned to Zendar. The young man clenched his fists and stared at Bassan in defiance. They were forcing him to choose.

Crap, either way they'll still say I'm soft. Can't make the hike or won't risk the scouts.

He glanced at the passage to the left. A couple more hours and they'd be in range to contact Zendar's clan? But what of the Lethan patrols?

The scene with Drent tumbling over the cliff entered his mind. Tarn took the risk and reacted. He and Drent could've both died. Bassan played it safe. Like he always did. No more.

"We should take the shortest route," he said, fighting to keep his voice steady.

Witz slapped his knee. "There you have it. We cut

through."

Zendar growled and jammed the map into his bag. "You two are crazy. We're going to wind up dead."

"Of course we're crazy. We snuck onto a prisoner planet when most would escape this damned place instead. If that's not insane, I don't know what is," Witz said.

Bassan rubbed dust from his face to hide his grin.

I can't argue with his reasoning.

A punch on his arm startled him. "You finally did something right, soft boy," Witz said, a wicked grin on his face.

Bassan scowled and rubbed his arm. To his surprise, a hint of acceptance trickled from Witz's mind.

Not enough to stop calling me soft boy, but it's a start.

They set off in a new direction. Zendar led them around the rocky hills, zig-zagging among the boulders. Earlier, it would've provided protection from the sun. Now straight above them, the rays burned right through Bassan's clothes. His scalp prickled, and he suspected the top of his head now sported a sunburn. He never burned at home. Of course, endless hours on the ancient Kintal ship meant slight time in the sun on Tgren.

I do need to get out more.

Zendar remained in front, silent since their last stop. He paused now and then to check a small device in his hand. Much smaller than the mapper. Bassan wondered at its purpose. He felt bad for going against Zendar's recommendation and decided to get the young man talking again.

"What do you keep looking at?" he said.

"It's a tracker," Zendar said, squeezing around a large rock. "It works better in open terrain, but hopefully it'll pick up a Lethan patrol before we stumble into them."

"That would be nice," grumbled Witz, roughly yanking his body around the boulder.

"You wanted to come this way."

Bassan pulled himself through the slender opening, his pack catching on the rocks. He almost stumbled to the ground when his pack came free. He reached out, grasping the nearest boulder, and regained his balance.

Witz cast a grimace his direction. "With all the noise we're making, that tracker better work," he said.

Probably need to switch to mental voices, thought Zendar.

Taking a deep breath and readjusting his pack, Bassan vowed to be quieter. He didn't appreciate being in the rear. Easy to pick off the straggler. Not a chance Witz would exchange places with him though.

They paused again not long after. Bassan sank to the ground, grateful for a break. He took a drink and realized his body pitched at an odd angle. He then noticed the sloping ground. So focused on the path, he hadn't noticed the gradual ascent. The mountains now filled his vision.

How close are we to sending a signal? Witz thought.

Zendar set down his water and retrieved the mapper. *Not far now. But at least another hour to get around this mountain. The terrain is about to get clearer, so we'll have to duck and cover where we can. Once we get out of Lethan territory, we'll be on level ground. Room for a ship to land.*

A ship! No more trudging across the desert. Bassan stretched out his left leg, the tired ache slithering up and down his muscles.

First chance I get, I'm putting my feet up.

Zendar slung his pack across his back. *Come on. The sooner we're clear of the Lethan, the better.*

They started the final leg of their journey around the small mountain. The path no longer rose in elevation, but cover grew sparse. Zendar sprinted from boulder to boulder, his head low and checking his tracker constantly. Stooped over, Bassan and Witz followed.

As if it wasn't already difficult enough. I wonder if we'll be crawling next?

Bassan panted from the effort to remain crouched. Sweat trickled down his forehead and dripped into his eyes. Using his shirt sleeve, he wiped away the salty sting. The wind had picked up, blowing sandy grit into his face. He wondered how much of this planet he would inhale by the time he escaped.

I'll be coughing dust. Never thought I'd miss the recycled air of space station.

Zendar paused behind a slender rock and Witz slid in beside him. When Bassan joined them, the sunlight dimmed, casting gloomy shadows across the landscape. Concerned, Bassan inspected the sky. Dark clouds billowed behind them.

Storm is coming, Zendar thought. He scanned his tracker. *We need to keep moving. Stay low.*

Bassan pressed his body against the dusty rocks.

Any lower and I will be creeping along the ground.

Gusts pushed them from behind, prodding them forward. The cooler air was a blessing, but Bassan knew the dangers of desert storms. On Tgren, they rose without warning over the mountains, resembling an invading army of ships. The larger ones could create a wall of sand and swallow towns whole. Taking shelter was always the best option. But here on Ugar, they were out in the open—easy targets.

He scanned the mountains.

Storm's almost around it. We've got to get out of here. Down!

Zendar's order sent Bassan and Witz to the ground.

What is it? Witz thought.

Bassan lifted his head and peered at Zendar, expecting the worst.

I've got movement to our left. Not far from here. High chance it's a patrol.

How many? Can we take them if we need to? Witz thought.

They tend to travel in groups of five or more. Not likely we could take them.

Do you think they saw us? Bassan thought.

I don't think they did. But they are headed in this direction.

Witz grumbled and shifted his position. *Are we close enough to signal yet?*

Yes, but they'll catch the signal as well.

Bassan glanced behind them. Light flashed in the approaching clouds, now closer than ever. *We can't stay here. That storm's gaining on us.*

I know we can't. Glancing down again at the tracker,

Zendar nodded. *All right, stay with me and stay low.*

Zendar got to his knees and scrambled forward to the next boulder. Bassan followed, hot on Witz's feet. They inched closer to the border and freedom. The wind beat at Bassan's backside and he chanced a glance over his shoulder. Black clouds filled the sky, billowing at a frightening pace. In the distance, a bolt of lightning struck the ground. A beast of a storm chased them.

It's about to get ugly. What if the ship can't land to rescue us?

They jumped three more boulders and paused. Zendar checked his tracker and scowled.

They're moving in our direction. Fast!

Then we've been seen, Witz thought. *Send the signal.*

But they will know our position.

Does that matter now?

Bassan shimmied closer. Zendar met his gaze and nodded. Pulling another device from his pocket, Zendar pressed several buttons. He hesitated and then hit one final button.

Signal sent. And now they definitely know we're here.

Time to run for it then, Witz thought.

Zendar pulled himself into a crouch. *On my mark. One, two, three!*

All three sprang into action. Bassan's feet strained to find hold in the loose rock but he managed to stay behind Witz, who also struggled to keep up with their agile guide. Zendar led them to the next boulder but he didn't stop. Running so low they were almost on all fours, they continued to dart between the low-lying rocks. Bassan's heart pounded in his chest, loud enough to drum in his ears and drown out the wind, which now mixed with thunder, vibrating the air with force.

As he dove behind a boulder, something exploded behind him. Thrust forward, he landed hard on Witz. Bassan's ears rang and he shook his head.

Off me, Witz thought, shoving Bassan aside. *Now move.*

Despite his cloudy thoughts, Bassan lurched forward. Driven by terror, he overtook Witz and clung to Zendar's backside while racing to the next outcropping. Another explosion rocked the ground behind them. Bassan didn't bother to look back. A bump on his foot told him Witz still ran with them.

They made it another hundred yards before an explosion rocked the ground in front of them. Zendar jerked back and slammed into Bassan. The three collided behind a large boulder.

They know our exact location. Now we're trapped, Witz thought.

Bassan pushed his back against the boulder. Witz dropped beside him and produced his weapon.

Give me their position. I've got to take that bomber out or we don't stand a chance.

Zendar leaned against the rock and held the tracker over Bassan's head. *To our left. Two clicks back. Crossing open ground.*

Perfect.

Witz spun around and held out his gun. Bassan's breath came hard and fast while the man took aim. Time froze and he waited for the next explosion that would kill them all.

Lowering his head, Witz fired several times. His finger moved in rapid succession, the shot resonating with a hiss after each. He dropped behind the rock and shoved Bassan.

I got him. Move!

Bassan scrambled after Zendar. The slope of the ground made running awkward, but they needed some distance between them and the Lethans before dropping to more even ground. Loose rock spun out from under his boots, but forward momentum kept him upright. The ache in his legs faded and Bassan sprinted for his life.

Lightning lit their path, followed by a monstrous clap of thunder. Bassan didn't miss a beat, though. He continued to hang with Zendar and they tore across the rocky terrain.

If the Lethans don't get us, that storm will.

Smaller shots hit the rocks around them. Bassan ducked lower, nearly doubled over in his efforts. Over his ragged breath, Witz grunted. Bassan chanced a quick glance back. The man remained right behind him.

We should be crossing their border now, Zendar thought.

Will they stop chasing us? Bassan thought.

Maybe. I'm not slowing down to find out though.

Shots continued to fire around them. An explosion rocked the ground above their heads. Debris flew everywhere and several rocks rolled down the hill. Bassan leapt over a small boulder as it sailed past them.

I thought you took out the bomber, he thought.

That wasn't from a gun, Zendar thought. *The Lethans plant mines around their borders.*

You didn't tell us about the mines.

Would you be running so hard if I had?

Zendar veered to the left. Lightning lit up their surroundings and Bassan realized they were on level ground now. No longer running at an odd angle, his strides grew easier. They tore across the desert floor, dodging small rocks and stubby vegetation. Bassan caught his pant leg on a twisted plant. His forward momentum freed him, leaving a shred of his clothing behind. The three continued to place distance between them and their attackers. And the approaching storm.

After several minutes, fire consumed his legs. His lungs burned with an equal intensity. Despite what lay behind them, Bassan couldn't maintain such a fast pace.

I don't think I can run much farther.

Zendar eased his pace. More than happy to slow down, Bassan caught up with him and matched his strides.

Zendar held up his tracking device. *They're not pursuing us. I think we're about out of range for their weapons.*

Still in the lead, Zendar slowed to trot. After a moment, he stopped and turned around. Wheezing for breath, Bassan staggered to a halt. He dropped to his knees. Every part of his body pounded with pain.

Don't let me throw up.

Witz dropped beside him. Zendar remained on his feet, bent over and grasping his kneecaps. The three gasped for air, their desperate breath deafening even over the thunder. Bassan closed his eyes and focused on pumping air into his lungs. Gritty, sandy air. But better than not breathing at all.

How long do we have to wait? Witz thought. Bassan turned to Zendar, eager for the answer.

Zendar straightened his back and reached in his pocket. He stared at the tiny device, his breathing still heavy. He clicked a button and nodded. *They're en route. Maybe ten minutes, tops?*

For a moment, lightning illuminated him. Bassan looked back at the storm clouds. Thunder rumbled behind them. But not so close now. The storm appeared to circle over the valley, pounding it with wind and lightning.

Did we outrun it?

Several minutes passed. Bassan's breathing returned to normal although his heart still beat fast. Nerves tingled from the experience. He wondered if he might relax once they reached Zendar's settlement.

I doubt I'll relax until I'm off this planet.

We still have the damned storm behind us, Witz thought.

I think it's shifted, Bassan thought.

It's circling the mountains. We might get wet, but I don't think it will pass directly overhead, Zendar thought.

Witz grunted and shifted his arm. Bassan turned to him and caught his breath. Blood coated Witz's left arm.

You were shot.

Nicked me in the forearm. I'll live.

Let's wrap you up. No need to attract a predator, Zendar thought, digging through his pack.

Predator? Bassan thought, sitting up straighter. "There's something bigger out here than a xert?"

Zendar produced a thick gauze from a white pouch. *We call them crenks. Giant lizards. Not as large as a man but those suckers can run fast. They hunt mostly in rocky terrain. Fresh blood might draw one out here though.*

Bassan hauled himself to his feet and scanned the mountainous area behind them. *You didn't tell us about giant lizards.*

Again, would you have crossed the land if you knew?

CASSADARK

The rumble of thunder echoed Bassan's annoyance. No longer running for his life, he realized the full danger of their journey through the Lethan's lands. Zendar protested their trek through that area, but he didn't divulge all the hazards.

"Anything else you're not telling us?"

Zendar finished wrapping Witz' arm and glanced up, his lips pressed in a thin line. The shadow over his face spoke of more secrets. Bassan tightened the grip on his pack harness, waiting for the young man to respond. Another rumble, this one with a higher pitch, distracted him. In the distant sky, lights appeared.

"And there's our ride," Zendar said, securing his bag.

"About time," Witz said, rising to his feet.

The ship approached at a rapid pace, the lightning illuminating her pointed nose. Judging by the wide body and wings though, it was the only sleek feature. Bassan tried to place her origins. Torbethian fighters sported a similar trim line around the cabin, but the body suggested a Fesell transport. The mix of pale yellow and rust splashed across her surface confused him further.

Reminds me of old Tgren ships. Which means we're lucky the damn thing's in the air at all. Great!

The ship slowed and adjusted its course. Dropping close to the desert floor, it angled to land. Her giant wheels hit the surface. Engines screamed, switching to reverse to slow her headlong flight. Dust and debris kicked up. A plume of dirt billowed out behind her similar to smoke pouring from a fire. The propulsion system drowned out the thunder. She rolled to a stop not far from their position. The dusty cloud kept moving and billowed around them. Bassan covered his mouth and turned away from the thick, dirty haze.

A dirt bath. Just what I needed.

He squinted through the swirling dust while the oncoming storm pushed it back in his face. As the dirt settled, a flash of light shot out from the rocky range they'd crossed moments ago. Lightning? No, too steady.

Bassan, come on, Zendar thought.

Wait! Bassan scurried to catch up with the others.

He grasped Zendar's shoulder and spun the young man around. Bassan pointed. *What is that?*

Zendar peered toward the mountains and his eyes widened. *We've got company,* he thought, and broke into a run.

Witz paused to look but Bassan needed no further prompting. He sprinted ahead of Zendar and toward the safety of the ship.

I guess they didn't take to me shooting their big gun, Witz thought.

A door opened midship, swinging out into the open air. A chain ladder fell out and hit the ground ten feet below. No ramp or steps? Bassan ignored the inconvenience and leapt at the device. Momentum caused him to swing and he clung for dear life. He reached for the next rung before the ladder stabilized. Easier to grip than the rope, he scaled his way to the open doorway in seconds.

"Come on!" someone shouted, seizing his arm and hauling Bassan inside.

Clawing forward with his hands, Bassan kept himself from tumbling into the ship. The base of a seat halted his forward progress. He swung around and pulled his feet out of the way, then hauled himself to his knees.

Zendar's head appeared in the opening. The man who'd hauled Bassan aboard grasped Zendar's pack and pulled. Bassan leaned forward and seized Zendar's arm and the young man made an abrupt entrance. Zendar spun around and crawled to the entrance.

"Come on, Witz. You can do it."

Damn, we probably shouldn't have left him for last.

Bassan reached for the seat closest to the door and rose on unsteady legs. The ship shimmied below him and he fought to maintain his balance.

And damn, I hate to fly.

At last, Witz's head appeared. Zendar and the other man hauled him inside and Witz grunted when he hit the floor of the ship.

"Grab a seat and strap in, now," the man said and pulled the ladder inside.

His voice struck more fear than the exploding mines

and was almost as loud. Bassan darted toward the nose of the craft. Startled by the view, he realized no barrier divided the cockpit from the rest of the interior. He dropped his pack to the floor and, free of his burden, he slid into the seat behind the pilot. A clear view out the cockpit greeted him. The storm filled the sky, but it could not obscure the approaching ships. Not the observation point he desired.

"Get your harness on," shouted Zendar, fastening his own in the seat across the aisle from Bassan.

Bassan peeked over his shoulder. Witz sat in the seat behind Zendar, but three seats remained open. Bassan started to rise, but a hand on his shoulder slammed him back into the seat.

"I said strap in!" the man said, towering over him. Dark eyes and skin even blacker loomed over Bassan. His craggy features spoke of zero tolerance for disobedience.

Body rigid, Bassan managed to nod, and fumbled with the shoulder harness. The man slid into the copilot's seat.

"Go, go, go!" he said.

The plane lurched forward. Harness half secure, Bassan rummaged for the fastener on his right side. Zendar reached over and slammed the clasp into place. Locked in place at last, Bassan grasped the straps across his chest and turned to Zendar.

Thanks, he thought. *Damn, we made it.*

Not if those three Lethan ships catch us.

Bassan stared out the cockpit window. The ships grew even closer.

Oh, crap, they are moving fast.

The ship spun to the left. Bassan clung hard to the harness and his whole body shifted. His unsecured pack pushed against his legs. The crude wheels picked up every uneven patch and rock on the ground and the ship shook in an unnatural and violent fashion. Between the gravitational pull and severe tremors, his stomach spasmed.

No, no, no, don't throw up now.

Teeth clenched, Bassan closed his eyes.

The force on his body shifted and pressed him into his seat. The shaking continued and increased. Bassan's innards turned to soup and he kept his eyes closed.

"This is going to be close," someone said.

Was that the pilot? And how close?

Don't shut your eyes, Zendar thought. *Makes it worse.*

I open them and I'll throw up.

You'll throw up if you don't.

"No one is throwing up on my ship!"

Bassan's eyes shot open. Outside the cockpit, the world raced toward them. The ship jolted hard and the shaking ceased. The dark sky filled their view and Bassan held his breath. Airborne at last.

"Incoming port side!"

The ship lurched to the right. A second later, an explosion went off on the other side of the hull next to Bassan. The force rocked the ship. His heart leapt to his throat. Only the straps prevented him from flying to the far side of the craft.

"I'll hold them off the best I can," the copilot said, his deep voice penetrating the ringing in Bassan's ears.

"We're no match for three. If we can't outrun them, we're dead," the pilot replied.

"I'll have to take a couple with us, then."

We are going to die.

All hope sunk to Bassan's feet, oozing out his toes.

The pack under his legs shifted, and he pressed it back against the seat. His entire body shook but he focused on the scene outside the cockpit. In the distance, lights appeared and grew brighter.

"Come to me," the copilot said, laughing at his taunt.

A round of shots went off. Not laser fire—actual shots. How old was this ship, anyway? No one had used shots in a hundred years except for the Tgren.

The approaching ship returned fire. Their pilot sent the ship into a dive. They hurled toward the ground and Bassan's rear end left the seat. The other man continued to fire. A small explosion appeared in the far upper corner of their view. The copilot let out a whoop.

"Got his engine. Unless he's crazy, he won't bother us anymore."

Their ship rocked and a boom echoed throughout

the cabin. Bassan gritted his teeth, his grip tightening on his harness. He glanced at Zendar. Eyes wide and mouth open, Zendar's expression didn't boost his confidence.

"Got our tail," the copilot said. "That's going to make flying this thing a real pain in the ass now."

Another ship flew overhead and the copilot fired. Shots pinged off their hull.

We need to get out of here. Why aren't we jumping?

"Doesn't this ship have a teleporter?" Bassan said.

"A what?" the copilot said, his attention on the ship approaching them.

"A teleporter!" Bassan said, projecting his mental voice to be heard over the rattle of the ship.

"Yeah, and it's got no juice. A lot of good that will do us now."

Another explosion rocked them from below. Witz's agonizing exclamation pushed through the din. Bassan chanced a quick look at him. Face scrunched in agony, the man gripped his left arm tight.

Father, I wish you were here now. You could jump this ship. So could mother.

Bassan caught his breath. His parents were jumpers. What if he could jump as well? With no interest in flying, he'd never tested for it. Especially with his connection to the Kintal ship so strong. That was his talent. But if he could jump, teleport the ship to safety...

Another explosion sounded outside the cockpit and the ship lurched hard to the left.

I know how to teleport when there's power. Father's explained how he funnels energy into the teleporter when there's no power. I've got to try.

What does your settlement look like from the air at this time of day? he asked Zendar.

Why?

Just show me.

Without waiting for an answer, he pushed at the man's mind. Zendar hesitated before dropping his shields. A respectable-sized town came into view, its low-lying structures spread out around small fields. A thousand colors glistened, a kaleidoscope of materials and lights. A wall made of metal surrounded the buildings, forming an off-shape circle. Sinking low in the sky, the sun cast deep shadows across the buildings. But it was enough to go by.

The image burned in his mind, Bassan closed his eyes and reached out to the teleporter. As expected, the device sat empty but still intact.

Come on. All you need is a little juice...

Still clinging to the image of the village, Bassan focused on the teleporter. Dead without any power. He concentrated on the device, eyes clenched tight. Its silence gave way to a sound, one that penetrated his skull. It grew in intensity, filling his head and chest. The sensation warmed Bassan and wrapped him in a blanket of security. The power flowed through him and the teleporter. The tingling sensation grew in strength until he thought he would explode.

"Brace yourselves!" the pilot said, his voice hitting a high note.

Jump! Bassan thought.

For a second, the shaking stopped. Bassan floated in a darkness so complete, it threatened to absorb him. The teleporter still connected him, though. His mind wrapped around the image of the town, and he forced the teleporter's energy to respond. As if he'd snapped his fingers, the darkness evaporated. The ship returned to him and he pressed his back against the familiar seat.

"What the...?" The pilot's exclamation filled the cabin.

"What happened?" the copilot said.

Bassan's eyes flew open. Stretched out before them sat Zendar's village, exactly as he'd pictured it.

"Who the heck jumped the ship?" demanded the copilot, turning to look back at them.

Bassan continued to stare at the town in awe, his heartbeat increasing.

Damn, I did it! I really teleported the ship.

A firm grasp on his arm brought him back. "Did you jump the ship?" Zendar said.

He knew Zendar's incredulous expression matched his own. He took a breath and nodded.

"But how?" Zendar said, shaking his arm. "We had no

juice."

"Kid's a jumper," the pilot said.

Those words caught Bassan's attention and he gazed at the back of the man's head. His wispy yellow hair appeared to stand even taller as if electrified by the observation.

"A jumper?" demanded the copilot, turning his attention to the man beside him.

The pilot nodded. "Yup. Someone who can teleport without any juice to power it. And damn, just in time."

"Never heard of such a thing. Handy trick though," the copilot said, staring at Bassan. His scrutiny caused the hairs on Bassan's neck to tingle, but a measure of respect drifted from the man's thoughts.

Zendar released his arm. "You didn't tell me you could do that."

Bassan held up both hands. "I didn't know I could. Until now. But my parents are jumpers. I thought, maybe..."

A hand slapped his shoulder and Zendar laughed. "Well, damned lucky you are. Crap, I thought we were dead."

"We were real close to it," the pilot said, angling the ship to circle the town. "Damn Lethans. Nothing but bloodthirsty scum."

Bassan finally allowed a smile to spread across his face. Zendar matched his silly grin. Bassan looked back at Witz and detected a hint of admiration on his face. The man nodded at him.

"Well done, soft boy," he said.

I will never outgrow that damned name.

"Chancer, we're coming in hot," the pilot said. "Have a team ready."

"Will do, Panvet," came the reply over the com. "And how the heck did you appear out of nowhere like that?"

"Seems one of our passengers has a special talent. We'll see you on the ground."

Bassan dropped his head against the seat.

I did it. Won't my parents be surprised? If I ever get a chance to tell them.

The pilot made his approach, and the ship shifted

several times. Bassan stared at the ceiling, unwilling to let the rough descent ruin his mood. A bump jarred him, and then the engines screamed to slow the ship. When the craft stopped shaking, he chanced a look out the cockpit. A large, open hangar filled the view. On the ground at last.

"Everybody out," the copilot said, clapping his hands with force. "Move it. Now!"

Bassan unhitched his harness and seized his bag. He followed his companions to the exit and Zendar threw open the door. They waited while men pushed a set of stairs into place with haste.

Good, because I didn't feel like climbing down. Or jumping from another damn ship.

He followed Witz and Zendar down the uneven steps. The moment they hit the ground, Zendar hustled away from the ship. Bassan followed with Witz bringing up the rear. Clothed in twilight, the compound blazed with lights across the crude airfield. Zendar led them into the large hangar and his pace slowed.

Sorry, we needed to get clear. Although it looks like they have the fire under control now, Zendar thought. *Welcome to Jaree.*

Bassan turned to look. Three crewmen sprayed a white substance over the fading flames on what remained of the tail fin. He swallowed hard.

We flew while on fire?

"Zendar!"

Two men approached them. The older of the two moved with authority and Bassan stood straight. To his surprise, the man embraced Zendar.

"Good to have you home," he said, slapping Zendar on the back. The man turned to Bassan and Witz. "Did you find what we needed?"

"Yes. This is Witz. He helped us set up everything. His brother is here in Jaree. This is Commander Cartent."

The commander shook Witz's uninjured arm. "Good to meet you, son. Who is your brother?"

"Hetz."

The commander smiled. "Our weapons expert. Pain in the ass but a hard worker."

Witz gave a bark of laughter. "That sounds like Hetz."

"Sir," Zendar said, "Witz was injured during our escape from the Lethans."

"We'll get you patched up. Gent!" He turned to the man beside him. "Get this man to medical right away."

"Yes, sir! Follow me," he said, gesturing to Witz.

Once on their way, Zendar pointed at Bassan. "Sir, this is Bassan. He's a Kintal with a special connection to the original Kintal ships. And he's a jumper. He got the Panvet out of a nasty dogfight."

The commander extended his hand. "Welcome, Bassan. Your presence here is most appreciated."

"Thank you, sir," Bassan said, shaking his hand. Skin rough to the touch, which didn't shock him. Although the man's bluish complexion suggested something softer. Blond curly hair poked out from under his cap. A bit of Lorvendera mixed in? "I'll do what I can to find a cure."

The commander glanced at Zendar, who simply nodded. Cartent smiled broadly at Bassan, his slanted eyes becoming even more so.

"I'm sure you'll do everything you can. Now, I bet you could use with some food and rest. Zendar, once he's settled, report to me."

"Yes, sir!" Zendar punched Bassan's arm. "Come on. Let's get cleaned up before the evening meal is over."

The commander had already stepped away, so Bassan simply followed Zendar. They crossed a large hangar, dodging personnel. The lights shone on several other ships, all in ragtag shape like the one that had rescued them. Shapes and colors mismatched. Bassan swore the one in the corner boasted a Cosbolt body. An older model like his father flew? Burns across the nose suggested better days.

I wonder if they dumped the Cassan pilot with his ship?

Bassan shuddered at the thought.

They passed through a checkpoint leading into the compound, and Zendar vouched for the new arrival. Once past the guards, Bassan paused to take in his surroundings.

Tall lights illuminated the town. No building appeared

more than one story, so he couldn't see past a couple rooftops. The glint of metal in a multitude of colors met him at every angle. Repurposed scrap metal. The entire town—constructed from the garbage dumped on this planet. Fitting and yet sad.

At least Tgren is uniform in its clay and sand structure. And reinforced with Cassan technology. I hope a strong storm doesn't come through while I'm here. The whole settlement might blow away.

We'll dump the packs at my place, Zendar thought, giving Bassan a nod and a grin. *Then we'll catch a bite before cleaning up.*

On cue, his own aroma wafted in his nostrils. Ugh. *Any chance we could clean up first?*

You want to go hungry tonight?

No!

Zendar nodded at a man as he passed. *No one will notice anyway. Trust me.*

Bassan offered the strange man a smile. Cracked lips turned upward even though the man's eyes narrowed. The man pulled his cloak closer, wrapping it tight around his body. His gait faltered. Bassan turned his head to follow the man's movement, concerned he might fall. The stranger lurched forward, crouching low to regain his balance. He continued on, one foot dragging behind him.

I wonder if he's affected by the plague? I hope I can save them.

Over here, Zendar thought.

Tearing his gaze from the older man, Bassan realized he'd fallen behind. He trotted to catch up with Zendar and the young man rounded a corner. He almost ran into him when Zendar stopped to fumble with a crude lock on a corrugated door. He shoved hard against the surface and the metal sheet gave way. A broad smile appeared on his lips and Zendar led the way inside.

I'm sure it's not what you're used to. But this is how my people live, Zendar thought. *And it's the best I can offer you.*

Bassan stepped into the doorway and halted, unable to see any farther. A bright light appeared a few feet in front of him, swaying back and forth, blinding him. Closing his eyes, he ducked his head. He counted to three and opened his eyes with care. The glow of a single lantern hung a few feet from his face, dangling from the ceiling. Focused on the warm glow, he stepped forward.

"It's not much," Zendar said, his pack hitting the floor with a resounding thud. "But it's a safe place to rest my head."

Bassan surveyed his surroundings. A bed to his right. A counter and many shelves to his left. A large dresser pressed against the wall with the door. Despite the simplicity of the room, many items covered the available surfaces. Those on the left appeared practical in nature—food, weapons, etc. On the right, a variety of items decorated the room, ranging from crude photos to old relics from other planets. Nothing matched—just a hodgepodge of styles and colors, not to mention races.

Like the rest of this place.

"You live alone?" Bassan let his pack slide from his shoulders to the floor.

"I do. No mate. But I'll work on it someday."

I need to work on that someday as well. When I get back. If I get back.

"Come on," Zendar said. "Let's go get some food."

His casual attitude pressed hard against Bassan's chest. "What about your ill? Shouldn't I begin accessing a cure as soon as possible?"

"Are you up to doing it tonight?"

Bassan's body ached from days of hard travel, and the last traces of coherent thought had left him hours ago. "Probably not."

Zendar nudged his arm. "We got you here much faster than expected. We desperately need your abilities, but they can wait until morning. When you are recharged and ready to go."

Bassan's stomach growled, the sound dispelling the silence of the room. Embarrassed, he wrapped his arms around his midsection.

Zendar chuckled. "Then let's get something to eat. The problems of the world can wait until tomorrow."

Winding through the narrow streets, Zendar led him deeper into the town. They passed several residents, old and young. A couple offered a warm greeting to Zendar while giving Bassan a curious but not unfriendly stare. The rich variety of races represented in each person spoke to the years of interracial blending. The result—a settlement comprised of Kintals, some of the purest in form. It comforted Bassan to see so many of his people.

The lights grew brighter, and they stepped into an open area. Large awnings stretched overhead, providing cover for the assortment of tables and chairs arranged in neat rows. Thirty or so people occupied the space, taking less than twenty percent of the seats.

Good, we're not too late.

The aroma of food hit his nostrils and Bassan followed Zendar with a bounce in his step, weaving around the tables. Several people welcomed Zendar back and eyed Bassan with curiosity. They didn't stop to chat though and approached a long building with open windows. An assortment of food bowls sat on tables inside, level with the windows and providing easy access from the outside. Zendar grabbed two metal plates and handed one to Bassan.

"Not a lot left, but enough to fill the hole in my gut." He dug a large spoon into a bowl of cooked vegetables.

The bowls were mostly empty, but enough remained to sample each. His hunger gnawing deep at his stomach, Bassan was ready to try everything.

Please no herren roots. Cruel twist of fate if that nasty Tgren plant grows on this planet.

Plates full, they took a seat at the nearest table and dove in. Bassan hardly tasted the first few bites, impatient to fill the void inside. By the third dish, he began noticing the tastes and textures. Most of it was new to him. The one meat entrée featured a tangy spice with a dash of sweetness, tingling his tongue. It pleased him though.

He scanned the other diners. No one race jumped out at him.

They're a mix of many races. I guess it shouldn't surprise me the food is as varied. At least it's all tasty.

While they ate, the others present stopped by their table before departing. All greeted Zendar and asked if he'd brought help. Each time, he pointed and grinned, introducing Bassan as his new friend. Bassan paused long enough to say hello and assure them he would do everything he could to save them. Several touched his shoulder, as if to prove to themselves he existed. Everyone offered their thanks before departing.

I hope I don't let them down, Bassan thought, washing the last of his meal down with water.

You won't. You possess the knowledge that will rescue us.

I don't, but the Kintal database might hold the answer. He patted the tablet still nestled against his chest.

Zendar's eyes narrowed. He smiled, erasing the shadow across his face. *Between you and your tablet, I'm sure the solution is there.* He grabbed his plate and glass and stood up. *Now, ready to get cleaned up and catch some sleep? It'll be an early start tomorrow.*

Bassan rose, his knees stiff from sitting after a long day of hiking. And running. *Yes! The moment I lie down, I'm going to be out.*

6

Roused at dawn, Bassan struggled to pull himself together and get dressed. His body ached, protesting the recent use of muscles that rarely saw much action. Even his toes throbbed when he pulled on his boots. Bassan realized he needed to change up his routine when he got back to Tgren. Witz was right about being soft.

They grabbed a plate of food and joined the small group gathered under the awnings. This time they reached the servings early rather than late, the food fresh and bowls piled high. Too tired for conversation, Bassan focused on his meal. Seated near the edge of the tables, he stole glances up at the sky. A faint light rose on the horizon, but darkness covered most of it, and he could even see a couple bright stars.

You weren't kidding about early, he thought, scooping another mouthful of creamy cereal.

Commander Cartent's request. And I imagine a tradeoff for starting today rather than last night.

Bassan yawned and arched his sore back. *I offered. This works.*

They finished their meal in silence. Zendar nodded at Bassan, his brows pulled tight together, and grabbed his plate. More awake now, Bassan hesitated, contemplating Zendar's intense look. He reached out, but a shield blocked Zendar's mind. Before he could form any semblance of a question, Bassan found himself alone at the table. He pulled himself to his feet and hastened after Zendar.

I guess it's time to get serious. These people are facing death.

Zendar led him through the desert city. Many of the residents had risen and begun their day. Those he encountered paused when Bassan and Zendar passed. Most of their expressions remained guarded. Bassan couldn't blame them for caution when it came to an outsider. He detected hope though. Where shields faltered, optimism flowed his direction. So did a certain level of expectation. A modest bit of pressure. As expected.

It's up to me and they know it.

A weight settled on his shoulders. Bassan dropped his chin and avoided making eye contact with anyone else.

He halted abruptly when Zendar stopped before a large set of double doors. Rocking on his heels, Bassan drew himself up straight. The guard looked him over before turning to Zendar. Bassan waited while the two exchanged private words. He scrutinized the building, startled by its height. Its mismatched metal siding reached several levels above the rest of the settlement.

Looks like a hangar. Is this where they keep the sick? Damn, should I be going in there? I can't help them if I fall ill...

"Bassan."

Startled to hear his name out loud, he turned around. Zendar stared at him, his face frozen and unmoving.

"Remember, you are here to save us. You hold the key."

"Well, I hope the database holds the key—"

"No." Zendar grabbed his shoulders and gave Bassan a gentle shake. "You hold the key. The answer is in you. And it will set all of us free."

"Set you free?" Bassan reached for his mind, hoping for clarification, but met a wall of resistance.

"Yes, that's why we selected you. I was desperate. I promised to bring back our salvation. I just..." His hands fell from Bassan's shoulders, and he stepped back, shaking his head. "I trust you'll understand."

Understand what? Bassan thought, alarms ringing in his head.

The doors slammed open. Bassan jumped. His hand went to his tablet, pressed tight against his chest.

Come on, Zendar thought. *I'll show you.*

Bassan followed Zendar inside. He took one step through the door and halted.

He stood in a hangar, all right. A massive one. And occupying most of the available space sat a ship both alien and familiar.

The doors closed behind him.

What is this? Bassan thought, glancing at Zendar.

The young man turned to him, lips pressed in a thin line. Zendar stared up at the ship without answering. Bassan followed his gaze.

A craft of impressive size filled his view. The massive ship boasted rounded corners, although she was anything but smooth on the outside. Numerous exterior devices covering her hull, the colors and shapes imitating the settlement. Bassan had no idea of their function, but one device stood out. Weapons. Located in several places. Whatever her purpose, this ship could defend herself.

Movement caught his attention. Men and women scurried about, working on the ship. Sparks flew from several locations, welding pieces to the surface. The acrid stench of melting metal hung on the air. It stung his nose and he shook his head.

His view altered, he stared straight ahead. A portal lay open before him, leading into the ship. He focused on that welcoming entrance. Two men carried some equipment inside, vanishing into the brightly lit corridor.

But what caught his attention was the overall color scheme inside the vessel. Blue. A brilliant blue. Similar to the ancient Kintal ships...

"You have a Kintal ship?" he demanded, grabbing Zendar's arm.

"No," Zendar said, straightening his shoulders. "We are building a Kintal ship."

Bassan released him with a growl. "How?"

"Apparently the Narcons don't value their Kintal ship, and they've dumped countless pieces of it over the past ten years. We've scoured the planet to find those pieces, sometimes at the loss of life, so we could put together this ship. We lacked one thing, though."

"What?"

Before Zendar could answer, someone called their names. They turned to see Commander Cartent and another man approaching. Bassan wanted answers, but he knew better than to disrespect authority.

"Hope you are rested now," Cartent said to Bassan, offering a courteous nod.

Bassan squinted at Zendar, stifling his aggravation. "Yes, sir."

"Good, because we need your wits about you today." The commander gestured to the man beside him. "Barnenden is the chief engineer and scientist working on the Freedom. You'll be working directly with him."

The shorter man nodded and shifted the tablet in his hand. His yellowed skin marked him a Narcon and one of the few non-Kintals Bassan had encountered so far in the compound. Narcons often lacked friendly personalities, but this man offered a genuine smile.

"Bassan, correct?"

When Bassan nodded, the man's smile grew. "I have read about you. I must say, finding you was most fortunate, considering your unique experience."

What does he mean unique? How does he know me? Why am I here?

"Sir, thank you, but I don't understand. Zendar said your people were dying..."

"We are dying," Cartent said, emphasis on the second word. He gestured toward the ship. "This way. Better if we show you."

Bassan turned to Zendar but the man fell in step with the commander. Barnenden clasped his shoulder and prodded him forward. Annoyed to find a Narcon dictating his actions, Bassan kept his gaze forward and ignored the man.

With each step toward the ship, Bassan's boots grew heavier. What was he really here to do?

If Zendar lied to me...

Inside the ship, the lights bathed him in a familiar gentle indigo. Muscles tightening, he followed. He knew this path. He'd walked it thousands of times on Tgren. The curve of the Kintal ship welcomed him while warning signals erupted in his head.

They're building a Kintal ship. How? Even if the

Narcons dismantled their ship, how did they get all the parts? And where are the sick people? What is going on?

They wound through the passages to a familiar ramp. Bassan trailed the group, his breathing forced. When they reached the landing, he grunted. The room overlooked the pod room in the Kintal ship back home. Same layout, including the consoles. Yet no windows overlooking the pod room. What was this place?

Commander Cartent turned to Bassan. "Zendar told me you've made critical progress in accessing information on Kintal ships due to your special connection with them. We need your skills to help us complete this ship."

Bassan flashed Zendar a look he hoped conveyed his growing agitation. "You tricked me into coming here by convincing me people were dying?"

"As I said, our people are dying," Cartent said. "Larger tribes are forming and threatening our existence. Many aren't interested in cohabitating. They want to conquer and take the best in resources and people, condemning the rest to die here."

Fury erupted in Bassan, and he took a step back. Focused on Zendar, he let his frustration pour from his mind. "You lied. You told me there was sickness. Why didn't you tell me the truth?"

Zendar leaned away, his hands up. "I had to get you here no matter what."

"No matter what? Including lying to me about your people being sick? And your sister dying? I bet you don't even have a sister! Damn it, here I thought Witz was the scum for drugging me."

"Bassan," Cartent said, his voice cutting the air with force. Biting his tongue, Bassan turned to the commander. "I instructed Zendar to use any means necessary to bring us help. While I regret the circumstances that brought you to Jaree, you are here now, and we are still in desperate need of your assistance. We need this ship operational. If we don't get off this planet soon, we'll be wiped out. All of us. Would you condemn the children and innocents to die such terrible deaths? This ship is our only chance."

The man's words prodded his conscience and struck

a chord. Guilt butted into his thoughts. Despite his anger and indignation at the deceit, the rage within subsided a few notches. He held the means by which they might live. That is, if he acted. He did nothing to save Drent, but he could save these people.

There's no disease, but if the other tribes are as aggressive as the Lethan, then it's only a matter of time. Damn it, I can't do nothing. Not again. Not to mention it's my only ticket off this planet. But if Zendar is still lying to me...

He peered at Zendar, still irritated by the deception. "Sir, I do have a connection with the Kintal ships, and I've conducted a lot of research based on my ability, but there's no guarantee I can help you. I don't know every system on the ship."

"You don't need to know every system," the commander said. He moved to a console, its panel dark, and placed a hand on the frame. "But we're hoping you can access the systems on this one and get the rest of the Freedom online."

Bassan frowned and moved closer. Lights shone from two of the controls, but all else remained dark. The two control panels beyond it blazed with the glow of information and life. *Only two?*

"Wait a minute," he said, spinning to his left. A wall greeted him, control screens occupying a small portion in the center. The rooms containing numerous other consoles were absent. "Where are the rest of the control panels? There should be more."

"The Narcons disassembled a portion of their Kintal ship and discarded it, but not everything. We've had to duplicate and compact where necessary," Cartent said.

Bassan stared at him. Few knew the layout of a Kintal ship. "How would you know how to do that? You've never seen a Kintal ship."

Barnenden cleared his throat, drawing everyone's attention. "I worked on the ship on Narcon for twelve years. It was my life, so I am quite familiar with it. I also know exactly what parts they discarded. At least those components prior to three years ago."

"And what parts we couldn't ever find," Cartent added. "As I said, we've duplicated what we could and merged it with other technology. This ship is a bit of a mongrel, but she's Kintal at heart."

A thousand questions pinged around inside Bassan's head. *How much merging? What parts did they recover? Why is this Narcon here? What if I can't access the panel...?*

He swallowed hard on that last thought. A chill swept through his body.

"I help you access the systems, or I don't get off the planet," Bassan said, voice cracking. He scanned the faces of those present. "No one does."

The commander nodded. "Only those skilled and athletic enough to sneak aboard a garbage transport."

Bassan's gaze settled on Zendar. The man shifted his feet. Bassan's gut churned and he flexed his fingers. *Skilled and athletic, of which I am neither. And that was your plan for getting me off world? I don't know why I believed you.*

I could still get you on one of those ships if need be, Zendar answered, straightening his chin. *But I won't need to because you're going to get this working in no time.*

Bassan's jaw dropped.

I'm stuck. Completely stuck. I fix this console or I never see Tgren again. Never see Sirella again, or my parents.

A sadness swept over him. With it came reluctant resignation. If he wanted off this planet, it was up to him. Bassan reached into his jacket and produced his tablet. "I guess I need to get to work, then."

* * *

"We reconfigure this connection," Barnenden said, his fingers a blur over the panel, "and route the power through this converter. Correct?"

"Yes," Bassan said, glancing at his tablet. "From that point, you'll have enough to power the secondary reactor."

"One step closer to turning on life support," the other assisting technician said.

Barnenden made the adjustments, pausing on occasion to check his calculations. Bassan leaned back and rubbed his temples. His head throbbed from repeated connections all day with the Kintal ship. General information was easy to find. Specific panel connections—much more challenging. He hoped no more melds with the ship were needed today. His brain craved a break.

"Got it," the chief engineer said.

Bassan opened his eyes and peered at the screen. The code aligned as predicted. And if his calculations lined up, the life support system sat at the ready.

"That should do it," he said, mustering what enthusiasm his aching head could manage.

"Well done," the other technician said, slapping him on the back. Bassan managed a weak smile.

"We need to run a full diagnostic first," Barnenden said, eagerness broadcasting from his mind.

"Let's get started." The other man spun away to the nearest console.

Now? I'm starving.

As if on cue, his stomach rumbled. Loudly. Bassan covered his midriff with his free hand.

Barnenden leaned away from the screen. "Why don't you go get something to eat before the evening meal is over? Obviously, no one is bringing us food this evening. The diagnostics might take hours and even if it doesn't, we can't turn on the system until there's a full crew here tomorrow morning."

Too tired to object even if he wanted to, which he didn't, Bassan nodded. He tucked his tablet into his shirt, retrieved his cup of water from the floor, and wished the men good luck. Feet dragging, he trudged down the ramp.

He knew his way out of the ship and found the correct hangar doors without a problem. Despite the dusky sky, the complex appeared equally lit. But once outside, his pace slowed even more. Which way to the mess hall again?

I think it's in the middle of the complex. Should I ask the hangar guard?

A breeze blew, cool and refreshing. It carried with it a hint of roasting meat. His stomach growled again at the prospect of a filling meal.

Follow my nose it is.

He wove among the buildings, sniffing the air with each turn so he didn't lose the scent. Bassan passed several residents coming from the direction he headed, so he took it as a promising sign.

Please let there be some food left. I'll lick the pan if I must.

The glow of lights grew brighter. He rounded a corner and it opened onto the dining area. The serving building sat on his left and he approached, prepared for disappointment. He realized a nice selection of entrées remained. The bowls were barely a quarter full but better than the scraps he'd eaten the night before. He grabbed a plate.

That reminds me. I wonder where Zendar got to? I have no idea how to find his place again. I still want to give him a piece of my mind for deceiving me.

Piling his plate high with a bit of everything, Bassan went for it all. He found the closest empty table and dove into his food. About halfway through he slowed enough to begin tasting each bite and enjoying it.

Considering their limited resources, their dishes are amazing. Or am I so used to Tgren food it makes anything else taste exotic? Shame I can't take any of it back with me—if I go back, of course.

No longer focused on his meal, Bassan observed the complex. A few more stragglers entered, but twice the people occupied the dining area as the previous evening. Several families ate together, old and young alike. Generations trapped on this planet.

Such a shame. Living one's whole life a prisoner even though innocent. Never to know any other life.

He scooped up another bite of food and guffawed as a thought occurred to him.

Like I'm any better. If not for the code in my head and the probe, I never would've left Tgren when I was younger. I certainly didn't want to leave this time. And look where it landed me.

The joyful laugh of a little girl caught his attention. She scampered around the tables, a young woman in pursuit. Wrapping her arm around the child's midsection, the woman caught her. She lifted the girl in the air and spun around twice. They laughed and the woman set the child on a bench and gave her a hug. The girl threw her arms around the woman's neck, giggling. Holding her tighter, the woman turned her head in Bassan's direction.

He started. The woman's slender, pale face held a hint of blue. Her ivory hair blew in the wind, pulling the long curls out behind her. For a moment, Bassan saw Sirella, her ashen face more beautiful than a full moon rising over Tgren. It struck him then how much he missed her. The ache spread through his body reminiscent of a chill.

Sirella, I promise, if I get off this planet, the first thing I'm doing when I get back to Tgren is asking you to be my mate.

Laughing, the child broke free and ran in Bassan's direction. He smiled when she drew near, her face full of delight.

So free and innocent. I hardly remember that feeling.

Boom! An explosion rocked the compound.

Bassan dropped to his knees, as did everyone else. The child clung to the ground in front of him, her face twisted in terror. Without another thought, he jumped up, slid next to her, and threw his body over hers.

I've got you, he thought, holding her close.

Distress emanated from her, but a sense of security also sparked in her mind. Bassan stroked her hair and looked up.

Is it an air attack? Someone storming the walls? Should we get under cover?

A series of short blasts arose from the sirens, breaking the eerie silence. Unsure of their meaning, Bassan remained in position.

What happened?

Underneath him, the child squirmed. Bassan lifted his body and she sat up. The girl gazed at him, her dark, wide eyes conveying gratitude more sharply than even her thoughts. He stared at her, surprised by the depth in her gaze.

Liron!

Bassan glanced up and the woman swooped down on the girl. She scooped her up in her arms and held the child close. Bassan sat back, unsure of his response. The woman opened her eyes and offered a gentle smile.

Thank you for protecting my daughter.

The woman and child returned to their family. Bassan stood and dusted off. He continued to watch them, unsure of his next course of action.

I still have no idea what happened.

Forcing himself to move, he spun around. Several people bustled away, pausing to clear their plates. Others remained at the tables, though. As if nothing had taken place.

A thought struck him.

Did I really just throw myself over the girl? Crap, where's Witz? The one time I do something heroic...

"There you are!"

Zendar appeared in his line of sight and Bassan jumped. The young man glowed with energy and a vigor Bassan could no longer remember. Head still throbbing from a full day of connecting with the Kintal ship, Bassan resented Zendar's rejuvenated state.

"What just happened?" he demanded.

"The blast? A drone explosion. The Lethan sometimes send drones to spy on us. We shoot them down of course, but there is usually a bomb attached. We take out their drone, they take out something of ours."

Bassan's heart still pounded. "You're sure that was it?"

"You heard the siren blasts. Drone detonated. All clear."

And I'm supposed to know that?

Grasping the table, Bassan slid back into his seat. Zendar dropped to the bench across from him. After retrieving his fork, Bassan stabbed a small root.

"And where have you been all day?" he asked, taking a small bite.

"Working for part of it. My captain arranged for me to get back into the patrol schedule. I leave tomorrow for two days. You all right with that?"

"If I can find your place again I am."

"I'll make sure you can find it before I leave tomorrow. If you get lost, ask someone. We all know where each other lives."

Bassan nodded. Still poking at his food, he asked, "Why did you lie to me?"

Zendar took a deep breath and glanced at another table before clasping his hands together and leaning closer. "I could say it was Witz's idea, but I'd be lying. Telling you we were dying of disease was all mine."

Bassan offered a snort of contempt, his attention shifting back to his plate.

"In my defense, it was better than Witz's plan. He wanted to knock you out and kidnap you."

Sounds like Witz all right.

"That's actually what you guys did."

"Well," Zendar said, running fingers through his hair, "at least I talked Witz out of keeping you out until we reached the containment room on the trash ship. It didn't seem right."

Bassan poked again at his food, his appetite gone. "But why not tell me the truth? Tell me about the Kintal ship and your plans to escape?"

Zendar shrugged. "It didn't sound as convincing."

"What about the scene you showed me? The one with all the sick people?"

"That was...a half truth. A virus swept through the compound two years ago and about forty people fell ill. I just amplified the vision to make it look show more. It's a Fesell ability."

A robust breeze blew through the open dining area, carrying with it the strong odors of sand and overcooked food. Bassan sighed and dropped his fork. He lacked the energy to argue further. The situation remained the same regardless. Get the ship operational or remain here forever.

He stared at his plate. Half of his food remained. "I hate to waste it, but I'm not hungry anymore."

"We waste nothing," Zendar said, slapping the table. "Come on, I'll show you where to dump it."

Bassan followed him to the building serving food. To the right, a large metal can marked "compost" sat in the shadows. Zendar lifted the lid and gestured for Bassan to clear his plate. A rank smell emitted from the container and Bassan dumped his food in haste. Zendar closed the lid with a flourish.

"You should smell the compost pit," he said while Bassan set his utensils with the other dirty dishes. "It's at the far edge of the complex and for the most part downwind. Some days though, everything stinks. But all organics, from food to waste, goes into the pit to be used as fertilizer for the food we grow. Without it, we couldn't feed half this many people."

"Be nice if the wind doesn't shift while I'm here," Bassan said.

Zendar grinned and punched him in the shoulder. "Come on, I'll take you back to my place."

They meandered down the narrow streets, the lights from the buildings providing minimal illumination. Zendar pointed out landmarks so Bassan could find his way back again. Head still impaired, he tried to remember the details. No two buildings looked alike, so the landmarks were distinctive. A dwelling with red metal panels. A taller building with strips of green wood in between the silver and black steel sheets. A wide structure with a seascape painted across the front. Bassan paused to gaze at it. His sole experience with the ocean resided in a brief glimpse from a shuttle. Despite twenty-five years on Tgren, not once had he visited any of her oceans.

I wonder if Sirella has ever seen an ocean? I can't remember Piten taking his family on a trip like that. When I get back, we're visiting the ocean whether I enjoy flying or not.

Once they reached Zendar's place, Bassan realized he did indeed recognize it. The door was a simple, silver metal sheet, and the rest of the building sat awash in a mixture of yellow and orange. He didn't recall seeing another comparable door, so Bassan anticipated its distinct makeup would stand out tomorrow night. Otherwise, he might circle the compound for hours.

Zendar shoved the door open. "You didn't lock it?" Bassan said, following him inside.

"I rarely do. I locked it when I was off world because around here, if you're gone for very long, some people start to assume you're not coming back. I didn't want to return to an empty shack."

Bassan sank onto the stool by the makeshift table. The sole light in the room dangled from a wire above it. He yawned and pulled out his tablet.

"I forgot to ask. How did it go today?" Zendar said.

"We rerouted the connections for life support. I think they're going to test it tomorrow morning."

"That was fast." Zendar moved to the opposite side of the table. "You are a genius when it comes to Kintal ships."

Bassan rubbed his forehead. "Not a genius. I simply know where to look. Right now, I want to look for some sleep."

"Right. Well, I won't keep you. In the morning, I'll show you the washrooms and lead you to the hangar before I head out. Then you're on your own for two days. But if you get lost, ask anybody for directions."

I'm sure I'll have to do that more than once.

Bassan dragged himself to the makeshift bedding on the floor. Boots off his feet, he collapsed. His tablet poked at his chest and he slipped it out and under the edge of his pillow. Nestling in, he closed his eyes. Zendar stirred a couple times but otherwise the room fell into silence. Only the hum of the distant generators and a stray voice penetrated the calm surroundings. His head no longer throbbed, and he suspected sleep would drive away the remaining ache.

May the life support come on tomorrow. It has to.

7

"Diagnostics complete," Barnenden said.

Bassan leaned forward, grasping the edge of the console. His left foot drummed out a rapid beat.

Please let it be right this time.

Barnenden tapped the screen and brought up the results. Bassan held his breath and read through the lines of code. No red. No blinking numbers. It was a go.

"Finally," he whispered.

"I'll alert personnel. Ready to turn on life support," Barnenden announced.

Bassan stretched his back, aching from hours spent bent over the console.

It better come on.

Despite a day of frustration, the small room now buzzed with anticipation. Three other technicians had assisted them today, pooling the compound's resources to find a solution. Last night's diagnostics indicated a power issue and the one today revealed a routing problem. After several attempts to route the signals correctly, they completed the third diagnostic. With everything checking out and no other issues surfacing, Bassan hoped nothing else went wrong.

Come on! Work. I want off this damned planet.

A distant hum oscillated in the air. Bassan glanced around the room. No one else responded to the sound.

Can no one else hear it?

The hum increased in volume. Bassan scanned the consoles in the room. The monitor in the corner flashed information across its screen. Bassan moved closer. The ever-changing numbers drew him in, enticing him, and he loomed over the console. The figures made no sense.

"Life support still not operational," one of the

technicians said.

Bassan stared at the screen.

What are you trying to tell me?

Tired, he didn't relish another plunge into the computer's history. If they were to find the solution, no other option remained. He drew a breath, closed his eyes, and placed his hand across the connection orb.

Life support. Show me life support systems on the Kintal ship. Show me those numbers.

The darkness dissolved and his view shifted. A Kintal console came into view. He stood to the side as two other men, olive complexions marking them Tgren, worked on the console. They punched in codes and waited. Bassan leaned closer, hoping to catch the combination of numbers. One man slammed his fist on the edge of the console.

"We're so close." He turned to Bassan. "What are we missing?"

Startled to be part of the equation, Bassan took a step back. The men stared at him, awaiting a response. Bassan approached and examined the screen. Every connection appeared correct. Except...

"This is routed wrong." Bassan tapped the screen and entered new coordinates. "You need to route these three auxiliary BUS modules in the correct sequence."

The numbers flashed on the screen. Within seconds, the lines all exhibited green.

"That was it," the man said.

The correct sequence of the modules. Of course.

His hand lifted from the connection and Bassan rocked on his heels. One of the technicians appeared at his side.

"Are you all right?" the woman said, grasping his elbow.

Bassan shook his head to clear the confusion in his mind. What had he seen? Life support. Three auxiliary BUS modules. That was the answer!

"It needs to be routed in the correct order," he said, staggering toward Barnenden. "It won't work otherwise."

The man frowned. "I thought it was."

Bassan reached the main console. "It's not. But I know how to connect it."

Barnenden moved aside. Bassan focused on the screen, his mind still reeling from his vision. He'd not witnessed the actual solution, but he knew what to do. Sure of the direction, he inputted the commands, adjusting the routing.

"There," he said, hitting the final computation.

Another hum reverberated the air. This time, everybody searched the room with their eyes. Bassan gripped the edge of the console, his body quivering. This had to work.

"Life support is on," a voice called across the com.

The entire room erupted into cheers. Bassan closed his eyes and let his head droop. Two days of intensive research and work. Success at last!

"Son, you did it," Barnenden said, slapping him on the back.

Bassan lifted his head and offered a weak smile. Barnenden grinned from ear to ear, his eyes drawn into mere slits. Bassan laughed at the sight. In all his years dealing with Narcons, not once had any of them cracked even a faint smile. Despite his initial hesitation, he liked Barnenden.

Here I thought all of you had a Vindicarn stick up your rear.

Once the excitement died down, they ran another diagnostic. This time, no issues turned up.

"Bassan, you did it," Barnenden said, grasping the frame of the main console with thin fingers.

Bassan rubbed his tired hands on his thighs. "We all did it. We were men on a mission."

The Narcon laughed, his lean frame shaking from the effort. Again, it struck Bassan how this man resembled nothing he'd ever learned about Narcons. Where was the cold and calculating attitude? And the reserved demeanor? Barnenden's pleasant nature sat at odds with other Narcons.

"Why are you here?"

The moment the words left Bassan's mouth, he regretted them. They hung in the air like an accusation. Barnenden cocked his head, eyes narrowed, and Bassan braced himself for a reprimand.

Barnenden's shoulders sagged. Remorse drifted from his mind. He rubbed his forehead and turned his gaze to the screen.

"I was one of the first scientists to access the Kintal ship on Narcon. We worked day and night uncovering her secrets. With the enforced peace, our leaders focused on the ship. Information was slow in coming though. Eventually they grew bored by our lack of output. The sections we'd already been through, they deemed unnecessary. Military personnel began stripping the ship, discarding what wasn't needed. I stood and watched countless databases of information ripped from the foundation and sent out with the trash."

"Commander Cartent said a lot of the ship came together from discarded elements of the Narcon ship," Bassan said, putting the pieces together.

No wonder so much of this ship resembles an actual Kintal vessel. It really was.

"Yes, it was all consigned to be dumped on Ugar."

Grief echoed in the man's words. He was dedicated to the Kintal ship. As dedicated as Bassan. Yet they were both here...

"Were you dumped as well?"

Barnenden's eyes closed. "Yes. I protested the needless waste of resources. We still had so much to learn. But those in charge wanted to remain ignorant. They grew obsessed with a way to counter the probe. The war they aspired to win had been denied them. They wanted to find an answer in the Kintal ship, a way to defeat the probe. My protests against such a futile effort fell on deaf ears. Three years ago, they felt my unrest a problem. Before I could even speak to my mate, I was sent here."

Bassan recoiled internally. "To rot and die," he finished.

Barnenden turned to him, his eyes dark. "Yes. Their way of silencing me forever."

Moments ago, everything had hinged on the life support coming online so he could escape. Now Bassan realized the implications of breaking free from this prison far greater than he imagined. Despite what he'd gone through to get here, others endured far worse fates.

"This ship means everything to me," Barnenden said, his hand stroking the edge of the console. "If I can't make her fully operational and get her off the ground, not only will a lot of people die, but I'll never see my mate again."

Bassan sucked in his breath. "Neither will I."

Barnenden offered a weak smile. "We are on the same page, then. And we'll do whatever it takes to succeed."

"Yes, we will." His chest tightened at the conviction in his voice.

"We're done for tonight. Why don't you knock off for the night, go get something to drink?"

"A drink? As in, alcohol?"

Another technician snorted. "Of course. A good, stiff drink now and then is what's kept us sane all this time."

After receiving instructions for where to find the bar, which sat off the dining area, Bassan offered his thanks and departed. He exited the hangar with a spring to his step.

Damn, I did it! Life support on. We can leave soon.

This time, the route to the dining area came easy. The bar resided at the opposite end, radiating a warm, welcoming glow. The man handing out drinks recommended a light brew. Trying one couldn't hurt, could it?

He grabbed his mug and eyed the tables. Witz sat to his left. Bassan froze. Their gazes met, and Witz waved him over.

Really? Better not call me soft boy.

A man sat across from Witz, and Bassan took the open spot next to him. Settling on the bench, he glimpsed the man to his left and did a double take. Witz sat across from him, didn't he? Bassan gawked from one to the other.

"Seeing double?" Witz said, crossing his arms and leaning forward on the table. Clothed in a green, shirtless vest, the bandage around his left arm stood out. Definitely Witz. And the stranger beside him...?

"I'm Hetz," the man said, offering his right hand.

Bassan returned his grasp, trying not to stare. Dark eyes gazed at him. The wild edge, a hint of crazy adding a sparkle, was a mirror match to Witz. Twins. They were identical twins.

Great! Two of Witz. Just what I needed.

Hetz bore the same pointed chin and high cheekbones, although his darker skin revealed extended time in the sun. Red hair hung in long, twisted locks from his head. A long, winding serpent tattoo spiraled down his arm, the head positioned on the back of his hand. Startled by the realism in the artwork, Bassan released the man's hand. The men laughed.

"Don't like snakes?" Hetz said, his grin twisting at the corners of his mouth.

Feeling foolish, Bassan dropped his hands into his lap. Hetz slapped him hard on the shoulder. Bassan grabbed for the table to keep from tumbling off the bench.

"Maybe some time out here in the desert with the rest of us vermin will change your mind."

Bassan steadied himself and faced Hetz, his mind searching for a suitable response. None came to mind.

"Now you know why I was so adamant about coming here and finding my brother," Witz said, lifting a large mug to his lips.

Bassan nodded, his gaze still on Hetz. "I didn't realize he was your twin brother."

"Twins, but I was firstborn."

Witz erupted in laughter. "So you enjoy reminding me. Didn't help you when the Narcon shipment went south."

"And I lied my ass off so they wouldn't trace anything back to you. I knew you couldn't handle life here on Ugar."

"Think I'm too soft?"

Don't say it...

Witz pointed a finger at Bassan. "That's soft boy right there. If the desert is going to swallow anyone, it'll be him."

Bassan gritted his teeth. He scooped up his mug and held it to his lips.

"I'll keep the desert from eating you," Hetz said, elbowing Bassan.

The jostle caused part of Bassan's brew to spill. Suppressing a grumble, he mumbled a thanks.

Hetz leaned back, flexing his thick arms. "After all, you're supposed to save us."

Apprehension pressed against Bassan's chest.

Memories from his tenth year flooded his thoughts. The Kintal code in his head—the key to the survival of all ten races. Eleven now. While that responsibility weighed heavier, somehow the prospect of saving one small group of people scared him more.

"Yes, I understand you've been working on the ship," Witz said. He gestured with one hand. "Progress?"

No one told me it was classified. Besides, they already know about the Kintal ship.

"The issue was life support. It's working now," Bassan said.

Hetz let a whoop and slapped Bassan hard on the back. More liquid sloshed out of his cup.

At this rate, I'll lose all my drink.

Witz rapped his fist on the table. "Excellent job. Damn, Zendar was right about you. You're a genius. I had my reservations."

Bassan dried his fingers and cleared his throat. "Not a genius. I have a connection with Kintal technology and know where to look for answers."

"Why is that?"

Bassan sat bolt upright. How to answer? Zendar knew. Bassan had disclosed his secret in the session on the space station. Not willingly though. But how many here knew his identity?

"I..." he began, focusing on the mug in front of him. "I'm the one who carried the code to the Vindicarn home world when the probe threatened all of us fifteen years ago."

Witz gasped. "The code that stopped the probe from destroying the home worlds?"

Bassan nodded and glanced up. The men stared at him. The shield around Witz's mind evaporated and astonishment broadcast loud and clear. Hetz echoed a similar sentiment until his shields locked back into place. But in that one brief moment of exposure, their respect rang pure. Bassan gathered it close, letting the feeling boost his confidence.

"Damn!" Hetz said. "I'd heard it was a Kintal child, but that's it."

"I heard he was the son of a war hero," added Witz.

"Yeah, well, I guess my father is—"

"Something about the war between Cassa and Vindi fifty-some years ago," Witz said. "Something big."

Ha! Something big all right.

"My father is the one who destroyed the Vindicarn disrupter ship that led to the end of the war sixty years ago."

Hetz pounded his fist on the table. "Your family is destined to save the world. Is that it? Did your mother do something heroic as well? Bet my ass she did."

Bassan's shoulders sagged. He detested bragging. "When the probe first appeared and threatened Tgren, she was the one who stopped it from destroying all life on my planet."

His response sent the men into colorful calls of exuberance. Those gathered at the other tables grew still and stared. Bassan shrank in his seat.

"Bassan, I underestimated you," Witz said, a wicked grin plastered across his face. "You might not be physically tough, but you and your family have guts where it counts." He turned to Hetz. "Did I tell you the kid's also a jumper?"

"No!"

"Yes! Got our ass out of a tight spot and brought us to Jaree."

Another thump across his shoulders. More drink spilled. Bassan gave up and set down his mug.

"You're all right in my book, then," Hetz said, curling his thick fingers around his half-empty mug. He leaned closer and nudged Bassan's elbow. "Man, you've hardly touched your drink. I'm on my third one."

Placing both hands on the table, Bassan turned to him, eyes open wide.

Witz laughed and rapped his knuckles on the table. "That's because you keep shoving him. Let's let the poor guy drink. Besides, you were telling me about the raid last year. Finish the damn story."

Thankful for the diversion, Bassan took a long draught. As promised, the drink slid smoothly down his throat, bubbling and quenching his thirst. He set down his mug and turned to Witz. The man winked.

You're all right, kid.

* * *

Used to an alarm, Bassan worried he'd sleep late the next morning. After a restless night, he roused with a start. Did he hear something? He dragged himself to the lone window, covers and all, and peeked outside. A hint of dawn permeated the dark sky. He yawned and rubbed his face.

Might as well get up. Gives me time for a shower before eating.

He reached the dining area in full swing of the morning meal. After finding an empty spot, he ate his food quickly.

As he departed, he noticed Barnenden alone at the nearest table. The man rose, a small personal tablet in his hands. Bassan approached him. Barnenden looked up and offered a tired smile. The man's crumpled clothes and dark shadows under his eyes suggested a long night.

"Did you sleep in the ship?" Bassan said, comfortable enough now to poke some fun at the senior technician.

Barnenden chuckled. "No, I left shortly after you did. But I spent half the night in my shack going over our calculations."

"Is something amiss?" Bassan racked his brain for any oversights and nothing came to mind.

"No, everything checks out. I just wanted to be sure before I released you. There are other areas of the ship the commander wants you to check."

"I thought life support was the main issue?"

"The one system that wasn't working. But with your connection to the Kintals' technology, every section wants confirmation. This ship must be a hundred percent or we don't get off this rock."

I can appreciate that. I really want to leave this rock.

He fell in step with Barnenden, and they made their way to the ship. The compound bustled with activity as people moved past them with a purpose. Strangers nodded at the pair and several even smiled. Their response buoyed Bassan's spirits and he walked a little taller.

"Bassan, you've given me hope."

The words startled Bassan and he responded with his mind. *By fixing the life support?*

You fixed more than the life support, Barnenden thought, glancing at him. *After working on the ship for almost three years, I'd reached the point where there wasn't anything else I could do. None of us knew how to fix the issue, and we'd run through hundreds of scenarios. I slipped back to depths I'd not known since my arrival here. All chances of seeing my mate again evaporated in the desert heat.*

Barnenden's candid admission came with a heavy weight of emotions. Unused to such outpourings, Bassan's shields rose in defense. The moment he cut off the man's pain, a frown touched the corners of Barnenden's mouth.

Damn, what's the proper etiquette with the Narcon? Or here for that matter?

Afraid of offending the senior technician, Bassan eased back on his shields. Their connection reestablished, Barnenden cocked his head.

You're a very private person.

Bassan's shoulders sagged. *Yeah, probably the Cassan in me. Or my father.*

Your father? The one who destroyed the Vindicarn disrupter ship?

Bassan's whole body jolted. *Yes. How did you know?*

News travels fast around here and Hetz likes to talk. But then, I already knew. After what you did on the Vindicarn home world during the probe's attack, information about you and your family traveled across the galaxy. On Narcon, we were privy to the information due to our alliance with the Vindicarn.

I don't remember much about that day. My father told me later that the leader, Cherzta, knew what my father had done to the Vindicarn people during the war and feared Cherzta wouldn't let us go. But for some reason, he did.

Cherzta is ruthless and not easily swayed. You were fortunate.

Lips pressed tight, Bassan nodded.

My memory might be fuzzy about what happened, but I'll never forget his cold face and dark eyes. Cherzta scared the crap out of me.

Although I think there is more than luck at play, Barnenden thought. He balled his free hand into a fist. *Everyone has a gift. Most people never find theirs. But your special ability is right there in your talent of connecting with the Kintal ship. I think that is only part of it though. You are the result of two talented and skilled parents, a blend of their unique abilities. Who knows how deep the gift runs?*

Mouth open, Bassan stared at the senior technician. Him, talented? Sure, he had a connection to the Kintals' technology. More a freakish knack though. The younger students coming through the Kintal training program viewed him as an aberration. One trick no other could emulate, so why try. Then it hit him.

Maybe it had nothing to do with the code in my head. It might be a gift, a talent born from gifted parents. Look how much I discovered in the past five years alone due to my ability to connect.

Plus now I have a second unique ability.

"I can also jump ships with my own power."

"You can what?"

Bassan's neck snapped around, startled he'd spoken out loud. He opened his mouth, but no sound emerged.

"Did you say you can teleport?"

Bassan glanced at those passing by but none paid them any heed. "Yes. I'm a jumper, like my father and mother."

Barnenden threw back his head and uttered a bark of enjoyment. "What did I tell you? You are talented on many levels."

You said news travels fast. I'm amazed everyone doesn't know I jumped the rescue ship here before the Lethan could blow it to bits.

No, I'd not heard that. Then again, I've been holed up in the ship for the past two days and only spoke to Hetz for a moment this morning. Jumping ships—now there's a rare but useful talent. I'm sure Commander Cartent plans to implement that skill when we depart. One more weapon in our attempt to get off this planet.

"I don't know if I could jump something the size of the Freedom. Does it even have a teleporting system?"

Barnenden winked. "You bet it does. Once we're away from this planet, we can purchase fuel for the system. But if you can jump the ship, even better."

I've only jumped once. What if I mess it up? We all die, that's what.

"As soon as we reach the ship, I want to run one more check before I turn you over for new placement."

I'm sure the teleporter is one of the systems they want me to inspect. Hopefully it's intact and I don't have to go searching the database. Of course, it might not even be Kintal technology. In this sector, it's possibly Cassan.

When they reached the ship, Barnenden ran a full diagnostic on the life support system. Operating at peak capacity, life support functioned without an issue.

"Did you want me to check on the teleporter?" Bassan said. Despite his reluctance to try jumping a vessel of this size, he needed to know if he could even connect with the device. One jump didn't make him an expert.

"That's next on the list. I can run a diagnostic on it while we're there."

He led Bassan down a level to the main control room located at the bow of the ship. Unlike the actual Kintal ships, this control room featured three outside views. The eleventh race's craft flew by radar and external sensors, producing a detailed, three-dimensional hologram of their place in space. No such device appeared to be present here.

We're close to replicating the system. But I'm sure it's beyond what these people can build. And in this ship, I'd rather we weren't flying blind. I'm all right with the view as long as I'm not here when we're flying.

"We can access the teleporter from the hallway on the starboard side," Barnenden said, leading the way.

A worker called for the senior technician and Barnenden excused himself. Bassan waited while the men discussed the information on the screen in front of them. Not wanting to listen in on their conversation, he focused on the rest of the control room. Smaller than the one on Tgren's Kintal ship and not even a quarter of the size of a Cassan flagship, screens and workstations lined every available space, including the floor. The narrow rows allowed for the passage of one person and that was about it.

Wow, so small. The other room is also much tinier compared to a real Kintal ship. Of course—they didn't have the resources to build anything larger. But not much room to spare. All those people must fit on this ship. And it's not that spacious to begin with, either.

A man attempted to pass him and Bassan squeezed out of the way. He retreated to the edge of the doorway and trusted no one needed access to the panel behind him. From his vantage point, the whole room lay in front of him. Lights and screens glowed from all angles.

There's room for a least twenty workers. I guess that's a good thing. Hopefully all the pilots are stationed here. Between the bunch of them, one must know how to fly a ship of this size. Not to mention navigating it using a mix of technology.

A flicker of light caught his attention. At the rear of the control room, a thin, clear panel revealed pulsating energy. Curious, Bassan drew closer until he stood in front of the narrow window. A liquid tinged with green swayed in front of him.

The orb!

On cue, white bursts of power shot through the device. His senses sparked in cadence, his skin and nerves quivering right down to his toes. Now closer, the rhythmic hum reached his ears. So faint compared to the device in the Kintal ship on Tgren.

Did it lose power when the Narcons dumped it? Or is the barrier shielding the sound?

He pressed one hand against the synthetic glass. The surface vibrated, tingling his fingertips. Another burst of power shivered the glass and his whole hand quivered. After growing up with the ship on Tgren, the sensation comforted him.

Maybe they wanted to shield everyone. I bet few have ever experienced a power source similar to this one. Still can't believe the Narcons dumped it. Here I thought Vindicarn the ruthless ones.

"Ah, Bassan," a voice said at his elbow.

He jumped and discovered Commander Cartent beside him. Bassan spun around and stood straight at attention out of habit. His gaze strayed to the smears of grease across Cartent's face and suppressed the urge to ask about the streaks in his short-cropped hair.

A commander who's not afraid to get dirty. That's honorable.

"Admiring our power source, I see."

"Yes, I..." Bassan trailed off, unable to voice his concerns over the reduced power of the orb. The gleam in Cartent's eyes spoke of pride in the device. Who was he to deflate the man's joy?

"Commander Cartent," Barnenden said, joining them and providing Bassan a diversion. "We were on our way to the teleporter compartment."

"Excellent. With life support running, I want Bassan to look at that component before we move him to the next system. Proceed."

Barnenden led them out of the control room and a short distance down another hall before stopping at a panel surrounded by controls. "The teleporter resides here. You should be able to access all information on these two monitors."

He punched several buttons and brought up the schematics on one screen and the coding on the other. Bassan listened while the engineer ran through the system. He wasn't familiar with teleporters, but he followed Barnenden's narrative as the man explained the various connections while he operated a diagnostic. When the dimensions flashed on the screen, Bassan sucked in his breath.

It's bigger than the one on the Kintal ship.

"Where did the teleporter come from?" he said, glancing at the commander.

The man's steel eyes darkened. "A Fesell destroyer. What remained of her. By some miracle, the teleporter survived the drop intact. And we got to it first with only one loss of life. The others didn't fare so well."

Puzzled by the man's final words, Bassan opened his

mouth to speak. Then it hit him. Another tribe wanted it. Or they entered someone else's territory.

I wonder how many people died retrieving parts for this ship? Never mind, I don't want to know.

"We were concerned its power might be too strong, so we altered the configuration to match this ship," Barnenden said, tapping on the screen. "All levels were acceptable when we turned it on."

"Except no fuel for a jump," Bassan said, rubbing his chin with his knuckles.

"That's where we anticipate you come in," Cartent said. "At least until we can purchase fuel."

"Sir, I..." Bassan's hands dropped to his sides. *How do I tell them I have no idea how I jumped the other night?* "Jumping a ship of this size might be beyond my capability."

Barnenden pressed his lips together and frowned. "We need to test it. Perhaps we can perform a trial run before we depart."

Cartent placed his hands behind his back. "And risk detection? Unacceptable. We were lucky the Panvet's jump didn't draw attention. Other options?"

"Well, we need to confirm Bassan's ability to connect with and fuel the device. I think we can perform an adequate test here on the ground. I'll monitor the system while he performs a trial connection."

Bassan met his gaze and nodded. "No actual jump. I just charge the device."

"Precisely."

"A quick charge," Cartent added.

Barnenden's fingers danced across the screen. "What settings do you need?"

What settings do I need? I have no idea. Crap, think.

Bassan dropped his chin, his gaze aimlessly wandering the floor. Focusing on the jump three days prior, he tried to recall any detail that might help now.

I know how to tap into the power to jump. And I've watched my parents perform jumps without using the component's energy for years. But how did I do it?

"Bassan?"

The engineer's voice jerked him back to the corridor and the two men awaiting his answer. Chest tight, he blurted the first thing that came mind. "I don't think it matters."

"Very well." Barnenden stepped back and gestured for him to proceed.

Afraid to even look the commander's direction, Bassan moved into position in front of the screens. The data held steady save for a few changing figures. He stared at them, still trying to find the connection. The readouts stared back, mocking him.

There was no data. The desperate jump in the old ship played through his head.

I don't even remember any data. I reached out with my mind and connected with the teleporter.

He shifted his attention to the access panel. Behind that small opening resided the device capable of jumping a ship much larger than this. Fully charged, it would emit a tremendous amount of energy. At the moment, silence greeted his ears. But not his senses.

I know you're in there, waiting.

He placed his hand flat across the panel. Closing his eyes, he reached out for the teleporter.

Like I need to make a regular jump. Just juice it myself.

He focused on the one location he wanted to see more than anything in the world. Tgren and the city of Ktren. It was too far of a jump to perform, but that made it a safe destination. He wouldn't accidentally jump the ship for real. Bassan pictured his home spread out across the valley, the sun low, and lights beginning to appear. An ache formed in his chest.

I want to go home.

Something surged on the other side of the panel. It coursed through Bassan's mind, fueling the cycle of energy between man and machine. It continued to swell, growing stronger and stronger.

"Bassan!"

He jerked back and opened his eyes. Dazed, he glanced around. Barnenden hovered over the main screen, mouth open. Cartent stood beside him, brows drawn together in disapproval. Bassan sucked in a quick breath. The commander's expression eased although his eyes remained hard.

"Easy, son. I said a quick charge."

Panic gripped Bassan's guts. "I didn't teleport us, did I?"

"No, we're still on Ugar."

"But now," Barnenden said, excitement filling his voice, "we have a full teleporter."

Bassan turned to the screen. The charge indicator sat a full strength.

I did it!

"That's a handy talent you have there," Cartent said. "You are going to save our asses in so many ways."

"I hope so, sir."

He stared at the indicator bar with renewed optimism. As he watched though, the power began to drop in strength. His confidence fell with it.

"What's happening?" he said.

"There's no fuel to sustain the charge," Barnenden said. "Your power recharges the cells, but without any fuel, it's temporary. Don't worry. I knew it wouldn't remain at full strength."

"Which is why it's so important we acquire fuel soon after we get off this planet," Cartent said, clearing his throat. "Besides, we don't know how many jumps Bassan can perform."

Bassan snapped his fingers. "My father once told me he could perform twelve jumps in rapid succession in his Cosbolt. That might give me a starting point."

Cartent squared his shoulders. "Before I send you to your next assignment, I want you to run some calculations. Based on the difference in size and strength, estimate how many jumps you could perform and how close together. Get that information to me the moment you have it, Bassan."

"Yes, sir."

The commander spun around and returned to the central control.

"I have other pressing duties," Barnenden said. "I'll leave you to your computations."

Alone in the hall, Bassan stared at the screens in front of him. The energy bar continued to drop toward empty. In minutes, nothing would remain.

But I did it. Twice now. It's not a fluke. Won't Father and Mother be surprised when I tell them?

The power reached zero and he pressed his lips together.

I will tell them because I am going to get home. Even if I have to jump this damn ship all the way back to Tgren.

8

"One jump per hour?"

"Yes, sir." Bassan fidgeted. He knew the commander wanted a different answer. But based on the size of the ship and the teleporter, he couldn't jump it more often. Unless his powers exceeded his father's.

Which I seriously doubt.

"I'm sorry it's not more," Bassan added.

Cartent dropped his tablet on the console in front of him and stood straight. "It's more than we expected. With no ability to teleport, we intended to run hard and fast. You've given us options."

"I...I won't be able to jump far. And I'll need to see clearly where I'm going. Especially since I've done it only once."

The commander leaned back and crossed his arms. "Only once?"

I didn't mean to say that.

Bassan shrank back. He tried to swallow, but his throat went dry. Unable to speak, he resorted to mental communications.

The Panvet was the first ship I've ever jumped.

Cartent's expression remained firm. "Hetz said your parents are jumpers. Were you not also trained to jump?"

Bassan's shoulders dropped, along with his composure. "No, sir. My studies were on the Kintal ship. We never tested my ability to jump."

"The son of two jumpers? I find that hard to believe."

Hoping the floor would swallow him whole, Bassan grappled with the truth. "I...I hate to fly."

A bark of laughter startled him and Bassan glanced up. A ripple of curiosity stirred in the minds of those present. He remained still, focused on the commander

133

and ignoring the inquisitive minds around him. Cartent brought his hands to his head and ran fingers across his scalp, effectively spreading the grease more. The man shook his head and grasped the console, leaning against it.

"You hate to fly," he murmured. The commander lifted his chin and gazed hard at Bassan. "The son of two talented pilots and jumpers has an aversion to flying?"

Heat rose to his cheeks. His fingers stroked his tablet, hoping to summon a suitable answer. "That's not where my talents lie."

Cartent smirked. "You are talented in too many areas to know where your true talents reside."

The commander's response confused Bassan. While he struggled to find a suitable response, his mouth open in hopes one would emerge, the man cut him off.

"Well, I think my final assignment for you will determine your true talent."

"Sir?"

"Our most pressing need awaits you," Cartent said, stepping away from the console.

"Wasn't life support your most urgent need?"

The commander shook his head and gestured for Bassan to follow. "It was, and your ability to jump will certainly fill in the gaps, but we have one more concern when it comes to getting off this planet and safely away from the Narcons."

Curious yet wary, Bassan trailed after Cartent. They exited the control center and walked past the teleporter. Bassan focused on the panel, now keenly aware of his connection to the device. The commander led him to a steel ladder extending down to the next level. Bassan secured his tablet and followed him into the depths of the ship. He reached an alcove and realized it fed into a central tunnel running down the center of the ship.

I wonder what's down here?

His stomach growled. Bassan regretted working through the midday meal. He hoped he wouldn't miss the evening meal as well.

The two moved toward the prow of the ship and Cartent

led him into another small control room. A dozen men worked on various components, including Barnenden. They all looked up and stood at attention.

"We've worked long and hard to assure this ship has the strongest weapons possible. We need to beat the Narcon drones waiting to blast any ship that tries to escape Ugar. We've achieved that. At least by our best calculations. But"—the commander turned to Bassan—"there is one more threat we must manage during our escape. And you are the key to finding the solution."

One more threat? Bassan pressed his tablet to his body.

"Barnenden?" Cartent said, swiveling to face the engineer.

The man cleared his throat. "According to our calculations, at the time of our departure, the Tgren probe will be in this sector."

Bassan fumbled with his tablet. "What?"

"The probe will be making a long and leisurely sweep through this sector during our projected departure."

The probe! The ship that nearly wiped out Tgren before he was born. And then returned to systematically destroy all the races when he was ten. The probe that required the code stuck in his head to dismantle the annihilation order, almost killing him in the process. Bassan's mind reeled.

"Well, you have to change your departure time, then," he said, blurting out the first thought in his mind. "No weapon exists that can counter what the probe can do."

"Bassan," Carteret said, his tone demanding attention. "The probe will be in this sector for weeks. We are days from departing. If we delay, we might not get another chance."

"What do you mean?"

Carteret assumed a commanding posture. "Our intel says the Lethan intend to attack us and soon. We need to be gone before that happens, and before they discover the ship we've built. Otherwise, everything we've worked for over the past seven years will die here on this planet."

Bassan's empty stomach churned. If they could escape without conflict, the probe would ignore them. But if they drew the fire of the Narcon satellites guarding the planet and engaged, the probe would come to investigate and destroy them because they broke the treaty of peace now programmed into it.

"You—you don't realize what you're asking," he said, fumbling for words. "The probe is set to enforce peace. It will attack any ship defying that."

"Which is why we need you to access its designs and come up with a plan or a weapon to counter the probe."

"Counter it? Do none of you remember when it threatened to destroy all the races? The one thing that countered it was a code in my head. And it's long gone."

The room fell silent. No one moved. Blood pounded in Bassan's ears and he gazed with stunned belief at those gathered. Barnenden stepped forward.

"But your connection to the ancient technology is still intact. You can access the database and find the Tgren schematics on the probe."

"No one's come close to finding those plans though."

"Because they haven't accessed you," Cartent said, his low voice carrying tremendous weight.

Bassan staggered back. "Me?"

"You have a direct contact with the basic technology of all the races. Hidden within the Kintal database is the schematics for the probe. And you can find it. Your ability will find it."

Dread gripped Bassan's innards so tight, he couldn't breathe. Access the designs for the probe? Impossible! Even if they existed, finding them changed everything. The probe enforced peace on all the races. No more wars. But if another entity came along that matched the probe or disabled it...anarchy.

"It would destroy peace among the races," he said, wheezing for breath. "We'd be open to wars again."

The room fell silent.

"Only if we had to use it," Barnenden said in a soft voice.

Bassan spun away. But if they used it...

"It's a risk we have to take," Cartent said.

Bassan turned to the commander. Hands behind his back, Cartent exhumed total confidence. Bassan's exasperation melded into pure shock. "You're willing to risk a galaxy-wide peace, millions of lives, to get off this planet?"

The man's eyes drew to slits. "Peace? There is no peace here. This planet's inhabitants have warred for centuries. Lives taken on a grand scale. Where is our protector? Where is that peace everyone else was promised?"

Cartent's words came out controlled and logical, but a hint of resentment flowed from his mind. It echoed throughout the room, assaulting Bassan's head. He shielded his mind to block the charged emotions in those around him.

I know it's not fair you're trapped here. I get it. But you have no idea what you are asking for. Most of you didn't experience the war fifteen years ago. And I nearly died to bring it to an end.

Grappling with his own anxiety, Bassan shook his head. "Even if I find it, you said we have days. There wouldn't be time to build a weapon or anything."

"Not from scratch. This ship is equipped with several unique and powerful weapons. If we knew how the probe operated, we could adjust ours to match. A long shot, yes, but if we don't have a proper defense, we fail. And if we can't, perhaps knowing how the weapon works will show us a way to disable the probe. We need every advantage at this point."

A hush settled over the room. Bassan glanced around. The group watched him, faces drawn and solemn. He rubbed the back of his neck, attempting to forestall the coming headache. So much at stake...

If we damage or disable the probe, it will change everything. And in the aftermath, every race will be after this ship. If they discover how the information was obtained, they'll be after me. But what if I can't even find that information? The probe will destroy us.

Even worse, what if there's another reason they want to know how the probe works? What if this is just another lie?

No matter what, I'm screwed.

Bassan sighed. "This is the real reason Zendar brought

me here, isn't it?"

"The primary reason," Cartent said. "Once we realized we couldn't get life support online, that function became equally important. And you've also solved the issue of no teleporter. Now we need you to access that weapon. Find out how it works. Find a way to deactivate it. Ultimately, we need a solution."

Resigned to his fate, Bassan nodded. Cartent departed, leaving Bassan surrounded by anxious engineers. He pressed his tablet firmly against his chest and studied the men around him.

"How do I access the database down here?" he said, trying to contain his agitation.

"Over here." Barnenden gestured to an oversized console. It didn't look Kintal, but once Bassan drew closer, the controls matched the one on the upper level. Annoyance simmered faster in his mind.

"Did the Narcons throw out all of them?" Bassan spat. "The fools."

His attention snapped to Barnenden, remembering his audience, and he realized his words were rather harsh. The chief engineer gazed at the console and grasped its edge.

"A few that we know of. And yes, they were fools. They tossed this console in the same drop with me. Stripped of its shell, it might've been missed had I not seen where it landed."

Sorry, thought Bassan, unsure of what else to say.

Barnenden nodded. "Most of our focus has been restoring its functions. The weapons and shields are a mix, but they're all controlled by this console."

I'm astonished you got any of it to work at all.

Some days I wondered if we would. He offered a wink. "The memory bank suffered some damage, so if you can't access what you need here, we'll try with the other console. I'm still amazed at how much data these Kintal units hold. No other ship functions like them."

"That's what makes the Kintals so special," Bassan said. "We are the best of all races."

Barnenden chuckled and smacked Bassan on the

back. "They are the result of what happens when we all work together."

Bassan set his tablet on the edge of the console. He leaned forward, taking in the technology before him. The familiar layout offset the crude casing. The main control knob glowed, inviting him to access her secrets. He pressed his lips into a thin line, contemplating his next move. Was he ready to do this?

Bassan, Barnenden thought. *I know this is asking a lot of you. And I do understand the implications. I don't want to do anything that would bring the races to war again. But once we get off planet, the sentries will fire on us and we'll have to return fire. Even if we jump, using your ability, there's a chance the probe will investigate. We need to be ready when that happens.*

I know. It scares me though.

It scares me as well.

He turned to the engineer. Despite his yellow skin and strange, offset thin eyes, the man's dread showed in his tight face. He understood the implications. What Bassan was about to attempt could change the whole scenario connecting the eleven races. Forever.

"All right," he said, his hand hovering over the orb. "Let's see what I can find in there."

* * *

Hours later and with next to no results, Barnenden called a halt.

"Everyone, take a break. Time for the evening meal. Go eat and recharge."

The men murmured and disassembled. Soon only Barnenden and Bassan remained in the room. Bassan's head ached from repeated connections with the device.

"You should take a break," Barnenden said.

He shook off the engineer's suggestion. "I'm so close."

Then find it.

Bassan took Barnenden's order to heart. Find it. Yes, he had to find it.

He pressed his hand on the orb yet again.

The connection sparked. He reached out, desperate to connect with the console's database on the Tgrens.

The link led him down the same path. Tgren history. But nothing on the probe.

It doesn't want to connect via the normal channels.
Then try something different.

Bassan took a step back and crossed his arms.

Searching for Tgren information turns up their basic history, but that's it. What am I missing?

He dropped his chin to his chest. After hours stooped over the console, the movement sent a jolt of pain snaking down his spine. He lifted his head and arched his back instead. His joints popped in protest.

I've searched for mention of the probe, but the information doesn't cover it. Or any specifics. Just the basics about their life before the migration. Before the probe changed everything. And searching for weapons turns up Kintal devices. Impressive, but not what we need.

He glanced at Barnenden, going over data on his tablet. "What if the information isn't there?"

The Narcon shook his head. "After everything else you've found? It must be there somewhere."

"It's not with the information on Tgren. Or weapons. Or anything else I can think of."

Barnenden set down his tablet and rubbed his temples. "What else might they have called it? Is there a name for the probe itself? Or the events surrounding it?"

"Ironically, we've never found one. You'd think an extinction level event would have a name for the history books."

"Maybe they wanted to wipe out that part of history. That's why they sent the races out across the galaxy—so they could change it."

Something stirred in Bassan's memory. "Change..."

He moved to the console. He tapped on the screen and waited.

"What is it?" Barnenden said.

Bassan's search brought zero results, which didn't surprise him. But he knew what would help him find it.

"I'm going to try again," he said, placing his hand on the orb and closing his eyes. He reached back for the memories of his ancestors.

Say-vee. Show me Say-vee.

The room shifted. Where was he? A control room. A large control room. Dozens of people working at computer stations. The energy in the room sparked of anticipation.

What are you working on?

Bassan approached the closest computer screen. He turned to the man working at the station. Dark hair and an olive complexion, as he'd expected.

You're Tgren. Are you working on the probe? If you only realized what it will one day do.

The man tapped some keys. Computations filled the screen. The man nodded, hit one more key, and then tapped the screen twice.

Schematics flashed across the screen, forming a shape that could only belong to one thing. A jolt of enthusiasm shot through Bassan.

That's it!

The man stepped away. Trembling with excitement, Bassan willed his fingers forward. They touched the screen. A ripple of electricity emanated from the figures and image as if they knew of their importance.

Back out slowly. Layer by layer. Find out where this information is hidden.

He moved with care and closed the first file. Hundreds more, all concerning the probe's functions, flashed across the screen.

One more...

He closed the master file. There it was. Passcode protected, of course.

But I know the passcode now.

Bassan continued to back out of the files, noting the name of each level. When he reached the primary data level, he pumped his fist in triumph.

There you are.

In a flash, Bassan disconnected from the memory. He returned so fast, he rocked back on his heels from the disconnect. A hand gripped his elbow.

"Bassan!"

Opening his eyes, the Freedom's weapons control room greeted him. Lurching forward, he fingered the screen. *I found it.*

"You found it?"

Yes. Bassan typed furiously. *Now to access it before I forget.*

He pounded down in levels, hesitating once. At last, he hit the correct file. Passcode required to access it. Without missing a beat, he typed Say-vee.

The file opened.

"There," he said, pointing at the screen. Files scrolled across the monitor. "That is the entire database on the probe."

Barnenden gasped. "Everything?"

"Yes. Everything."

"You did it!" He thumped Bassan on the back. "How did you find it? And how did you acquire the passcode?"

Bassan smiled with pride. "Tgrens have a word for change that no other race uses. Say-vee. I searched for a moment with that word and found the Tgren scientists working on the probe. It did have a name, which was also its password—Say-vee. Change."

"It did change everything."

"It did." Bassan gazed at the screen. So many files. "We have a ton of information to sift through. This could take days."

"We don't have days. I'm calling the team back right now," Barnenden said. "And I'll instruct them to bring some food for us. We'll be busy for the rest of the evening."

Despite his throbbing head, a surge of elation rushed through him.

I found it. Damn, I found it! And I bet others have searched for it for years. Bet that's why they dumped these consoles. The Narcons grew frustrated when they couldn't find the file.

Was that part of Barnenden's assignment? "Were the Narcons looking for this information when you worked on the ship?" he asked before losing his nerve.

Barnenden held up his hand, his eyes unfocused. Bassan waited while the man completed his mental conversation with his team. Finished, the engineer's body rocked.

"Indeed. We hit the same obstacles you did, which aggravated our leaders. They wanted to counter the probe."

Of course they did. It stole victory from their war.

"Anything to destroy peace," Bassan said, the memory of Narcon and Vindicarn ships attacking Tgren rippling through his unshielded mind.

The engineer stiffened. "I know you think the Narcons are nothing but bloodthirsty warriors, ready to go to battle at a moment's notice. But we have spent most of our existence under the influence and domination of the Vindicarn. When Cherzta ordered his people to stand down after the probe nearly destroyed their world, it was the first time Narcons experienced any amount of freedom. While I don't condone what they were after, our leaders wanted to find something that would prove us stronger than the Vindicarn. The secrets of the probe were certainly worthy and more than enough. That information would've changed our position with the Vindicarn forever."

Taken aback by Barnenden's unexpected raw honesty, Bassan dropped his hands to his side and stepped away from the engineer. "I'm sorry. I always thought your races were allies."

"We were, more or less. The Vindicarn always called the shots though. And ever since their defeat at the hands of the Cassans about sixty years ago, they have pressured the Narcons to join them in any and all aggressive ventures."

"Because two races are stronger than one."

"Precisely."

Bassan nodded, his thoughts trailing to his home world. "The Tgren have been guided by Cassa but never dominated by them."

"Ah, but no one enjoys a fight more than a Vindicarn."

Don't think I'll repeat that in front of Zendar. Although I still want to pound him for tricking me. Twice.

Two engineers appeared. Barnenden nudged Bassan's arm.

Don't worry about it. Now, let's start dividing out these files and get to work.

* * *

Many hours later, Bassan staggered toward the

hangar exit. Somewhere behind him, two other engineers shambled along, their boots scraping the floor. In the stillness of the hangar, the sound reverberated in an odd fashion.

I'm so tired, I hope I can find Zendar's again. Otherwise, they'll discover me curled up in an alley corner somewhere.

He reached for the door, fumbling with the handle. It flung open, knocking Bassan's hand away, and someone smacked into him. The smell of dusty sand filled his nostrils.

"Hey!" Bassan said, putting his hands up in defense.

"Oh, sorry. Wait, Bassan?"

The light outside the hangar door prevented him from seeing the face, but he knew the voice. "Zendar?"

"Yeah." He stepped back into the light. Dirt covered Zendar's face, blending with the sandy clothes and hat he wore. "Wow, you're working late."

His way no longer blocked, Bassan shuffled forward and nodded at the lone guard in passing. "Yes, and right now I want to find your place and collapse."

"Come on, I'll take you there," Zendar said, falling in step with him. "I'll probably pass out soon as well. Want to wash two days' worth of hard trails off me first."

The lights lining the paths between the buildings were fewer and far between. No people either, which meant it was really late.

"You just get back?" Bassan said.

"Reported in and then stopped by my place to grab some clean grubs. When you weren't there, I thought I better come find you. I didn't want you wandering all over the compound."

"No, I've been in the Freedom all day."

"Still working on life support?"

The question ignited Bassan's earlier agitation. "No," he said slowly, "I've been working on the primary reason you brought me here."

"Huh?"

Bassan cast a scowl his direction, not that Zendar could see it in the dim light. "The probe. You brought me here to find a way to counter the probe. Or more specifically, to find the probe's schematics in the database and unlock her weapon's secrets."

"What?" Zendar glanced around after his thunderous exclamation, but all remained still. He pressed closer to Bassan. "Look, I brought you here to get the ship in working order, get the life support on."

"And counter the probe's weapon."

"Is that what they have you doing now?"

"Oh, come on," Bassan said. "Don't pretend you didn't know."

Zendar spread his arms. "I didn't. They told me life support and a few other issues needed to be fixed. Find someone who knows where to look in a Kintal ship."

"Find someone who knows where to look? Find someone who can dredge up details on the largest weapon in the galaxy."

Bassan! Zendar patted the air. *Crap, Cartent might not want everyone to know yet.*

A retort died on Bassan's lips. Despite his anger, talking about the probe in public probably wasn't prudent. Bassan lowered his chin. *Well, that is exactly what I have been working on for most of the day. They want to know how to disable or destroy the probe's weapon.*

I had no idea, Zendar thought, making a left. *I guess the commander is planning ahead.*

Planning ahead? Bassan grabbed Zendar's arm and spun him around. *Don't you get it? If we can neutralize the probe, the Freedom will become the most hunted ship in the galaxy. All the races will want that information. Plus, we'll destroy the one thing keeping the races at peace right now. And I almost paid for that peace with my life fifteen years ago.*

Zendar shook himself free and stepped back. Despite his exhaustion, Bassan's body trembled, pulse speeding through his veins. No one grasped the real situation. Barnenden understood, but the engineer's drive to escape this planet negated all considerations. He supposed it didn't shock him. Certainly, no one thought twice about luring a Kintal expert down here to fix all their problems.

Can we escape without it? Zendar thought, his mental

voice hesitant.

Oh, possibly. Bassan rubbed his neck where it ached from hours spent over the console. *If none of the drones fire on this ship and it doesn't fire back. But should a real skirmish begin with the probe in such close proximity, it's going to come investigate and shoot to kill.*

But you can jump the ship. Can't you? There's a teleporter on board.

And we calculated I can jump it once an hour and then not too far. If at all.

But you jumped the Panvet.

One jump doesn't make me an expert jumper.

Zendar balled his hands into fists and stared up at the sky. *So, it all hinges on what you can find? I guess we either die here or die in space.*

The words settled heavy on Bassan's mind. The thoughts emanating from Zendar matched in seriousness. So much disappointment. And beat-down desperation. Everyone projected it. The weighty views wore on his conscious.

Zendar inclined his head. *Come on. You need rest. So do I. Maybe it will make more sense in the morning.*

Bassan rubbed a hand through his disheveled hair.

No, I'm sure it will sound even crazier tomorrow.

9

Boom!

Bassan jolted out of a restless sleep. Dazed, he scanned the dark room. Zendar also roused with a start and a sharp intake of breath. In the distance, a siren grew in strength.

"Zendar, what the—"

Boom! A nearby explosion shattered what remained of the peace.

We're under attack.

Another explosion sounded. Bassan rose to his feet before his brain had a chance to tell his body to move. Fingers still on his tablet, he shoved it into his shirt and groped for his boots.

Who's attacking? he thought, jumping on one foot while he secured his second boot.

Based on our recon yesterday, it's probably the Lethan. Determined to take this settlement. And pissed we slipped through their lands.

Zendar threw open the door. Bassan staggered out after him. A blast two rows of buildings over sent them cowering. Pieces of debris rained down around them. Uncovering his head, Bassan glanced at the sky. The lights of a ship trailed away from the compound.

"Come on," Zendar said, grabbing Bassan's shirt and yanking.

Propelled forward, Bassan regained his footing and hurried after Zendar. *Where are we going?*

To the wall. I need to man the guns.

A rumble echoed overhead and Bassan ducked. He recognized the sound though. The Panvet. Jaree's fleet, however small, was in pursuit.

Do they need me to teleport or anything?

I don't know. Zendar pushed past a group headed in the opposite direction. *Ask the commander.*

Another nearby explosion sent Bassan off balance.

Crap, I imagine he's busy. I remember my father, strained to the limit when the Vindicarn and Narcons attacked Tgren. Should I?

He dug in his heels to catch up to Zendar and reached out to Cartent. As expected, the man's mind spun like a whirlwind. *Do you need me on any of the ships to teleport them?*

No. You're too important. Stay on the ground and watch for incoming.

Bassan caught up to Zendar and climbed a makeshift ladder to a platform against the border wall. Four oversized guns sat on the platform, their barrels pointed at the sky. Someone manned the one at the end, and its heavy artillery spewed out a deep drumroll of sound. Bassan tried to cover his ears, but Zendar hauled him to the next gun in line.

Where is everyone? Damn it, probably not the safest place for you, but we need a body on every gun.

On a gun? I've never shot anything in my life.

Here. Zendar turned on the weapon and slapped Bassan's hands into position. *It pivots in all directions. Point and watch the screen. When the target turns green, fire.*

Bassan gripped the handles, noting the buttons at the end. The screen on top shook with static for a moment before it cleared. Mostly. He peered skyward and cringed.

Watch for the enemy. When he's close and within range, aim and use the screen. It's an air attack at the moment, but that could change, so watch the ground as well. And watch your ass.

Bassan peered over the wall at the horizon. The dark obscured any approaching enemy. Only the immediate area around the compound revealed the desert below. Would he even see someone approaching?

Zendar slapped his back. *Got it?*

He jumped but retained his hold on the gun. *I got it.*

And if you see an incoming about to hit you, jump. I'd

be in so much trouble if you got splattered.

Zendar seized the next gun in line. Bassan concentrated on the weapon in his hands. He adjusted the position of the barrel. Its sluggish movement reminded him of the ancient transports on Tgren.

Ship's going to fly right over me before I have a chance to aim.

A distant hum caught his attention. He swiveled around. A dim line of lights approached the compound.

How can I be sure it's not one of us?

Listen. Reach out with your mind and touch the crew. You'll know if it's not one of us. Just pull back quick and shoot before they pinpoint your location.

Smoke from a nearby burning building wafted their direction. Its acrid smell filled Bassan's nose and the smoke obscured his view. Following Zendar's instructions, he reached out to the crew. Confusion and rage met his mind. Bassan withdrew quickly.

Not ours! He spun his gun around and pointed it at the lights.

Make your shot count.

Bassan turned to Zendar. The man's attention and gun focused on another position in the sky. The man on the other side aimed in the same direction. The fourth gun remained unmanned. It was all up to him.

I've never killed anyone before.

The smoke blew a different direction. Illuminated by the lights of the city below, the ship came into clear view. Aiming straight at him, Bassan expected a volley of lasers. Instead, the vessel dropped lower. A small explosion rocked her wing. She tipped to the left but remained on course.

Pointing his gun at the ship, Bassan lined up his shot and checked the computer screen. No green. His aim was off a bit. He adjusted his shot and looked up again to verify the ship's trajectory.

As he did so, several items fell from the ship. An invisible force wrapped tight around his throat. Bombs!

Recalculating his aim, he stared hard at the screen. The ship grew larger in his view, closing in on his location.

Come on, give me the green.

More bombs fell from the ship. The ensuing explosions shook Bassan to the core. He had to do something.

It's like playing grav ball. Sometimes the wild shots make it.

Lining up the ship one more time, he ignored the screen. Pressing his thumbs hard against the trigger, he let loose a volley of firepower against the invading craft. He continued to fire, keeping the lights of the craft and the end of his gun in sync.

An explosion rocked the underside of the vessel. The ship listed to the left even more. No longer coming straight at them, it swerved off course and dropped lower.

Bassan ceased fire. *Oh, damn.*

The vessel skimmed over the compound wall not far from the platform, a plume of smoke trailing behind. It continued for a few more seconds before hitting the ground. The ship erupted into a giant fireball. The glow illuminated the scrubby desert for quite a distance. Bassan stared in disbelief.

I brought that ship down. I did it. *I did it!*

Great! Keep shooting.

A volley of shots from another ship overhead punctuated Zendar's thought.

Bassan lost track of the ships passing over them. Many were theirs. A familiar pilot and copilot's banter went through his head more than once. But after witnessing the death dropped on the compound by the one ship, Bassan was relieved few other vessels seized the opportunity to repeat the attack. Despite the invader's numbers, Zendar's people held their own.

Dawn broke. The ships overhead echoed back as their own. The ache in his arms grew, and Bassan leaned back from his weapon. The skies, once busy with aircraft and fire, boasted few ships. It appeared no enemy vessel sailed through their airspace.

A horn blasted three short pulses, and Zendar let loose a tired cry. *The attack is over.*

Bassan released the gun and dropped his arms to his sides. No longer in use, they shook from exhaustion. He glanced to his right and realized a woman now manned the fourth gun. So busy with the fight, Bassan had never noticed her arrival. But for who knows how long, the four of them defended their section of the compound.

We lived through it. All right. Now I'm officially beat.

* * *

Bassan followed Zendar through the torn up streets of the compound. So many buildings sat in ruins, and smoke continued to billow from several directions. Urgency seeped from the minds of those they passed, prodding Bassan to action. He wanted to help those in need. He suspected Barnenden awaited him on the ship and reached out to the man.

I'll be there soon, he told the engineer. *These people need help. The ship isn't damaged, is it?*

No! We were fortunate.

The medical facility sat near the main dining area, but as the building became overrun within minutes, Bassan and Zendar escorted the injured to the open area. Tables were pulled back and blankets placed on the ground. People poured into the expanse to attend to the victims of the attack. Lacking any medical training, Bassan continued checking the damaged buildings with Zendar.

At least I'm good for something besides working on the Freedom.

He maneuvered around a pile of shattered metal. Its form twisted up, reaching for the sky.

I hate to think of people trapped under this mess.

The next street over, they came upon two men trying to lift the fallen roof of a dwelling. Zendar dashed forward to help and Bassan followed.

This is where Rence's family lives, Zendar thought, bending down to assist.

"Careful, lads," one man said. "Lift with your legs."

Bassan grasped the edge, the thin metal pressing into his hands. Adjusting to lift from the underside instead, he bent his knees and straightened his arms. With four of them, the large piece of corrugated metal raised.

"Slide it to the left."

Muscles strained as he lifted. Bassan helped shift it along until the damaged wall of another building prevented them from going any farther. They set down the roof and the second man, whom Bassan presumed to be Rence, leapt toward the exposed remains of the home.

"Navent! Liron!" he called, tossing aside a tangled piece of metal.

Bassan and the others moved in to assist. Stepping with care, he reached for the remains of a door. Underneath, he discovered cabinets, smashed and twisted. Zendar joined him and they dug through the rubble. Rence continued to call the two names, his voice frantic. The panic emanating from his mind overwhelmed all, forcing Bassan to shield. He focused on removing the cabinets.

"One more," Bassan said, yanking on the splintered wood. With a grunt, he lifted the piece and swung it over to Zendar, who took it from his grasp. Bassan turned back to survey what he'd unearthed and caught his breath.

Tiny fingers poked out from under a flattened table.

A chill shot through the pit of his stomach. He stared, frozen to the spot, at the small hand.

"Navent! Liron!"

The man's desperate cry jolted him to life. Bassan dropped to his knees and wrapped his hands around the tabletop. *I found someone.*

Zendar appeared at his side. By the time they'd lifted the table away, Rence knelt on the ground.

"Navent, Liron, can you hear me?"

Bassan turned and saw him stroking the bloodied head of a woman. Clutched in her arms, a little girl's thin body curled tight against the woman's chest.

"We need to get them to medical," the first man said. "Move them carefully."

Rence pulled his hand away from the woman and curled his arms around the child. Lifting her from her mother's grasp with care, he straightened his back and held her out to Bassan.

"Please carry my daughter," he whispered.

Bassan accepted her, his own arms shaking. The man adjusted the child's hands before turning his attention back to the woman. Bassan rose to his feet, cradling the tiny load to his chest. She weighed nothing. Zendar grabbed his elbow and led him out of the wreckage.

You got her?

Bassan nodded. Zendar guided him through the streets. They reached the dining area and Zendar took him to the first available blanket. Bassan knelt and eased the girl to the ground. She stirred as he placed her on the blanket.

"Mama?"

Sleepy eyes stared at him in confusion. Now that he had a close look at her, Bassan recognized the child. Pale skin and hair, like Sirella. She and her mother had played in this area a couple nights ago.

You were so content that night. And now...

"Where's Mama?" she said, her raspy voice rising in pitch.

He squeezed her tiny arms. "She's with your father. They'll be here in a minute."

Her eyes narrowed and she scrutinized him. "Why are you here?"

Before he could answer, a woman knelt beside them. "Liron, sweetie. Where do you hurt?"

"My head hurts."

"We'll take care of your head." The woman turned to Bassan. *Thank you for finding her. I'll take it from here.*

He nodded and released Liron. His body stood after much effort and he staggered back a step and stared down at the pair. She appeared in far better condition than the woman. Navent's injuries scared him. The child might lose her mother. It wasn't fair.

A slap on his back reminded Bassan of Zendar's presence. *She'll be all right.*

What of her mother though?

Hopefully, they can save her.

Bassan shook his head. Why was he here? The girl's words troubled him. Why had he risked everything to come to this planet?

He scanned the compound, filling by the minute with injured, innocent people, desperate for a better life. That was his purpose. He was here to save these people. And the sole way he could do it resided in the schematics of the probe.

I'm going to get cleaned up and return to the Freedom. Surprise emanated from Zendar, and Bassan turned to face him. *Your people are dying. I need to find the solution to the probe issue and get them safely off this planet.*

Go, then.

Bassan balled his hands into fists and strode away from the makeshift medical facility. He didn't get far though. Upon reaching the last row of tables, he spied a familiar serpent tattoo, partially covered by bandages. Concerned, Bassan approached the man where he sat slumped forward on the table.

"Hetz?" he said, pausing at the end of the table. The man glanced up, eyes bloodshot, and face lacking any emotion at all. "Are you all right?"

Arching his broad shoulders, Hetz leaned away from the table. He rubbed his face, the motion slow and deliberate. "I'll heal."

"What happened?"

Hetz stared across the compound, eyes unblinking. "Damn bomb landed next to our weapons platform. Threw my ass right to the ground."

Bassan sucked in a quick breath. "After the damage I've seen today, you're lucky to be alive."

"Yeah, lucky," Hetz murmured.

A flash of extreme distress escaped his mind, suppressed in an instant. Bassan's muscles tensed. The anguish had nothing to do with the man's injuries. Then he noticed the absence of Hetz's brother. His chest tightened further.

Where's Witz? he thought, his mental voice but a whisper.

Hetz didn't move. Bassan toyed with repeating his question. A soft sigh escaped the man and he dropped his chin. In that instant, Bassan knew the answer. He stepped forward and placed a hand on Hetz's shoulder.

I'm sorry.

Yeah, so am I.

Bassan's insides twisted.

What do I say? Crap, Witz was a nuisance, but he

didn't deserve to die here.

"Witz..." he began, searching for the words. "All Witz wanted was to find you."

Hetz snorted and peered up at Bassan. "And he did, crazy sot."

The agony in Hetz's eyes bore into Bassan. Unable to endure the man's pain and at a loss for further words, Bassan retreated. He strode from the dining area, placing distance between him and the suffering. A new purpose rose in his spirit.

I can't help Witz, but I can help the others. I don't want to condemn the rest of us in the process, though.

* * *

Bassan leaned away from the console, his fingers clinging to frame. He almost lost his grip and one foot shot back to keep him upright. Steady at last, he released the console and rubbed his face.

We've been at this all day. I need some sleep.

He scanned the room. A dozen others huddled over consoles and tablets, all working in earnest. Although judging from the stooped postures, exhaustion gripped all of them.

Commander Cartent is on his way, Barnenden announced to the room. *We have one minute to organize our findings.*

And hopefully it's enough. Or at least makes sense after almost no sleep last night.

The commander entered the room, his step slower than usual. His disheveled and dirty clothes gave evidence to a long and tiring day. Bassan could only imagine the day's demands on the man.

"What have you found?" Cartent said, foregoing any greeting or formalities.

Barnenden cleared his throat. "We've spent all day analyzing the probe's weapon. While we've learned much, one thing is clear. We cannot duplicate the weapon. Not here. I'm not sure anyone could."

Cartent dropped his chin to his chest. "That's unfortunate. Do you have any good news to report?"

The engineer glanced at Bassan. Taking the hint,

CASSADARK

Bassan stepped forward, tablet in hand.

"We might be able to counter the weapon."

The commander's head jerked up and he fixated on Bassan. "Elaborate."

"We discovered the code for firing the weapon. When the probe determines a target, this code travels to the ignition sensors. Along the way it picks up trajectory and speed. All of these things combine into a deadly and accurate blast of energy."

"One we can counter?"

He gripped his tablet tighter, reluctant to admit the truth. But he had no choice. "We have all the schematics on the code and its route through the probe's system. We can send a targeted blast of energy at the signal and scramble it."

Cartent stood straighter, his eyes aglow with expectation. "We can stop the probe from firing?"

"Yes, but," Bassan said, loath to drop the dreadful news, "we have two issues."

"Which are?"

The question smacked Bassan in the chest. His father's commanding tone and presence filled his head and he hesitated. Glancing at his tablet to regain his composure, he took a breath and forced the unease deep into his gut.

"We are going under the assumption no one has adjusted the probe's programming since its commission over a thousand years ago," he said, daring to glance up. The stoic face of the commander stared him down and Bassan swallowed. "The blast of energy we send will contain its own programming, designed to interfere with the specific firing code. If it's been changed or someone else has challenged the code, it won't work."

"Why would it be different than what's in the data?" Cartent said.

Barnenden came to Bassan's rescue. "The probe isn't a simple machine. Within its core lies artificial intelligence, similar to that of the original Kintal ships. It can adapt and change its programming. If someone else has targeted the weapons in this manner, the code will need to be different to counter the attack. Which leads to the second issue."

Cartent pivoted to face the man. Tensions rose and the air around Bassan grew heavy.

Crap, he's not going to like the answer.

"If this works, it will work once, that's it. The probe will readjust its code and we won't be able to counter the changes. We'll knock her down once, but after that, we're an open target."

Silence beat at Bassan's eardrums. Or was it the anger and displeasure pouring from Cartent's mind? Either way, he wished to slip away and never return.

The commander grasped his chin and rubbed the thick stubble. No one moved or spoke. Bassan even stopped breathing.

"So," began Cartent, still staring at the floor, "we have one chance to block its weapon."

He swung around to Bassan. "And one chance to teleport the ship."

Loath to add to the burden, Bassan kept his mind shielded tight.

And I can only teleport once an hour.

Cartent pressed his lips together, his cold stare still penetrating Bassan's heart. The man shook his head and removed his cap, running fingers through unkempt hair. "A week ago, we had no options. At least we have two now. It will have to suffice."

Jamming his cap on his head, he nodded at Barnenden. "Prepare the code. We're leaving the day after tomorrow."

The commander strode from the room. Bassan stared after him, tablet clutched to his chest. Leaving in less than two days? He could finally go home.

"All right, everyone focus on that code," Barnenden ordered, snapping his fingers. "We can get in a few more hours of work and finish up tomorrow."

The group burst into action and resumed their work. Bassan turned to the Kintal console and sighed. He stared at the display, its colors mesmerizing. They promised so much. He leaned forward, jaw clenched. There must be other options.

Something poked at his memory, a vision from a recent connection with the ship's past. The ancient Tgrens creating the probe. No, the Tgrens reprogramming the probe. Remotely. How did they do it?

What if there's another possibility?

Bassan whirled around. "Barnenden!"

The man gave a brief order to an engineer and approached. "Yes?"

Afraid to get the others' expectations up, Bassan switched to mental communication. *What if there's a back door?*

A back door? Another way into the probe's programming?

Yes. The Tgrens who built it accessed it remotely and changed its programming to attack their own home world. What if we found that open access?

Barnenden's eyes lit up and his mouth fell open. *We could control the probe.*

A chill trickled down Bassan's back. *Yes.*

The engineer stared at Bassan for a moment before casting a glance around the room. *We've enough to work on the code. If you think you can find it, search for the back door.*

Bassan nodded and Barnenden stepped away. *One thing!*

The man hesitated. Bassan reached out with his left hand, not quite touching the man's arm. *Don't tell anyone what I'm doing. Not even the commander. The fewer who know, the better. Just in case. If I can access the probe and control it, every race across the galaxy will want that information...*

Bassan didn't continue his thought. The engineer knew the implications. Barnenden nodded, his unguarded thoughts ones of acceptance and understanding. *No one else will know. And if you find the back door, don't tell me the details. Let the secret stay with you.*

The senior engineer returned to his station. The weight of his proposal dragged Bassan's shoulders down and he slumped, knees threatening to buckle.

Let the secret stay with me? It might have to die with me to accomplish that.

* * *

Zendar appeared at Bassan's elbow. Startled, Bassan

jumped.

"Sorry," Zendar said, reaching out to steady him. "It's getting late and thought I'd check on you."

Regaining his composure, Bassan closed out the screen in front of him. Zendar didn't need to know the details surrounding his latest project. "I think I'm ready to call it a night."

"Excellent, because they're going to stop serving food soon. And there's no eating in the dining area right now due to the wounded."

Images of Liron and her mother flooded his mind. Bassan rubbed his eyes, hiding the ache of that earlier moment. He wondered if Navent survived.

He checked with Barnenden, who continued to work without signs of ceasing. The man signaled for him to go. *Do you have a lead on the back door?*

Bassan pressed his lips together and nodded. A smile twitched at the corner of Barnenden's mouth.

Go, then. See you tomorrow.

Zendar led the way out. Bassan followed, his mind growing numb with each step. The long days caught up in a rush. His equilibrium teetered back and forth from so many connections with the Kintal console. By the time they reached the hangar doors, not only did his body shake but so did his head. He needed rest. Desperately.

"You going to make it?" Zendar said, grasping Bassan's shoulder.

With your help, it's a slim chance.

Come on. Let's get you some food.

The still air wrapped around him. Bassan grew aware of his body's odors and wrinkled his nose. *I need a shower or no one will want to be around me. Including me.*

Tell you what. I'll go get you a plate of food while you wash up.

Thanks. Bassan's mind wandered to the morning attack. *How's Navent and Liron?*

Liron will be fine. Navent... Zendar kicked a piece of rubble out of his way. *She's hanging in there. Broken ribs will heal but her head injuries might be too much.*

The news knotted Bassan's empty stomach further.

They'd looked so happy a few nights ago. *I despise war.*

So do I. We lost some good people today.

Bassan refrained from asking how many.

There's so few of them. Not even a fraction of the population of Ktren. Those lost were family to these people. Means it hurts more.

"Here we are," Zendar said.

Fewer lights glowed in this section, but enough shed illumination for Bassan to notice the damage. What remained of the shack on the other side leaned against Zendar's place and part of his roof drooped forward. Too close...

"I reinforced it on the inside as best I could. I wouldn't recommend sleeping on that side of the room though." He nodded at Bassan. "Get cleaned up and I'll get some food for you."

Fingers on the handle, he gave the door a light tug. Bassan sighed when it opened with ease. Thought he'd bring down the whole place.

Two more nights. I can do it. Two more nights and I'm getting off this planet.

* * *

The ship bustled with activity the next day. Each time Bassan ventured out of the control room, he passed dozens of workers carrying loads to various parts of the ship. The bulk appeared to be food, but judging from the makeshift labels, an abundant supply of medical equipment flowed into the vessel. Several people carried armloads of blankets and clothing. Whatever extra they possessed now made its way inside.

I guess the commander wasn't kidding about leaving tomorrow.

Determined not to miss the midday meal, he slipped out with another engineer to retrieve food for the six men working on the probe's code. The back door still eluded him, but Bassan remained optimistic. Several options remained.

I'll find it.

As the men exited the ship, Bassan noted a familiar character approaching.

"Hey, Bassan," Hetz said, pausing to deliver a sound punch to his arm. The blow knocked Bassan off balance and he winced.

Rubbing his arm, Bassan glanced at the engineer, then to Hetz. "What are you doing here?"

"Weapons," Hetz said, his chest out. "No one knows weapons like I do. I'll be manning the guns when we make a break for it tomorrow. I'm checking my station and see what modifications are needed. Don't want to get caught with anything hanging out."

Because you will shoot it right off.

Bassan cleared his throat. "You're the best man for the job."

"Damn straight!" Hetz punched him again. "I'm itching to kill anything that gets in our way."

After yesterday, no one is safe from you.

Bassan wished Hetz a good day, happy to get away from the repeated blows. He and the engineer continued toward the ship.

"I understand Hetz shot down three ships yesterday morning," the engineer offered.

"I bet he did."

Wonder if that was before or after Witz was killed? Damn, I feel bad for him.

They paused at the hangar door while a large cart of supplies passed. Bassan swung his arm, hoping the sting would fade soon. He pictured Hetz blasting the ship's guns left and right with an equal amount of force.

Blow up all the Narconian ships and sentries you want. Just don't shoot the probe. Please!

10

I got it.

Bassan stared at the screen, excitement bubbling up from the center of his being. After hours of searching, after countless dead ends, the back door loomed before him.

Barnenden appeared at his elbow. *You found it?*

Yes. Nine trips back to the past, but I found it.

The man heaved a sigh. *Can you access it?*

He typed in a command and a new configuration of code appeared on the screen. A jolt shot through his system and Bassan sucked in a quick gulp of air. *I believe I can. It'll take some time.*

Best news I've heard all day.

All day? What time is it?

Bassan jerked his body back and scanned the room. Three of the engineers still worked at their stations. *Do I have time?*

The evening meal will be served soon. Yes, you have time.

Bassan grasped the man's arm before he moved away. *Remember, tell no one. If I can't access it, no one will be disappointed. If I can...*

Barnenden's face dissolved into patient understanding and he clapped his hand over Bassan's. *The secret will stay with me.*

Bassan sensed the man's dedication and honesty in his open mind. The engineer meant what he said. Bassan offered a smile of appreciation. *Thanks.*

You worry about that back door, Barnenden thought. *We're almost done with the code. Let's wrap it up soon.*

Maybe I'll get a hot meal tonight.

Focused on the schematics in front of him, Bassan explored the options provided by the back door. The Tgrens once used it to alter the probe's programming, turning the weapon on their own people. Now he could access it to prevent the probe from blowing up their ship.

His elation waned when he pondered the last vision though. That moment in the past when he discovered the back door. At the time, his exuberance overwhelmed the other elements of the setting. Now they began to weigh on him. Something wasn't quite right...

He pondered the scene again. Although the moment presented itself as expected, those involved surprised him. Three Tgren scientists hovered around him while he accessed the probe. But a Kintal stood beside him. And his own hands, the body he inhabited in the memory, revealed a mottled blue skin. Yet the fingers lacked finesse. More like the thicker stubs of a Lorvendera than the slender digits of an Arellen.

I was a Kintal rather than a Tgren. There were two of us there. With the Tgrens. Why? The Tgrens claimed they created the probe. Did they?

Bassan pushed his thoughts aside and continued exploring the data. Coupled with the information they'd already uncovered, controlling the probe from the back door wasn't a distant possibility. It was real. Every aspect lay at his fingertips. The design as familiar as...

The Kintal ship!

Bassan staggered back from the console.

Why didn't I notice before? The probe's entire programming reeks of Kintal technology. The Tgrens designed it, but the Kintals programmed the probe. They created the weapon and the artificial intelligence. They gave the probe its power.

Sweat trickled down his forehead. Fingers clasped around the edge of the console, Bassan clung to the device while blistering tremors consumed his frame.

When the races sent the seeded Kintal ships out, the Tgrens stunted their own development to prevent a repeat of the probe. The recording from our ancestors a thousand years ago said the Kintals weren't included in the reseeding because they'd appear again naturally. But maybe they didn't want their technology to develop at all because they created the probe's weapon. The Kintals. My people!

The thrumming of his heart grew faster and louder. The pounding added to the dread surging through his system. The swell grew, threatening to drown him in shame and remorse.

A touch on his shoulder sent Bassan reeling backward. A hand caught him before he tumbled to the floor.

Bassan? Are you all right?

Someone pulled him upright and he stared at Barnenden. The man's narrow eyes and yellowish skin struck a wild thought in Bassan's mind.

You're Narcon. Your worst transgression is siding with the Vindicarn, killing hundreds of thousands. I'm Kintal. We designed the strongest weapon in the galaxy. And we killed billions with it.

I need some air. He pulled free from Barnenden, his movement more abrupt than intended.

The engineer let him go although his thoughts echoed confusion. Bassan ignored the stares of the other engineers and focused on a hasty retreat. He reached the exit and burst into the corridor. The presence of even more people slowed his headlong flight. He pressed against the wall and slid forward until he reached the ladder. The rungs grew oversized in his hands and he struggled to climb to the next level. A hand from above hauled him up.

"Hey, excellent timing. I was coming to see if you wanted to eat."

Feet finding the floor, Bassan staggered back against the wall and beheld the speaker. Zendar's easy grin greeted him.

I'm...I'm not hungry right now. He pushed away from the wall, forcing his feet to move faster as he careened down the corridor.

Whoa, Bassan! Are you all right? Boots pounded the floor as Zendar gave pursuit.

Just need some air.

The crowded corridors slowed his progress. Averting his gaze from curious onlookers, Bassan wove around the bodies. His heart pounded against his chest. The ship shrank and pressed the walls closer. Someone's shoulder slammed into his. Without pausing to apologize, Bassan redirected his headlong flight. He reached the ramp and let it propel him into the hangar.

Bassan! What's wrong?

The hangar doors in sight, he swung his legs harder. Arms pumped in unison. He crossed the busy hangar floor in seconds and burst through the double doors. A steady flow of people moved along the path and he turned down a narrow side street.

Slow down.

No longer surrounded by people and spent from his efforts, Bassan reduced speed. His lungs protested the outburst and he huffed. Time to halt and find air again. He shoved his back against the wall and bent over, hands grasping his knees.

"Bassan!" Zendar caught up and grasped his shoulder. "What's going on? What's wrong?"

Breath still labored, he used the moment to gather his head. Everything continued to swirl, spiraling down to one undeniable conclusion.

All this time we blamed the Tgrens...

The probe. His hands tightened over his kneecaps. *The Tgrens built it, but they didn't design the weapon.*

Then who did?

Bassan pushed his body upright, leaned his head against the metal wall, and met Zendar's gaze. "We did."

Zendar's eyebrows came together. "We?"

"The Kintals."

Mouth open, Zendar took a step back. "Kintals created the probe's weapon? But I thought the Tgrens claimed they did."

"They did." Bassan hesitated, gaze on someone approaching carrying a bag of goods. He waited in silence as the man passed. No one else could know the truth.

I've seen that ancient transmission hundreds of times, the one from those final people alive after the probe destroyed everyone else, he thought, keeping a tight lock on his mind. He replayed it in his mind again to be sure.

The Tgren scientist claimed they built the weapon and turned it on themselves after annihilating the other races.

Did they lie?

Something sparked in Bassan's memory. *Wait.* He held up his hand.

Sweat dripped down his face. Bassan closed his eyes and concentrated. He skimmed through the ancient message presented to all the races fifteen years ago, after he delivered the code—searching for what, he had no idea. But a clue had to exist.

The survivors created a fail-safe so Tgren technology wouldn't proceed at the same rate as the other races, hoping the next generation wouldn't create the probe again. But they didn't do the same to the Kintals.

Because they didn't make the journey.

Bassan wiped the perspiration off his face. The Kintals were supposed to be a neutral race, but they were wiped out with everyone else. And they never sent an eleventh ship. That was the fail-safe.

He opened his eyes. Zendar stared at him, hands spread wide, waiting.

The probe wiped out the Kintals when it destroyed the Tgren population. They killed off both races because they were equally responsible. And then the Kintals didn't send a seed ship. Either so we wouldn't make it or to scatter us. Either way, it makes sense.

Damn. Zendar pressed a hand to his forehead.

Damn is right. Bassan's shoulders slumped and he crossed his arms. *All this time we thought the Tgrens killed off all the races and the Kintals were collateral damage. But they worked together to bring the probe to life. We're not the poor race that got crapped on. We're as guilty of annihilating eleven races.*

News of our involvement will rock the galaxy when it gets out.

Bassan jerked to his full height. *It can't! Zendar, we can't tell anyone. Kintals have endured a raw deal for years. We are still considered second-rate on by many. Word gets out our ancestors created the weapon that destroyed everyone and we'll be sunk. We were hunted once—we'll be hunted again.*

Zendar's eyes widened. *You think so?*

I know your people get along here, but it wasn't like that on other planets. Before we were known as Kintals, we were branded Rogues, the outcasts of society. We can't take the chance it will disrupt our place now. You must promise me you won't say a word about this to anyone.

I won't, I promise. Zendar's fists dropped to his sides and he uttered an exasperated grumble. Blinking once, he eyeballed Bassan. *People will wonder why you raced out of the ship.*

I'll tell them stress and exhaustion got to me, especially from connecting so many times to the Kintal console.

That explanation works.

Bassan's whole body sagged. A breeze tousled his hair, cooling his face. He glanced at the hangar.

Did you want to go back? Or do you want to get something to eat?

Could he eat? He'd better if he wanted to remain functional the rest of the day. "I need food. It'll give me time to get my act together."

They joined the others for one final joint meal on the planet. Despite the scraps offered in attempt to clear the pantry of unneeded goods, everybody gathered to partake of the food. The wounded no longer filled the space and the change elevated everyone's mood. Eager to depart, they displayed their excitement without inhibition, mental shields down and minds open for all to hear.

They're still nervous though, Bassan told Zendar while they ate their food. The undercurrent penetrated the outward joy, radiating stronger than the smiles of those around them. He shielded his mind. *I'm worried enough without the whole town's concerns beating on my mind.*

Zendar brought his hand down on the table and cocked his head. *You can hear everyone?*

Sure. Can't you?

Zendar frowned. *I have to concentrate. And it's easiest on one person. Ah, must be the Vindicarn in me. Good thing I have a heavy dose of Fesell and Torbethian in me as well.*

Bassan shoved a mouthful of sugary mush into his mouth. *Be grateful you can't hear it, then.*

At least I can suppress and control minds.

Bassan noted the smirk on his tablemate's face. Zendar crammed a large piece of meat into his mouth. The juices overflowed from his lips, but it didn't suppress his smugness.

Oh yeah? Well, I can jump ships with a drained teleporter.

I can escape from this planet on a garbage ship.

Bassan allowed a grin to consume his face. *I carried the salvation code and can connect with Kintal technology and experience the past. Beat that.*

Zendar broke. His cackle became a choke as he tried to swallow while laughing. He hit the table with his fist, sinking into hysterics. Concerned, Bassan started to rise, afraid Zendar might expire in front of him. A gasp followed by maniacal chuckles eased his apprehension.

You got me, all right. Zendar reached for his water. *Still a better tracker than you any day.*

You can have it. If I never trek across the desert again, I won't be disappointed.

Ah, but doesn't your home world contain a large population of deserts?

Who says I'm ever going outside again when I get home?

Zendar grinned and leaned back, his gaze taking in the other diners around them. *Home. This place has been my home since I was born. After today though, I'll have no home.*

The observation struck a chord and Bassan set down his fork. He recalled a similar moment years earlier with another Kintal in need of a place to belong. Piten's family found sanctuary on Tgren. Perhaps Zendar could do the same.

You could always come with me. Tgren is a welcoming place for Kintals. Lots of opportunities there. And lots of familiar desert.

Zendar cocked his head, eyebrows drawn together. *Tgren. Where is her territory?*

It borders Cassa, with a portion of it touching Arella and Vindi. Tgren sits on the outskirts though. Beyond is unchartered space.

Are the Tgrens exploring it?

Bassan chuckled. *With help. Tgrens have begun venturing into their own solar system recently. Cassans have explored the immediate area, though. That's how they discovered Tgren and her people.*

Imagine, a whole race unknown to the rest of the galaxy.

They weren't the only ones, Bassan thought. *Until fifteen years ago, no one realized Rogues were actual Kintals and their own race.*

Zendar nodded and poked his fork Bassan's direction. *As you pointed out to me.*

Bassan's gaze took in the scene around him. Men, women, and children, blending as one people. Indeed, many claimed Kintal heritage. A race accepted now. What would happen to the Kintal people if the truth of their involvement in the mass extinction of the races surfaced? Tgrens possessed no significant technological advancements and posed no threat. Fifteen years of Kintals working on their ancient ships, not to mention their access to and training from other races, created a whole new situation.

I won't be the only threat. So will my people. Maybe we can't create the probe's weapon here. Even with the schematics, there's a chance none of the races can. But what if Kintals can recreate it? What if that back door is all they need? There's so much information stored there. I've barely scratched the surface. But if the Kintals find a way, if the other races even think they might be able to do it...

An idea struck him. *You said you have Torbethian in you?*

Zendar set down his glass. *Yes, why?*

Once we're free of this planet and the probe, I'm going to destroy all information and access to the back door. That includes what's in my mind, and I need you to do it.

Zendar dropped his palms on the table with force. *What?*

Torbethians can alter minds, right? They can erode and suppress memories. You can do the same, correct?

Zendar shook his head, his mouth still open. *To a degree. I'm not as precise with it as a true Torbethian, though.*

If you can suppress it enough, no one will find it again.

Bassan, you're not listening to me. I'm not terrific at it. The last time we caught someone on patrol and the leader decided to release him with no memory of us, I nearly scrambled his brain.

Did you?

No, but I removed a lot more than his memory of our encounter.

It's a chance I'll have to take.

"No!"

Zendar's verbal outburst shocked them both. Those around grew still and stared. Zendar ducked his head. "Sorry about that."

The unease dispelled and diners returned to their food and chatter. Zendar slumped lower in his seat. Bassan's muscles threatened to slide him under the table, but his mind clung to a calm and composed demeanor. He had to maintain control. And despite Zendar's protests, risking a mind scramble was the only answer.

I know it's a considerable gamble, but I must get that information out of my head.

Zendar rubbed his face and moaned. *I don't want to cripple your mind.*

I've faced worse.

What could be worse than losing half your mind?

Bassan lifted his chin, a smile tugging at his lips. *Losing all my mind on Vindi fifteen years ago.*

That broke the ice. A snort of laughter met his ears. Zendar's smile extended to his eyes and he sat up straight. *You can have that one.*

Thanks.

They stared at each other a moment. A week ago, Bassan hardly knew the Kintal across from him. Now he was about to entrust him with his life.

Zendar grabbed their empty plates while Bassan stood and stretched. *Thanks again*, Bassan thought, implying more than taking care of their dining ware.

I'd say you're crazy, but I knew you were a bit off when you agreed to come here, Zendar thought. *I hope nothing goes wrong and I don't screw it up like everything I've done to you.*

You don't screw things up. You just make life more interesting.

* * *

When he returned to the control room, several glanced his way. Barnenden frowned, but not in a disapproving manner, and he remained silent. Bassan resumed his place at the main Kintal console. Despite the startling revelation, they still needed to escape the planet. The back door lay open. He needed to explore it in depth.

Absorbed in his work, he jumped when Barnenden appeared at his elbow.

"Sorry, didn't mean to startle you," the engineer said. He gestured to the now empty room. "The others have retired for the night. We have the code ready for tomorrow. Why don't you get some sleep? We'll have a few hours before departing."

Bassan nodded and closed the back door. He already possessed the knowledge to override some of the probe's features anyway. Just not the weapon. Yet.

You all right?

Bassan rubbed his eyes. *Just tired.*

This past week has been hectic.

A laugh escaped Bassan's lips. *That's one way to put it.*

Barnenden leaned against the console and gazed at Bassan. *I imagine life-changing is a better word. Especially for you.*

Everything about the past few weeks has been life-changing for me.

It's so much to absorb, Bassan thought. *You think you know how everything works and where you fit in, and then bam—the façade falls away. I'm...I'm not sure I know who I am anymore.*

The words slipped from his mind with no chance of retrieval. Bassan froze, terrified by his naked disclosure.

Barnenden drew a deep breath, his gaze dropping to the console. *I remember when they first brought me here. I was a Narcon surrounded by Kintals held hostage by my own race. No one could've been more out of place. But despite my misgivings, these people welcomed me in as one of their own, even before they knew the knowledge I possessed. By all right, they should have screamed for my blood. But Kintals are very forgiving people.*

After what we did, we'd better be forgiving.

I found my place on this ship. Barnenden tilted back his head and offered a faint smile. *You'll find yours. With all your talents, your place will present itself. Trust me.*

Barnenden nudged his elbow. Allowing his posture to droop, Bassan relaxed and returned the man's smile.

Whatever my purpose, I'll be ready. Might be mentally unstable by then, but I'll be ready.

* * *

The next morning saw a flurry of activity. Bassan listened to the delightful shouts outside while he packed his few belongings. Unshielded exuberance bombarded him from all directions. Caught up in the excitement, he resisted the urge to shield.

Shame you can't hear this, Zendar. You're just the wrong mix of Kintal for strong telepathic hearing.

Bassan secured his pack and grabbed Zendar's heavier bag. He grumbled a moment before remembering it represented everything the man owned. A lifetime confined to one small container. Bassan shouldered the two bags.

You'll be stunned when you see my flat. And my place isn't that big.

He stepped outside the same moment Zendar appeared with breakfast.

"It's not much," Zendar said, holding up two odd-colored sacks, "but it'll fill us for a while."

They exchanged bags and trotted in the direction of the hangar. Despite the early hour, a stream of people surged toward the ship's open hatch.

"Not sure where I'll place my bag while I'm helping direct traffic," Zendar said.

"I can store it in the small control room with me. Probably be my sleeping quarters, as well."

"Thanks. I might grab some floor space there myself," Zendar said, handing over his pack.

"Might as well."

Zendar tapped Bassan's shoulder. "See you in a couple

hours. This is it. We're getting out of here."

The anticipation in Zendar's voice, and that of those surging around him, buoyed Bassan's spirits. A smile spread across his face as he boarded the Freedom.

I'm going home!

11

Everyone prepare for departure. All essential personnel to your stations. All others, secure your family and belongings in a location outside of high traffic areas.

Commander Cartent's orders echoed in Bassan's head. He gripped the console in front of him. The data on the screen stared back at him, daring Bassan to use it.

This is it. Hope I don't have to use this back door.

Zendar joined him. "Glad I can stay here. Up top, it's standing room only."

Bassan squared his shoulders, forcing thoughts of the ship's mix of elements away. "Better be enough power for liftoff."

"Be a short trip if we don't."

Bassan regarded Barnenden as the man frantically checked all systems. His team had worked so hard to prepare the code for the probe's weapon. He hoped they wouldn't need it, either.

When it comes to the probe though, we need everything we got.

Under his feet, a tremor raced across the floor. It grew with intensity as the ship roared to life. Bassan's fingers tightened around the console. His innards trembled independently of the ship, jarring his body from head to toe.

"Feel that power," Zendar said. "We're going to blast right off this damned planet."

I hate flying...

"The hangar's ceiling is retracting," an engineer said.

Zendar laughed. "Why? We won't be needing it again. Should blast right through the roof."

Maybe letting him stay here wasn't such a smart idea.

The rumble of the engines continued. Bassan tried to

focus on the information in front of him, but the tremors only added to his growing nausea. Closing his eyes, Bassan focused his thoughts anywhere but on the approaching launch.

Sirella, I'm coming home. I'm sure the past couple weeks have tortured you. If only we were mates—I could've let you know I was all right. My fault. I'll make it right when I get back. Promise.

Bassan reached out in a vain attempt to connect with Sirella. Silence greeted his efforts. An empty pit opened, pulling his hopes into the void. What if he never touched her mind again?

Commencing launch in three, two, one…

The trembling intensified. The engines one floor below roared. His body tensed, waiting for the jarring liftoff.

We're going to explode, I know it.

And we're off!

Bassan's eyes flew open. *That was it?*

What did you expect? thought Zendar, the waves from his mind far too excited for Bassan's tastes.

His death hold eased and he forced his body to relax. *I expected a rougher takeoff.*

No, that was awesome.

One hand on the console, Zendar gazed at the ceiling. The pure joy on the young man's face caught Bassan by surprise. Zendar's eyes glowed with uninhibited enthusiasm as he sported the largest grin possible. The feelings pouring from his unshielded mind matched his body's exhilaration. Despite his short reprieve from the planet while seeking help, this moment marked freedom. And not just for Zendar. For everyone.

Wait until you all taste real freedom.

"Look!" The engineer at the console beside him beckoned the group closer.

Bassan leaned over, curious. The computer screen showed a view from the underside of the craft. Far below, the settlement receded farther and farther from view. While impressive, what caught Bassan's attention were the ships racing toward Jaree. And them.

"Lethan," Zendar said. A wave of panic filled the room.

"Several are in pursuit and shooting at us," the engineer announced.

They're attacking? What if we don't escape the planet?

The ship trembled in response. One hit, then another. A warning light screamed.

No! We've come so far.

A siren wailed. It pounded at Bassan's head, threatening to drown out every last vestige of hope. He closed his eyes and lowered his chin.

"And we're shooting back," Barnenden said, his voice penetrating the panic. "One ship down already."

Eyes springing open, Bassan turned to Zendar. *Hetz.*

They don't stand a chance, then.

"Two ships down."

"And the others are losing ground," Barnenden added.

Bassan peered closer at the screen. The other ships grew smaller by the second. Their engines possessed no chance of keeping up with the Freedom.

We just might make it.

The ships vanished, along with the settlement, replaced by a blur of browns and greens. Their vessel rose quickly, leaving the planet's surface in a hurry.

"We outran them," someone said with a whoop.

I could've used without an attack during our departure. Bassan directed his comment at Zendar, keeping his grumblings from the others.

Now you know why the commander wanted to leave so soon. The Lethan were gunning for another attack. That one might've meant our doom.

"We'll hit the atmosphere's mantel in moments," Barnenden announced.

Bassan peered at the ceiling. He snorted at the gesture.

Dummy, like I'd see it that way.

"Damn, we're moving," Zendar said.

Bassan, I need you in position to teleport if necessary, Commander Cartent thought.

Yes, sir.

He closed the back door and secured his station. "The commander wants me at the ready to teleport."

"Go then," Barnenden said.

Bassan spoke to Zendar. *No one is to touch this console while I'm gone. No one.*

I'll guard it with my life. Zendar stepped closer and grasped the top of the console with a firm hand.

Zendar received a brief nod of thanks before Bassan moved with haste down the hall to the ladder. He pulled himself up to the next level, almost colliding with someone at the top. The man mumbled an apology, pulling his knees to his chest. Bassan stared at the mass of people huddled along the corridor. Most gawked up at him, their eyes wide with expectation.

"Excuse me," he said, picking his way through the bodies.

He reached the panel hiding the teleporter. A family of three clung to each other at its base. "I'm sorry, but I need to access that panel."

Pushing the youngster toward his mother, the man scooted to the left. Separated from his father, the boy cried out.

"It's all right," Bassan said, reaching out with his mind as well. He touched the youngster's head, the wild white hair soft to the touch. The boy looked up at him. The same terror of flying greeted his senses. How to calm the child? An idea struck him.

"Do you know what teleportation is?" he said, crouching down to the boy's level.

Face scrunched, the yellowed wrinkles threatening to take over, the boy shook his head.

"It's the ability to jump from one place in space to another. We're here, but I can take us someplace far, far away. Behind this panel is the teleporter. It doesn't have any power, but I can still make it teleport us. But I need to be close to make it work. Is that all right?"

The boy's eyes widened and his mouth opened. In less than a second, the wrinkles vanished, and he stared at Bassan in wonder.

"You'll take us far away?" he said, voice but a whisper.

"If I need to, yes. We'll cross millions of miles in seconds."

A gasp escaped the youngster's lips. A smile tugged at

the corners of his open mouth, reflected in his bright eyes. Bassan tousled his hair and nodded at the boy's mother. He stood and placed his hand on the panel. Behind the cold metal, the teleporter came to life. It hummed deep within his chest.

Father, you told me so many times about your gift, how it felt. I never understood, never cared. And I should've—it's like my connection with the Kintal ships. But I feel it now. And I know why you were so drawn to its power. Even without jumping, it fills me so completely. I can't wait to share the experience with you.

Eyes closed, he focused on the sensation as the electronic echo of the device rang in his mind. The rumbling beneath his feet vanished. Only the pleasant whirr of the teleporter remained. Soothed by the pulse, Bassan lost track of everything else.

A jolt, followed by cries, brought him back to reality. He grasped the wall and gazed around the corridor. Those taking shelter there clung to one another, eyes wide.

Zendar, what happened?

The security drone fired on us. We're returning fire now.

Another shudder flowed under his feet. Bassan pressed his hands against the wall. The ship lurched and the gravity fought to keep all contents aligned. His body pitched and he cast a wary glance at the others. Those in the hallway latched onto whatever they found. Whimpers and cries echoed down the corridor.

Two drones are on us now.

The ship lurched and he leaned heavy into the wall.

How large are the drones? And how much firepower are they hauling?

Below him, the boy sobbed in his mother's arms. An arm pressed against his legs and Bassan glanced down. The man hugged his mate, offering what comfort possible under the circumstances.

At least you'll keep me pinned to the wall.

Zendar, what's going on?

We dispatched one drone, but five more have appeared.

Are we taking damage?

A pause ensued. *Barnenden says yes.*

Bassan took shallow breaths. Concentrating on the teleporter, his energy flowed, and he brought the device to full power.

I can't just jump though. I need to know where.

He took a chance and reached out to Cartent. *Sir, teleporter is ready. If you want to jump, I need coordinates.*

No response. As he prepared to ask again, the commander cut him off with a reply.

Prepare for a jump. Coordinates coming.

A deep tremor vibrated through the ship, followed by an audible explosion. Bassan gritted his teeth.

Give me something. Now!

Bassan! Barnenden's thoughts interrupted him. *Here are the coordinates. Still in Narcon territory but closer to the border.*

Mind open, Bassan received the image. Concentrating on the location, he poured every last vestige of energy into the jump. The teleporter screamed in his head. Body pounding from the inside out, Bassan pushed the jump. The outside noise vanished, replaced by blissful silence and darkness. Then the shrieks of those around him resumed. The trembling did not though.

Barnenden, did I take us to the right place?

Yes. Well done.

We're away from the planet. A hint of concern colored the commander's words as he broadcast loud for all to hear. *Tend to damage control now.*

Bassan sighed and leaned against the wall. *Zendar, how bad is the damage?*

A small breach. Plus some other minor damage. But nothing major. We escaped intact.

We escaped total annihilation is more like it.

Bassan's legs shook as he tried to move. The man's arm still pinned him to the wall.

"We're all right," he told him, wiggling to free himself.

The man dropped his arm. "We are?"

Bassan stepped back. The family reunited with a quick hug. "Yes, we're outside of the solar system now. Well beyond the security drones' reach."

"You took us far away?"

Bassan smiled at the boy's question. "Far away."

"You're a jumper?"

The question came from the other side of the corridor. Bassan turned and faced the older man who stared at him. Now that he could see the others, he realized everyone gawked at him.

Commander, hope it wasn't supposed to be a secret.

"Yes, I'm a jumper. Like my parents."

Several cries of astonishment echoed down the corridor. Feeling the pressure, Bassan knew he needed to return to the control room. He nodded and moved toward the access ladder.

"He's the one who brought life support online," someone said.

"I heard he also worked on the probe's technology," a woman added.

Bassan quickened his pace. He seized the first rung of the ladder, hoping to escape without further revelations.

"You were the one who stopped the probe the first time, right?"

At those words, he hesitated. Glancing down, he met the gaze of a young man about his age. Despite his dark skin, his Fesell background showed in his gaunt and drawn face. Bassan's reply stuck in his throat.

"That was you, wasn't it?"

A few exclamations of surprise preceded a wave of appreciation from those gathered in the corridor. A hand grasped his leg and Bassan jumped.

"You're the Say-vee," the woman proclaimed.

Startled to hear the Tgren word, Bassan froze. "I'm the what?"

"Say-vee," a man said. Bassan turned to face him, mouth open. The older man held up his hand. "Savior of the races."

The awe emitting from those gathered rose in intensity. Bassan clung tighter to the ladder. A savior? Hardly. He almost let his best friend die. The code that stopped the probe years ago? A fluke, a result of his disobedience. He held no control over the events of his world. These people grasped for faith in the wrong place.

"I'm just Bassan," he said. Without waiting for a response, he shimmied down the ladder.

He hit the floor below with force. Ignoring the stares from those in the corridor, he returned to his station. Barnenden intercepted him and thumped Bassan's back.

"Perfect jump. I knew you could do it."

"Thanks," Bassan said, annoyed by the tremor in his voice.

He slid into position behind the console. Zendar let loose a victorious cry and shook his arm.

"You jumped us to safety. Amazing."

Bassan offered a smile, still trying to get his emotions under control. Mental shields locked tight in place, he trusted his anxious thoughts might remained contained.

"Looks like we're headed for the Narcon-Charren border," someone announced.

The room erupted in cheers. Zendar added his cry of victory and grabbed Bassan's shoulders, giving him a hard shake. Rattled but happy to hear the news, Bassan allowed himself to enjoy the moment.

For a while, the only updates coming through involved repairs. The hull breach secured, confirmation was sent that no loss of life had occurred. Engines remained at full capacity and sped them toward their freedom. The reality of their escape grew with each passing moment.

"You know, I might take you up on your offer," Zendar said.

Bassan cocked his head, a smile spreading across his face. "You want to join me on Tgren?"

"Why not?" Zendar shrugged and returned his grin. "Surely your people still need expert trackers, even with all the technological advancements."

Most of it was done with drones and ships now, but Bassan saw no reason why Zendar couldn't fit into the program. Someone needed to confirm what the drones sent back to base. "It's an enormous planet. Lots to track."

Zendar slapped the edge of the console. "Done deal, then. I'll go with you when you return to Tgren."

When I return to Tgren...

"Sir!" someone said from across the room.

Everyone turned their attention to the technician. Barnenden gestured for her to speak.

"It's the probe. It's within one sector of our position."

A wave of panic hit the chamber. Bassan's chest tightened.

"Is it pursuing us?"

"Not at the moment."

Bassan breathed a noisy sigh. The last thing they needed was the probe bearing down on their location.

"Wait," the woman said, staring at her console. Barnenden dived for his own station.

"A Narcon ship approaches."

The mood in the room took a nosedive. They traveled in an unregistered alien ship within Narcon space.

This can't be good.

Bassan resisted the urge to follow the updates on his own console. Instead, he reopened the back door to the probe and continued working. And waiting.

Minutes passed. No one spoke. Bassan's fingers gripped the console so tight they hurt. The woman announced the arrival of the Narcon ship within proximity of theirs. The minutes rolled by. Bassan wiped the sweat forming on his brow.

I hope Cartent has an answer for them. Not enough time has passed for me to make another jump.

The ship trembled and several people gasped.

"They're attacking," Barnenden announced.

Geared to protect against the probe, not a Narcon ship, everyone stood frozen in place. Bassan held his breath to suppress its raspy sound. Then he realized the sound emitted from Zendar.

We're so close, Zendar thought, a mix of desperation and fury flowing from his mind.

A tremor shook the ship. Bassan fought to keep his hold.

Can you jump?

The commander's request rang loud in his head. *Not yet*, Bassan thought.

Damn, I sure wish I could though.

Another shudder rattled the room. It ran deep,

shaking Bassan to the very bone. Panic emanated from those around him.

"We're leaking fuel," someone said.

Say-vee indeed! I can't save us now.

The ship shivered again. Bassan closed his eyes and held his breath.

"I don't think the ship can handle another blow," a man across the room said.

Crap, this isn't how I thought I'd die.

All their efforts, all the struggles and the losses—for naught. A sadness filled him.

I'll never see home again…

An eager whoop filled his ears. Bassan's eyes flew open.

"We destroyed the Narcon ship."

Relief flooded the room. Everyone cheered and clasped hands.

Despite the excitement, a new heaviness settled on Bassan.

The probe is near, though. It will sense the destruction of the Narcon ship. And come after us.

The thought weighed on his mind while reports on the damage filed in. The fuel leak was a huge problem and all efforts focused on fixing the issue. Otherwise, all else appeared cosmetic.

This will be one ugly ship when it finally limps into a port.

Minutes ticked by. The ship continued its course to the border and Bassan persisted with the back door. The threat of the probe refused to leave his mind.

Without looking up from his console, Bassan asked, "What about the probe?"

The question brought silence to the room. Barnenden's fingers danced across his screen. He sucked in his breath. "It's pursuing us."

Ice rained down over Bassan's head.

Of course, it is. We destroyed a Narcon ship. We broke the pact.

Barnenden hesitated, his hand over his screen. "Prepare the disruption code."

What does that mean? Zendar thought.

We have a code designed to scramble the probe's ability to fire.

Great!

We can only use it once.

What happens after that?

Bassan decided not to answer.

I don't know what will happen. How fast can the probe reconfigure and fire its weapon?

He examined the configuration for the back door.

While I can possibly write code to change its prime directive, can I do it fast enough?

His fingers raced across the panel.

What are you doing? thought Zendar.

I didn't have much time yesterday to explore the back door options, but I'm hoping I can rewrite its directive so it doesn't blow us up.

You think you can?

I don't know. There are so many systems. I must find the correct one.

"The probe is gaining on us."

"Is the code ready to send?" Barnenden asked the engineer.

"Yes, sir."

"Stand at the ready. We know her range. We have to wait until she hits that moment."

Bassan continued to work, urgency prodding his fingers to move faster than he imagined possible. The complexity of the programming impressed him even while it sent his nerves on edge.

"It's almost in range!" someone called.

Bassan held his breath.

How soon can you jump? thought Cartent.

He peeked at the time. *Five minutes.*

Get in position.

With a grunt of annoyance, Bassan pulled Zendar in front of the console. *Don't let anyone near this. And don't touch anything.*

Got it.

Bassan rushed for the open door. As he departed,

Barnenden's words rang in his ears.

"We're in range. Send the code."

Dread swept through him. Bassan forced his body to move faster and ascended the ladder at top speed. He burst into the corridor and staggered over to the panel. Those gathered around moved out of his way. Hand pressed against the wall, Bassan closed his eyes.

Seconds ticked by. His ears strained for any sound of destruction. Only the whispers of those in the corridor and the hum of the ship found him.

Barnenden, did it work?

It didn't fire on us. In fact, it slowed down.

Maybe the code did more than we thought.

He tapped into the teleporter. He was close. Another minute or two and he could jump.

The probe's moving again.

Give me coordinates near the border.

A configuration of stars flashed in his head. *That's right on the border. Cross over, and we're in Charren territory.*

Not safe from the probe but at least no Narcons will be firing on us. I hope enough time has passed.

The probe's almost in range again.

Bassan dug deep and connected with the teleporter. It roared to life, his energy pouring into it. He locked onto the coordinates.

It's in range, thought Barnenden.

We have to make it.

Bassan!

Prompted by the commander's frantic call, Bassan jumped. A rumble traveled through the ship. He focused on the energy connecting him to the device. The teleporter flashed bright and then all went dark. A tremor shook through his fingers and he opened his eyes. The drab panel greeted him.

We're in one piece!

The air rushed from his lungs and his shoulders drooped.

Closer than I wanted, but you got us out of there, Cartent thought.

Thank you, sir.

Head reeling from two large jumps so close together, Bassan moved on unsteady legs toward the ladder. He fumbled with his grip on the way down and hit the bottom with a resounding thud. Grasping the metal rungs tight, he regained his balance. Head still swimming, he staggered to the room. Anxious thoughts drifted his direction when he entered.

"That was close," Barnenden said, punctuating each word.

Bassan frowned and placed a hand on the wall. "How close?"

"It fired as you jumped and the blast clipped the engine," another man answered.

Jolting upright, he searched for Zendar. The young man shook his head slowly and held his finger and thumb close together. A chill rose within Bassan. The tremors from multiple jumps also amplified every nerve in his body. "Can we still fly?"

"At the moment we're limping along. But the blast didn't cripple the engine completely."

Bassan wobbled to his console. Several people touched his shoulders in passing, adding to his unsteadiness. He reached the console and grasped it tight. He heard Zendar chuckle.

"Some people know how to make an entrance. You know how to make an exit."

Bassan cast a sideways glance at him. "Very funny."

He stared at the data in front of him. The numbers jumbled and he rubbed his eyes.

No time to be exhausted. I've got to find a way to make this back door work for us.

Zendar leaned against the wall, arms wrapped tight around his wiry frame. With no one hovering over him, Bassan forced his mind to work.

Prime directives or weapons. I'll take either at this point.

He forced himself to focus and poured through hundreds of files and computations. The noise around him vanished.

A booming cheer jerked him back to reality.

"We made it!" one of the engineers cried. Everyone in the room either added his own cheer or sighed with relief. "We're in Charren territory."

"No Narcon patrol can stop us now."

But a Charren one might, Bassan thought, directing his comment at Zendar.

You think they might detain us? Or worse, send us back across the border?

This ship is a patchwork of many ships and resembles an ancient Kintal ship. The Charrens will ask questions when we cross their path.

We're refugees though. And you're part Cassan, one of their allies.

The observation triggered an idea in Bassan's brain. He turned to Zendar. *And a Cassan who's been missing for a while. That might work to our advantage.*

He reached out and found the commander's mind, busy with repairs and running a ship with serious issues. He hesitated, but if he waited until a Charren ship found them, it might be too late. *Sir?*

Just a moment.

He waited, still scanning the files.

Yes, Bassan?

Sir, when we encounter a Charren ship, it might help our position if they know I'm on board. I'm sure there are a lot of people out looking for me.

Noted.

Please play that card, commander. Might be the difference between a safe passage or a boot back across the border.

He flipped through more files. A section on the propulsion system caught his eye, but he knew nothing about engines. Regardless, he doubted slowing the probe would make a difference. But what if he missed the one thing that could help them because it was buried in an unremarkable file? He didn't have the time to explore every file. Other crew members might assist him, but Bassan wanted the back door kept a secret. He continued his search.

A segment of files on life support flitted past on the

screen. He shoved them aside.

Wait a minute. The probe has life support?

An idea jolted in his head. He scrolled back and searched the files until he found one outlining the extent of the life support. Familiar with the life support on the old Kintal ships, including the pods that carried their ancestors to this section of the galaxy, Bassan examined the information. He caught his breath and read the details.

It does have life support. And it covers almost five percent of the probe.

Excited even as uncertainty poked at his guts, he searched for that section of the probe. The tracks led to a new file and he opened it. A chill of anticipation tickled his skin and Bassan gulped.

What is it? Zendar thought.

Bassan stared at the information filling the screen. On the lower side of the probe, an entire section housed a control center. One with life support.

Can we access it?

He pulled up the blueprints, fingers working fast.

Someone touched his mind the same moment a physical presence nudged his shoulder. Startled, Bassan looked up. Zendar stood beside him.

Find what you were looking for?

Find what you were looking for? Something tickled Bassan's conscious. The directness of Zendar's question shot trepidation through his system.

Innocent enough question, and yet...do I tell you?

What if Zendar's role played into a more devious plot? Could Bassan trust him?

You already know about the back door. And the Kintals' involvement. You've lied to me several times already. What if you brought me here to find access to the probe?

Bassan stiffened.

Are you really my friend?

Mouth dry, he slid his fingers over the controls, prepared to wipe the information from the screen. Zendar turned to him and frowned.

What's wrong?

Bassan swallowed hard. *I need to know I can trust you.*

Eyes wide, Zendar nodded. *Of course, you can trust me.*

You've tricked me several times. Lied to me. Prove it.

Mouth open, Zendar leaned back. A flash of guilt coursed through Bassan. He shoved it aside, determined to know the truth. Too much was at risk.

Pressing his lips together, Zendar crossed his arms. *All right. I've opened my mind. Come see for yourself.*

Hesitant but determined to know the truth, Bassan reached out with his thoughts. True to his word, Zendar's shields remained down. Bassan braced himself and entered the man's mind.

Determination, tinged with concern, greeted him first. The current situation dominated his head, but the focus of Zendar's mind surprised Bassan. Zendar expressed desire to prove his worth and worried that Bassan thought little of him. Those feelings laid bare, with no attempt to disguise or deceive, in Zendar's mind. The man could adjust a past image, but he couldn't conceal an open mind.

I don't think little of you. Bassan's mental comment slipped out before he realized it.

I lied to you about why we needed you, Zendar admitted, his gaze steady with Bassan's. *But I'm not lying now. I'm not after any probe secrets. I'm not a spy, either. I was born on Ugar and the people on this ship are my family. I would die for them.*

Struck by the force of his words and ashamed of his suspicions, Bassan retreated from Zendar's mind. He reeled back, grasping the edge of the console for support.

I'm sorry. The past few weeks have been chaos and nothing in my life is stable anymore. I didn't know what to believe or who to trust...

Bassan trailed off and stared at Zendar. All the uncertainty in his life crashed down at once. His great-uncle's death. The upcoming changes when his father would step down. Drent's injuries. Sirella. Not to mention the possibility of not seeing Tgren again. Awash in a pool of doubt, Bassan reached out for a secure hold. Zendar grabbed his arm. Bassan met his gaze.

The corner of Zendar's mouth twitched. He slapped

Bassan on the shoulder.

Believe I'm your friend. And I owe you everything. If not for you, I might've died on Ugar.

Tension rolled off his shoulders. *You managed to escape the planet once though.*

Only because I was crazy enough to take on a suicide mission. Not to mention I did return to Ugar.

Would you have gone back without me?

Yes, Zendar thought without pause. *I would've continued to search, but eventually I had to return, if only to let my family know I hadn't abandoned them.*

The last of his unease drained from Bassan. *You are a dedicated friend.*

I fight for what I believe in and that includes every person on this ship.

As should I.

The connections in Bassan's life swirled in his mind. His parents. Sirella. Drent and Tarn. Officer Mevine. His Kintal heritage.

And my connection to our Kintal ancestors.

He turned back to the computer screen.

I need to access that control room.

There's a control center inside the probe. If I could access it, I could control the probe.

Really?

Yes. I need to find admission to the controls.

"A Charren ship approaches!" someone shouted.

Confidence leaked from Bassan. Would they prove friendly to the Freedom?

"It's a class five patrol ship."

Top of the line. Of course.

Bassan turned his attention to the data on his screen. So much to absorb. But there! His access point. He had it now. But could he enter the command from here? Entering one from within the probe—how could he accomplish that?

Bassan, report to the command center.

Prompted by the urgency in Cartent's voice, Bassan closed the back door. He nodded at Zendar. *The commander calls.*

I'll guard your station with my life.

Confident his friend would keep his word, Bassan bolted for the door.

12

Within minutes, he burst into the main command area.

The Charren vessel filled the main screen. Never had Bassan seen one in person, although he'd spent many weeks as a child studying the Cassans' allies. Awash in blue and green, the ship dwarfed space with her sheer mass. Her rounded edges did nothing to soften the impact. Instead, they filled out the ship, dominating the view and resembling a star glowing bright and fierce. Overcome by the sight, Bassan ground to a halt.

"Bassan!"

He turned toward the commander, breath held tight.

"Your safety is the bargaining chip. That's why I wanted you here."

"Yes, sir," Bassan said. His gaze returned to the Charren ship and he waited.

The crew verbally exchanged information with one another, but Bassan paid them no heed. The ship before him stood between them and freedom, and his presence might be the only thing guaranteeing their safety.

"Channel open," called Cartent.

Someone called all clear. Bassan straightened his shoulders and stood to his full height.

"This is the Freedom," the commander said, his voice deep and resounding. "We carry refugees from the planet Ugar. Women and children. We seek sanctuary in Charren territory."

Silence filled the room. Bassan clenched his teeth.

"This 589 heavy patrol. Confirm your origins. Ugar is a waste planet in the Narcon system."

"A waste planet for people and material," Cartent said, his voice rising. "The Narcons have been dumping people there for centuries. We represent generations of captives, held by the transgressions of our ancestors. We grew up on that planet, with no chance of parole or escape. Until now. And we seek asylum."

Another pause. No one breathed.

"We detected the probe firing on a vessel. Yours?"

"Yes," the commander said. "We had to fight our way across Narcon space and the probe gave chase."

"You broke the treaty of no war."

Spoken without emotion, those words fell with a resounding thud on the room. Bassan stepped toward the center of the room and glanced at the commander.

Mention me. Please. Surely someone is looking for me.

"In order to escape, we had no choice."

When no response came, Bassan began to fidget. Their opportunity slipped away by the second and he was powerless to do anything.

"Interfering will place us in danger of the probe."

Bassan spun around. *Sir.*

Cartent held up his hand. "We also harbor a missing person, Officer Bassan of Tgren. We believe you might be looking for him."

Please let someone be searching for me.

Bassan focused on the Charren vessel, willing information of his absence to appear in their databanks. What if his importance didn't matter?

"We have a report of a missing Tgren science officer from Procura Space Station. Can you confirm his presence on your ship?"

Bassan swiveled to face Cartent. The commander nodded. Bassan licked his lips and lifted his chin.

"Sir, this is Science Officer Bassan of Tgren. My father is Byron, commander of the Cassan base on Tgren."

"Switch to visual," the deep voice responded.

The image of the Charren vessel vanished. In its place, a red-skinned man with yellow-white hair filled the screen. His wrinkles extended beyond his skin, crinkling into his hair, and his purple eyes glowed in their sockets. He scanned the command center, searching for Bassan. "I am Commander Ohkaa. Identify yourself, Tgren."

"Sir," Bassan said, stepping forward. "I am Officer

Bassan."

The man stared at him, his expression revealing nothing. "You were reported missing from Procura Space Station several weeks ago. We can assist you. There are two Cassan ships in the area searching for you."

Two?

"Sir, the probe is approaching," a crewman called.

Already?

Bassan balled his fists.

"Commander Ohkaa, this entire ship needs your help," Cartent said with urgency.

"Freedom, you are a target of the probe. If we assist you, we will also become targets."

"We understand," Cartent said. "But if you could help us off this ship, the probe would only destroy it. Or perhaps you could at least help us outrun it."

"We cannot take that chance. We have notified the closest Cassan ship of Bassan of Tgren's presence. They might be willing to help you when they retrieve their officer."

Bassan whirled around and stared at those present. *How close is the probe?* he asked Barnenden.

It will reach us in thirty minutes.

A chill coursed through Bassan. They needed the Charrens' help and right now.

"Sir!" Bassan said, turning to face the Charren commander. "I might be able to stop the probe."

The man wrinkled his wide nose. "And how do you propose to do that?"

Drawing upon strength he didn't know he had, Bassan stood tall and proud. "I stopped it fifteen years ago when it threatened to destroy all the races."

Ohkaa's wrinkles vanished. Eyes wide and mouth open, he stared at Bassan.

Yes, I am that Bassan. Believe me. And believe I have a plan for our escape now.

"You are the Kintal boy who delivered the code and stopped the probe?"

Boy? At least it wasn't soft boy.

Bassan suppressed his annoyance and adjusted his

stance. "Yes, sir. And I know how to stop the probe from destroying either of us now."

"Explain."

Explain? Bassan's temperature rose.

But I can't. Word gets out, everyone will want to control the probe.

"Sir?" one of the Freedom's crew members said. His urgent plea caught the group's attention and Bassan held his tongue. "A Cassan vessel has jumped to our position. She's hailing us."

Oh, please!

Bassan took a deep breath.

"Let's hear it," Cartent said.

Bassan!

His name overrode all other sounds as his father's voice rang loud in his head. *Father?*

You don't know how relieved I am to find you. I thought we never would.

The emotional charge of his father's mental voice shocked Bassan. That wasn't the only amazing thing, though. *You're here? All this way from Tgren? Who's in charge of the base?*

You're worried about the base?

No. Bassan closed his eyes and focused on their conversation. *I'm stunned you would be among those looking for me.*

You don't think I'd come looking for my only son?

I didn't think you'd be able to get away from your duties.

Well, I did. I'll explain later. I'm so thankful we found you. Your mother is coming unglued with excitement back on Tgren.

I'm sure she is.

Thoughts of his mother falling apart placed a yoke of guilt around his neck. *Can she get word to Sirella? I don't know if she's worried about me or not...*

Sirella has checked with your mother multiple times a day since you vanished. I'll make sure she knows right away.

The load lightened, Bassan let a smile tug at his lips.

Now, we need to get you off that ship.

We need to get everyone off this ship.
"Bassan!"

He opened his eyes and spun around. The commander glared at him, his fingers clenching the console in front of him. *Father, hold on.*

"Sir, my father, Commander Byron, is on that ship."

"I'm aware. Right now, we need to either get everyone off this ship or perform another jump."

"I'd still like to hear more about your plan to stop the probe," the Charren commander said.

Startled, Bassan turned to the screen and caught his breath.

"But since time is not your friend and the Cassan ship is here, it will have to wait. I'm sure it involves another code, does it not, Bassan of Tgren?"

Bassan seized the opportunity. "Yes, it's another code. It'll cause the probe to cease its pursuit of us."

Commander Ohkaa waved his hand. "I will leave you to it. We will be watching from a safe distance and deal with your people afterward, Cartent."

The screen went black.

"Bassan, what's your plan, and do we have enough time?" Cartent said.

"It will be tight," Bassan said, calculating the steps involved. Too many.

"Then let's jump the ship to safety. Notify both vessels of our intent."

"Someone give me the coordinates," Bassan said as he raced from the bridge.

He leapt over stray legs and bags and reached the panel housing the teleporter. An acrid smell filled his nostrils. Concerned, he placed his hand on the wall but immediately pulled it back. Hot to the touch. He reached out to connect with the device. Nothing. Fear gripped the pit of his stomach.

Commander, have someone check the teleporter. I think it's been damaged.

He scanned the area and realized no one pressed against that section of wall. The family of three sat several feet away, huddled together.

We're detecting electrical damage to the unit, Cartent thought. *Are you able to connect?*

I can't.

A tremble flowed down his arms.

No way to jump and the probe's bearing down on us. What are we going to do? Think, dummy.

Could he get to the probe and program it in time?

Father, is there a Cosbolt or other two-seater ship there?

We have a Marr 3. It holds two people.

A jolt of hope shook him and he sprang into action. *I'll explain later, but I need you to fly me to the probe.*

He sprinted for the ladder and reached out to the commander. *Sir, I need to get on that Cassan ship. It's the only way for me to stop the probe.*

He hit the floor hard and dashed down the hall. Ignoring the occupants of the room, he raced to his console. Moving with a speed he didn't think possible, he connected his tablet and opened the back door.

"What is it?" Barnenden said.

"No time to explain."

"Attention!" came Cartent's voice over the system. "The Cassan ship is sending shuttles. I need everyone to prepare for departure. Leave everything behind—human cargo only."

Around him, people flew into action. Bassan focused on his task, securing the information that might allow him to access the probe from within.

Bassan? Zendar touched his shoulder.

The last bit of data downloaded into his tablet. *I've got a plan,* Bassan thought, unhooking the device and grabbing his bag.

Men and women moved toward the hall, blocking his path. Panic rose in Bassan's chest and he dug deep. "Let me through!"

His own voice startled him. The engineers froze. Bassan seized the opportunity and pushed through to the corridor.

If you're going to be on the first shuttle, I need you in the cargo bay now, Cartent thought.

I'm on my way.

What's happening?

Zendar's confused voice caused him to falter. Halfway up the ladder, he peered down the hall. Why didn't he bring Zendar with him? He couldn't let his friend miss a shuttle to the Cassan ship.

Come on. Get on a shuttle quickly. Don't alert the others, but it's going to be a race for time. Bassan continued climbing. *I'll do everything I can to stop the probe.*

Panic filled Zendar's mind and Bassan shielded. He needed to keep his head together.

People moved toward the small cargo bay. Ignoring protocol, not to mention manners, Bassan plowed through the crowd. Many recognized him and let him pass. Others jostled for a better position. Even worse, several latched onto his urgency and pushed forward harder.

I'll never make it through at this rate.

Please! he called, broadcasting wide for all to hear. *I can stop the probe and save us. I need to get to the cargo bay right away though. Please, let me pass. Say-vee!*

A path formed in front of him. Stunned by the response, Bassan stumbled forward. Regaining his composure and confidence, he pressed on, feet moving faster with each step. Within moments, his boots pounded the metal floor in a rapid rhythm.

Almost there, he told Cartent. *Someone please guide me so I don't go the wrong way.*

A mind locked onto his. A familiar touch, yet not one he recognized. He clung to the contact and followed it down a ramp and into the rear of the ship. The mob grew thicker and he issued his desperate plea once more. Again, the way parted for him. Slipping between two large men, Bassan stumbled into the tiny cargo bay.

"Hold it," someone said, pressing an arm against his chest.

"It's Bassan. The commander said let him through," a man replied.

The arm restraining him pulled away and he staggered forward. A group of men and women, many on gurneys, pressed against the right wall. The injured. Of course they would ship off first. He slipped in beside a man and an older woman.

A hand clasped his shoulder. *Glad you made it.*

He turned to view the person. Before his mind had time to register the man's identity, tiny fingers grasped his. His gaze dropped to the child beside the man. A young girl, her head and arm in bandages, gripped his hand. Liron! But where was Navent? Concerned, Bassan scrutinized Rence.

His pale face, eyes sunken with grief, told Bassan all he needed to know. Navent hadn't made it. He returned the man's clasp and Liron's, sympathy flowing from his mind. A nod of acceptance acknowledged him.

You helped save my daughter, Rence thought, caressing Liron's face. She released Bassan's hand.

A warning blasted from the double doors. Everyone pressed tighter against the wall.

There's barely enough room for a shuttle. How many can fit on a shuttle? Thirty if they stand? There are hundreds of people on this ship.

A clamp locked around his heart.

I must succeed. Or half these people will die.

Zendar, how close are you to the hangar?

Hard to tell. The corridor is packed.

Fight your way through.

Alarm stirred in his friend's mind. *We have to get off before the probe gets here, don't we?*

Yes. So don't miss the shuttle. And tell Hetz. There's nothing for him to shoot at now.

The inner doors opened and a Cassan shuttle slipped into the narrow spot. Her ramp dropped right away.

"Get the wounded on board," someone shouted.

Bassan lagged behind, letting those carrying gurneys enter first. He glanced at the cargo bay entrance. The guards linked their arms together, holding back the crowd. They were one step away from a total panic. He edged closer to the shuttle and stepped on the ramp.

Bassan!

His muscles froze. He scanned the masses hovering at the entrance and caught sight of a familiar face. Zendar!

"I need him," he called, pointing at his friend. "Let him pass."

Squeezing closer, Zendar reached the guards. They parted enough to let him through. He ran to the shuttle and almost plowed into Bassan.

You made it, Bassan thought, steadying his friend. *Come on, let's get to the Cassan ship.*

He hauled Zendar on board by his jacket. Bassan caught sight of three open seats. He dropped his friend into one before taking a seat beside him. A young woman plopped down on his right, filling the shuttle. As Bassan fastened his harness, he realized people still entered the shuttle.

I guess they're going to pack it to the top, he thought.

Will she still take off? Zendar thought, fumbling with his harness.

Shuttles are designed to hold far more weight than this. I'm glad we have seats. At least we won't be tossed about.

Good thing we instructed the medics to house the wounded here. They'd never make it otherwise.

I wondered how they got through that crowd.

Instructed to sit, the latecomers wedged themselves in between the row of seats. A woman with two children pressed against Bassan's legs. Unable to move, he grasped his harness tight and turned to Zendar. The young man finished with his clasps and clung to the straps across his chest.

You know, until a month ago, I'd never been on a ship, Zendar thought.

You never went out with any of the ships?

Zendar shook his head and stared forward. *I was always ground patrol.*

So, escaping on the Narcon garbage ship was your first experience?

Yeah. I know, crazy, huh?

Bassan shook his head. *Obviously, we're both crazy.* He shifted his mental focus. *Father, I'm on the first shuttle.*

All right, now explain why I need to fly you to the probe.

His father's commanding voice slammed against Bassan's chest. Gritting his teeth, Bassan reached for the courage to respond with an equal amount of force.

No one can know, he thought, stressing those words.

I found a back door through the command center inside the probe.

Inside the probe?

Yes. It's got life support and there's a small hangar. But the only way to reach it is to jump a ship into the probe.

The shuttle door closed and the entire vessel shook. Bassan's fingers tightened around his harness. *I have a clear view of it and all the details on accessing the controls are on my tablet.*

I can secure the Marr 3, but Commander Gentar is going to want an explanation.

If he must know, tell him I have another code to deliver and I need to be near the probe to deliver it. Father, if word gets out there's a back door, that the probe can be accessed from within, and I'm the only one who knows how…

The shuttle shook below his feet. Bassan suppressed his fear of flying and focused on the mental connection with his father. Determined to make him understand, Bassan opened his mind and let his father access his worst concerns. Under normal circumstances, the touch equaled an invasion. The moment his father understood the truth, tranquility flooded Bassan's body.

You are in a dangerous position…

I know, Bassan thought.

I will protect you and your secret with my life.

Bassan's head slapped against the headrest and he closed his eyes. *Thank you.*

I'll be waiting for you the moment you land.

The shuttle shifted. From experience, Bassan knew they were on their way to the Cassan ship.

My father will be waiting for me when we land, he told Zendar. *If everything goes according to plan, we'll stop the probe before it can fire on the ship. Help get everyone off the shuttles so they can return for more passengers.*

I'll do my part. Zendar shifted in his seat. *Thank you. For everything. I know I tricked you into coming to Ugar, and that was wrong. You had every right to refuse to help us. Thank you for doing so despite me screwing up.*

The man's mind opened and regret flooded Bassan's thoughts. Gratefulness accompanied those wisps, along with a deep respect. Bassan ducked his head, overwhelmed.

I couldn't let your people die, he thought, every muscle tensing. A notion crossed his mind and he chuckled. *I didn't want to die there, either.*

Zendar laughed. Those around them turned to stare. Bassan offered a grin.

"We're going to make it," he said, mustering every ounce of conviction. "And so will all of those on the Freedom."

"You're sure?" someone asked.

Before Bassan could answer, another voice piped up. "He's the Say-vee. He saved the universe once before. Saving one small ship should be nothing."

Startled to hear that word again, he glanced toward the speaker. Navent's mate gazed at him, his eyes steely and set. Bassan nodded and his fingers tightened on the straps.

What happens if I fail these people? What will the survivors believe in then?

A gentle shudder signified the shuttle's landing in the Cassan ship's hangar.

Take my bag. Won't have room for it. And help get people off quickly, he told Zendar and threw off his harness. *I hope Hetz and Barnenden make it.*

He stood and Zendar clasped his arm. *Thanks to your warning, Hetz is waiting for the next shuttle.*

Somehow that comforted Bassan. Despite Witz's involvement in his abduction and the man's attitude toward him, Bassan wanted the scoundrel to succeed in his mission as well. Rescue his brother. With Hetz about to board a shuttle bound for the Cassan ship, Witz would achieve his goal, even if he hadn't lived to see it happen.

May I see you again when this is all over.

Zendar held tight to his arm. *You better come back. You promised me a ticket to Tgren.*

Bassan offered a smile and opened his mind. *Even if I don't, I'll make sure you are shipped to Tgren.*

Before Zendar could say more, Bassan broke their connection physically and mentally. He pressed through to the shuttle doors and all but fell down the ramp when they opened. He regained his footing, reached the hangar floor, and looked up.

Not three feet away, his father stood waiting.

His chest tightened and Bassan staggered forward. His father closed the distance and embraced him in a fierce hug. Relief and affection flowed from his father and Bassan closed his eyes.

I'm sorry I scared you and mother. I had no way to send a message.

His father sighed in his ear. *I'm so thankful to find you alive. I don't know what we'd do if we lost you.*

Every doubt Bassan ever entertained regarding his father's love fled his mind. Despite the events when he saved the races with the code in his head, Bassan still held reservations. Those abandoned him in a flash.

Before he could compose a response, his father held him away and gave his shoulders a shake. *The Marr 3 is waiting. We'll fill in the commander en route.*

Still grasping his arm, Bassan's father pulled him away from the shuttle. Bassan glanced over his shoulder. Zendar emerged, his eyes wide.

Get everyone off the shuttles, Bassan thought. *And I promise you will see Tgren.*

Zendar sent words of thanks and immediately turned to help the next person. Confident his friend would follow instructions, Bassan focused on the direction his father led him.

The Cassan ship commander locked into their thoughts and Bassan relayed his plans, omitting the jump into the probe's control center. To his relief, the commander understood.

We'll focus on retrieving everybody from the Freedom, the commander thought.

Bassan didn't have time to thank him. His father hauled him into a fitting room and shoved a suit and helmet at him. He suited up, his fingers fumbling with the snaps. Already fully attired, his father assisted him.

You better be right about this chamber in the probe, he thought, jamming the helmet on Bassan's head.

I am and I can get us there.

Then let's do this.

Bassan assumed a straighter stance and managed to salute.

Let's go, his father thought, pulling him toward the exit.

They raced across the hangar toward a cluster of smaller ships where a crew of three stood at attention next to a petite vessel. Narrow and streamlined, its dark shape resembled a bird of prey. The similarity to his father's old Darten struck Bassan and he grinned. He might've flown Cosbolts, but father had always fancied his Darten.

His father shoved him toward the ladder, and Bassan ascended to the platform. A tiny spot behind the pilot's seat beckoned him and he dropped into position.

The Marr 3 can be flown solo, which is why I selected it, his father thought, settling into the pilot's seat.

Good, because other than jumping, I have no idea what to do.

Jumping?

His father's question filled his chest with its intensity. Bassan realized his father held no knowledge of his jumping abilities.

I can jump like you and mother. No transporter power.

A bark of laughter erupted from his father. *You're a jumper?*

Yes, Bassan thought, his mental voice soft.

You'll have to tell me how you discovered that.

Quite by accident. But it's how we got the Freedom so far from Ugar.

The hatch closed over them, sealing the ship.

Jumping the Freedom again wasn't an option?

The acrid smell surfaced in his memory and Bassan wrinkled his nose. *No, the teleporter was damaged.*

Then this plan of yours better work.

A rumble behind Bassan signified the ship's engine coming online. He grasped his knees and stared at the control panel in front of him. The vessel moved forward. Bassan's pulse increased. He'd endured many shuttles and countless other large ships, but never something so tiny as this Marr 3.

Similar to a shuttle. Only with an amazing view. And

much faster. Much, much faster.

The ship moved into position. The large hangar doors opened. A long flight deck and another set of double doors lay before them. Bassan clenched his knees even tighter.

This will be smoother than any shuttle, his father thought.

Before a response formed in his mind, the Marr 3 moved into the flight deck. It paused and Bassan scrunched down in his seat.

A jolt of power shot them forward. His head pressed hard against the seat and Bassan gasped for breath. The world flew by in a blur. In a fight against his rising nausea, Bassan closed his eyes.

The thrusting motion equalized. The sensation of being pressed into his seat vanished. Wary, he opened his eyes. Open space greeted him. Despite his fear, a peace settled over him.

What are the coordinates to this inner chamber?

His father's request snapped him back to reality. *This is the landing bay inside the probe,* he thought, conveying the image to his father.

His father's mind locked onto his. *You're sure about this?*

Yes.

Prepare to jump.

The Marr 3 reduced speed and came to a standstill.

A thought occurred to Bassan. *Let me jump with you. The image is clearest in my mind.*

Together, then.

As one, they touched the teleporter. Bassan visualized the open hangar, deep within the probe. Its tiny space and gentle blue hues beckoned. Closing his eyes, he made the connection.

Jump!

Bassan kept his eyes closed lest he'd calculated wrong. The excitement in his father's thoughts jolted him to the present.

You did it.

He opened his eyes, and a large inner control room greeted him. The size of a small hangar, the room glowed with a thousand lights. They lined every wall, pulsating in unique rhythms, as if in celebration. Dozens of consoles filled the floor space, their triangular shape different from the ancient Kintal ship. Tgren design? However, the plasma ball at the far end represented the Kintal. So did the three consoles surrounding it. Without a doubt, the inside of the probe. Laid out exactly as the blueprints showed. It was real.

"Ah!" Bassan unfastened his harness and jumped out of his seat. His helmet struck the hatch above him and he winced.

Hang on, his father thought. *Let me power down and open the hatch. Is the air breathable?*

Probably a bit stale, but yes. Life support is still operational.

He slipped off his helmet. Grasping the tablet wedged between his legs, Bassan's muscles tensed. The moment the hatch retracted, a metallic smell reached him. Its bitter edge filled his nostrils. He took a cautious breath and decided the air fit to breathe. He stood and swung a leg over the edge. The hangar floor loomed before him, many feet away.

We'll have to jump out, his father thought. *Getting back in will be interesting.*

Bassan pulled his other leg over the side, clutched the tablet to his chest, and slid down the ship's side. He landed hard but on his feet. He gazed up, concerned for his father's landing. Bassan caught his father's arm, Byron's boots thumping loud on the ground. His father staggered a moment before catching his balance.

Sorry, I'm getting too old for this.

You're not old.

Thank you, but I've almost fifty years on you.

I miss mental communication. Zendar's people need to remember to do it more often.

Aware of the time constraints, Bassan straightened his shoulders. *Now, let's get to work.*

His father gestured toward the control room and stepped aside. Bassan rushed forward to the first Kintal control panel.

He pulled up the information on his tablet. Accessing the back door, he entered the information into the system. The panel, dark upon their arrival, came to life. Confidence swelled in Bassan's chest.

How much time do we have? he thought, reaching out to Zendar. Powering down several levels, he searched for the main controls.

Ten minutes.

Bassan's gut twisted. *How many remain on the Freedom?*

A pause ensued. *At least a hundred.*

Bassan's fingers worked faster, fighting his tense muscles.

I can't let those people die.

On instinct, he followed a trail. It led to a security area. Plunging forward, he opened those files. Allowing no access to controls, the path appeared to be a dead end.

Damn it!

His father appeared at his side.

I'm still looking for the controls.

What can I do to help?

Bassan hit a few more buttons. *Give me ideas. Anything.*

You carried the code before. Would that help?

Bassan shook his head. *That was a one shot deal.*

He pounded down to the main controls. An option opened. Passcode protected.

I need a password.

Do you know what it is?

No!

Frustration rattled his bones. Sweat formed on his brow, threatening to trickle into his eyes. They were here, in the control room. So close. Why didn't he know the password?

Zendar, how many remain on the Freedom?

Shuttles keep coming in. No sign of the commander or any of the main crew, so I imagine quite a few remain. Maybe seventy?

Bassan closed his eyes. After all his efforts and a narrow escape from Ugar, those people would die at the hands of the one thing designed to protect all people. To come so far...

Damn it, we're here. In the probe. But there's a password and I don't know what it is. I'm going to fail everyone.

No, you won't. You can do it. You are the Say-vee.

A light exploded in his mind. Say-vee! Would it be the same code here?

He entered the word into the controls. In a flash, he gained access to everything.

I'm in.

Do your stuff, his father thought.

Fingers flying across the keys, Bassan entered his command. Stand down. Don't destroy the Freedom.

That's it, he thought, stepping back from the controls.

A hand pressed against his back. Bassan looked up and found his father staring at him. He swallowed hard. *What if it doesn't work?*

It will work.

Those words from his father buoyed his confidence. Fingers on the edge of the control panel, he stared at the readout. His command hung out there, waiting for a response or a rejection.

Why doesn't it recognize the command?

Barnenden, how much time before the probe reaches the Freedom?

When I last calculated, seven minutes.

Bassan closed his eyes. *Where are you?*

Waiting for the next shuttle.

He didn't bother asking how long ago Barnenden inspected the arrival time. They had minutes. He scrolled through the commands again, many encoded. The last one, entered fifteen years prior, piqued his interest.

The day I downloaded the code...

The command encoded, he couldn't read it. But it wasn't the code from his mind. It was the instructions entered afterward.

Protect.

Bassan, we have one minute before the probe is in range.

Commander Cartent's desperate voice resonated in his

mind. Foregoing a reply, he typed furiously. With enough experience in coding, he copied the key elements from the previous command and reconfigured them.

Protect...

He entered the command.

Please work.

The system acknowledged the order. In a flash, the screen proceeded through several displays. Bassan leaned closer, his fingers wrapped tight around the console. Zendar's panicked expression crossed his mind.

You brought me there to save your people. Damn it, this has to work. I can save you...

He scanned the ceiling, aware of the massive weapon above their chamber. A deep hum reached his ears. It grew in intensity, vibrating the air.

It's powering up, his father thought.

Bassan slammed his fist on the edge of the console. "Damn it, come on!"

The screen ceased its rapid-fire computations and settled on one readout. The list of commands. There, at the very bottom, sat his command.

Protect the Kintals.

The overwhelming drone ceased with an audible pop. An eerie silence filled the room. Bassan strained to hear any sound above, any indication of the weapon charging. Outside of a gentle hum echoing through his boots and up his legs, no other noise reached his ears. Everything remained quiet.

Uncertain of his judgment, he reached out with his mind, trying to connect with any part of the ship. No teleporter registered. At the speed the probe traveled, a teleporter wasn't needed. Something registered though. A concentration of power unlike anything he'd experienced. He focused on it, homing in on its intensity. It crackled with potency, a force stronger than anything in the known galaxy. Despite the energy radiating from the weapon, it remained in check.

You did it!

Still in shock, Bassan turned to his father. In a rare moment, his father grinned from ear to ear. Still not believing his luck, Bassan reached out to the commander.

Has the probe fired? he asked Cartent.

No, came the tense reply. *It's in range now but it's ceased all movement.*

Weeks of uncertainty drained from Bassan's body. Trekking across the desert, escaping the Lethan, fixing all the issues on the ship, their desperate escape... All over now.

A hand slapped his shoulder. *Commander Gentar confirms the probe hasn't fired and remains still. You did it.*

His father drew him in for a rough hug. Bassan let a cry of joy loose and returned the embrace.

I did it. I'm more than just the one who carried the code.

His father grasped his shoulders and held Bassan at arm's length. *Of course you are. Why would you ever doubt that?*

You doubted me.

Bassan suppressed the thought, but not soon enough. His father frowned and squeezed his shoulders.

I questioned your decision to remain on Tgren and train there. But considering your gift, your ability to connect with the Kintal ships like no other can, it was the right call. I've not questioned anything you've done since then.

Except maybe embarking on this crazy journey to save those people.

His father chortled. *I would appreciate a full explanation on how that came about.*

I'll fill you in on the journey home.

Sounds like a plan. Now, let's return to the Cassan ship. Unless there is something else we need to do here?

In answer to his father's question, Bassan scanned the room. Much larger than he imagined. And so full of secrets. How did the Tgrens build this ship? What did the Kintals use to power the weapon? So many things he wanted to know.

We can come back next time it's in the Tgren system if you want. I think I can manage to do that discreetly, his father thought.

That would be great.

They returned to the Marr 3. As Bassan settled in his

seat and took one last look at the control room, the gravity of what he'd done hit him full force.

Father, no one can know we found this room. If word got out the probe had a control center and I could control it...

Don't worry. Only the two of us know. And no one's accessing the information from me, not even your mother.

The Marr 3 powered up.

Zendar knows the probe contains a control center but no idea how I intended to access it or stop the probe. He won't tell anyone. I...I even asked if he'd be willing to erase it from my mind. He's part Torbethian and—

What? His father's indignation struck Bassan full force, pressing him into his seat. *Not a chance. Bassan, you don't want to risk losing your gift. Besides, your knowledge of this place might be needed again someday.*

Hopefully not. We'll have to keep it a secret. And...and no one can know the command of the probe has changed.

A jolt of surprise emitted from his father. *What did you change?*

Bassan swallowed hard and shrunk in his seat. *The command is still to protect. But it's to protect the Kintals. It was the only way I could prevent the probe from firing on the Freedom but still keep the general protect command in place.*

A pause ensued. Then his father laughed. *With the probe still patrolling the galaxy, I'm sure no one will be the wiser.*

You're not mad?

Why would I be angry? You did what you had to. You protected those people.

Thank you. I couldn't let them down. Not their fault they had to fight their way off that planet.

The Marr 3 lifted into the air. *You must introduce me to this Zendar though. He sounds like a scoundrel.*

Bassan chuckled. *He is. And I hope he takes me up on the offer to return to Tgren. He's an expert desert tracker.*

We do have a lot of desert to track...

Jump!

13

"Everyone is off the Freedom, Commander Gentar. And our provisions. Thank you," Cartent said.

Bassan stood at attention to the side, relieved to play a minor role in this meeting.

"The Charren commander still wants an account of your appearance in Charren space. He is willing to negotiate."

Cartent clasped his hands behind his back and stood at attention. "Sir, would Commander Ohkaa be willing to accept our ship as retribution for entering Charren space unannounced?"

The Cassan commander lifted his chin. "I believe we can convince him to take up your offer."

"We'd appreciate it. That ship's a bit ragtag, but it contains a lot of Kintal technology. All thanks to what the Narcons dumped on our planet."

"Yes, that issue will be addressed, along with your condemnation on Ugar. How many others remain there?"

"Thousands. Maybe a million. We were spread out across the planet."

"The Narcons have a lot to answer for, then." Commander Gentar surveyed the room. "Science Officer Bassan."

Startled to hear his name, Bassan stepped forward. "Yes, sir?"

"Once again, you have successfully transmitted a code to the probe that halted eminent destruction. Thank you for your dedication and continued research. Hopefully, we don't have to call upon your services a third time."

"Thank you, sir."

"Commander Byron." Gentar turned toward Bassan's father. "As agreed, this ship will return to Tgren. Do you wish to take these people with you?"

Bassan clutched his arms together.

Father, please say yes. Where else will they go?

"Yes," his father said, chest out. "Tgren continues to grow and would benefit from the skills these Kintals bring. A handful wish to return to Procura Space Station though. It is home to several, and others wish to seek transportation to their home worlds from the station."

The commander's brows came together. Bassan sensed a private conversation. His father nodded.

"Prepare a shuttle for the Charren ship. Then set a course for Tgren," Gentar announced.

Everyone began to disperse. Bassan slid his way toward his father. *What happened?*

Commander Gentar must clear the transport, and this entire incident, with Cassan Command first. However, he didn't seem to think any objections would change our plans. This ship needs to return to the Tgren sector regardless.

Relieved, Bassan smiled. *I'm glad most of the refugees are coming with us.*

These people will bring new industry to the Tgren economy. That may work out to my benefit in the long run. And please your mother.

A smile tugged at Bassan's lips. *Pleasing Mother is important.*

Yes, it is. Once you have a mate, you'll discover that truth.

Those words punched a hole in Bassan's chest. He had a mate, waiting for him. And he would finalize the deal once he returned.

If Sirella will have me, I'll have a mate.

His father grinned and slapped Bassan's shoulder. *I doubt she will say no.*

* * *

"I wish you were coming with us." Bassan willed his breathing to slow after a dash from the bridge to the landing bay. When Gentar announced the last shuttle, he remembered a certain engineer would be on that ship.

Barnenden straightened his jacket and took a deep breath. "I can't go anywhere without my mate. After speaking with her earlier, I believe with the Charren government's assistance I can get her out of Narcon space. If she can join me on Procura Space Station, we'll decide what to do from there."

"After your ordeal, may they get her out quick. If you opt to leave Charren space, a home awaits you on Tgren."

A smile pulled at the corners of the man's mouth. "I'll certainly consider your offer. Your father also assured me a position working on the Kintal ship awaited my arrival on Tgren."

"You know I'll vouch for you with Senior Officer Mevine. I don't have quite the pull of my father, even if he's stepped down as commander, but I'll do everything I can—"

Barnenden held up his hand and Bassan clamped his lips together. Appreciation flowed freely from the technician's mind.

"I'm sure you have a far greater influence than you realize, Say-vee."

A jolt of surprise shot through Bassan. He allowed a smile to form on his lips and shook his head. His new nickname now.

Wait until Drent and Tarn hear that one.

"You might see me again, Officer Bassan."

"I hope so." Regret tugged at his chest.

I'll miss Barnenden. He changed my perception on more than Narcons.

Remember to keep the back door a secret, Bassan thought.

I'll tell no one. It worked, and that's all I need to know. Barnenden grasped him in a bear hug and thumped his back. *Thank you for getting us off the planet. We owe you our lives.*

You owe me nothing. Just go find your mate.

The man leaned back, tears in his eyes. He gave Bassan's shoulder a final squeeze and stepped onto the shuttle's ramp. Bassan held his breath, and Barnenden entered and vanished from sight.

I'll be checking on you.

"Well, look who turned out to say goodbye."

Startled, Bassan turned to find Hetz approaching the

shuttle. "Headed for home?"

"Yes," Hetz said, slinging his bag across his shoulder. "I can get back to the family business. Remind everyone we are still a proper operation and throw my influence around. With force."

Not legally though?

Hetz's smile deepened. *Legal is boring. And not profitable.*

Bassan shook his head. *Whatever works for you.*

Hetz smacked his left shoulder. Bassan staggered back.

"Witz might've called you soft boy, but you sure delivered. Thanks for getting us out of a tough spot back there."

"Witz kidnapped me," Bassan said, his gaze steady but friendly, "to get you off the planet. I have delivered my end of the bargain."

"That you did."

"And I'm sorry Witz isn't here to enjoy the moment."

Hetz pressed his lips together, his chin dipping for a moment. *We had a few days together. That's more than I ever thought I'd enjoy again with my brother.*

The depth of the man's pain revealed itself for but a moment. Bassan sighed. *I wish it could've been more.*

It would've been none without you. I'd give anything for Witz to be here now. Running the business without him... it's going to suck. But I'd still be stuck on that damn rock if not for you. You made the impossible happen. Well done, Say-vee.

Bassan cringed. That name would haunt him.

"Thanks again," Hetz said, slapping his shoulder with force. "You're ever out this way again, look me up. You need a favor, it's yours for the asking."

A thought occurred to Bassan. "Barnenden needs help getting his mate out of Narcon space and to Procura Space Station. He's on this shuttle with you. He said the Charren government would help—"

Hetz's hearty laugh cut him off. "That sorry bunch couldn't find a bomb in a mine field with a tracking device. You leave it to me. I'll talk to him and make it happen."

Relief settled on Bassan's shoulders. "Thank you."

The man punched his chest and strode past Bassan. As soon as he entered the shuttle, Bassan rubbed the sore spot and stepped away from the craft. Despite the success of the mission and the delight still bubbling from the refugees, a touch of melancholy settled over him.

May you all find what you seek.

***

Bassan returned to the control room. His father spoke with Commander Gentar, their voices hushed. Resigned to wait, Bassan stepped aside. Byron met his gaze and nodded. A moment later, Bassan's father approached.

We'll depart the moment the shuttle returns.

Bassan nodded. *I saw them off. Several good men left on that shuttle.*

His father clasped his hands behind his back and stood next to Bassan. *Didn't you say someone else accompanied you down to the planet besides Zendar?*

Yes, Witz. He was looking for his brother. And found him. Witz didn't make it. Killed during a Lethan attack on the settlement. But his brother Hetz is on the shuttle and headed for home.

Very good. I'd still like to know how you ended up on that planet.

Their earlier conversation entered Bassan's mind. *I want to know how you were able to come looking for me.*

His father shifted and stood taller. *I told you I planned to retire soon. And upon hearing you'd vanished, I did. I called on some favors and chartered this ship to search for you.*

Bassan gasped. *You retired to come find me?*

I told you I was going to retire soon, regardless.

But you came looking for me...

You're my son. Of course I did.

In a rare moment of openness, love poured from his father. Bassan ducked his head and reciprocated the gesture.

Thank you. But the Charren commander said two Cassan ships searched for me.

Fortunately, you are important enough the Cassan

government saw fit to send a vessel out as well.
Because of what I did fifteen years ago?
I'm not that special.
No, because of what you can do now. Your connection to the Kintal ships is unique. They didn't want to lose you. And apparently, it's even more unique than anyone realized.

Panic rose is Bassan's chest. What if they suspected? *No one can know about the back door or the probe's chamber.*

And no one will.

The tone of his father's reply left no room for doubt. Unable to contain himself any longer, Bassan hugged his father. His embrace was returned with an equal amount of enthusiasm.

I know I don't say it often enough, his father thought, *but outside of your mother, you are the most important person in my life. I'm so grateful she insisted on having a child. You turned out to be the most amazing addition to our lives. I love you, son.*

Bassan closed his eyes. *I love you, Father.*

His father thumped his back and released him. *Now, I must set Ktren up for the arrival of these refugees.*

Thank you for offering them sanctuary. And coming to find me. I hope that didn't drain all your favors.

A smile spread across his father's face. *We'll be all right. After all, your mother is the niece of a prefect. There's a fair number of favors waiting there as well.*

Bassan guffawed. Of course. His great-uncle always considered his mother a daughter. She still held a lot of sway on Tgren.

His father departed. Relieved at the turn of events, Bassan scanned the control room. He noticed a lone figure by the front view portal. Zendar.

Curious, Bassan moved closer. *Zendar?*

The man startled and pressed against the glass. He shook his head and laughed. "Bassan!"

Moving closer, Bassan sidled up next to his friend. "What are you doing?"

Zendar sighed, his gaze shifting to the view outside. "Just admiring the view. I've never seen the stars like this.

It's amazing."

Bassan gazed upon the stars as well. He'd never considered them amazing, but to someone who'd remained planet-bound his whole life, the sight would be incredible.

You can enjoy this view all the way to Tgren.

Zendar crossed his arms and smiled. *And I just might.*

Bassan shifted his feet and searched for a proper response. *I'm glad you're coming to Tgren.*

His friend turned his head and smiled. *So am I. Thank you for getting us off the planet.*

That's what you wanted.

Yeah, but... Zendar gazed at the stars. *I never thought it would happen. I mean, I thought you could do it, but I knew it was a long shot. Especially since I forced you to come on this mission.*

A decision I've not regretted.

Zendar turned to face him. *Thanks. I'm forever in your debt.*

Make a good life on Tgren. That's all I ask.

Will you help me?

A wave of distress escaped his friend. Bassan reciprocated with thoughts of encouragement. *Of course. You'll dig Tgren. I'll introduce you to my best friends, Drent and Tarn. Both Kintals. You'll fit right in.*

Thanks, thought Zendar, offering a faint smile.

You'll be all right.

His friend nodded and returned to staring at the stars. Bassan followed his gaze. The dark expanse, once so terrifying, now brought him a sense of peace.

You'll all be all right. And so will I.

* * *

Upon landing on Tgren, Bassan exited the Cassan shuttle the moment the doors swung open. He made it two steps down the ramp before arms flung around his neck.

You're alive!

He smiled and returned his mother's grasp. *I'm alive. So sorry I made you worry. If I'd had a way to send you a message, I would've.*

His mother sobbed against his chest. *I was so worried. I don't know what I'd do if I lost you.*

You didn't. I'm all right.

He managed to pry himself free from her grasp. His mother gazed up at him. Wrinkles lined her eyes, ringed with tears. Grey streaks wove through her long, dark hair.

When did Mother age so? I need to spend more time with my parents.

She finally relinquished her hold and stepped back. That's when he noticed Sirella standing behind her.

Sirella!

Bassan closed the distance, grinning like a fool. Sirella fell into his arms and he held her tight, drinking in her presence. She uttered not a sound, nor any tears, but excitement radiated from her mind.

I've missed you so much, he thought, holding her close.

I've missed you, she thought, her mental voice above a whisper.

He grasped her shoulders and held her out at arm's length. *Be my mate. Please.*

Her expression broke into one of incredulous joy and her thoughts radiated the same. *Yes!*

Bassan pulled her close and held on tight. *I don't want to be another day without your voice in my head.*

Whenever you're ready.

The sweet smell of her hair in his nose, Bassan sighed. *Tonight.*

Despite the commotion around him, Bassan focused only on her answer.

Yes.

* * *

A week later, a special assembly commenced. Unlike the previous gathering for Bassan's great-uncle, this one radiated eagerness and joy.

The crowd surged close together at the steps of the city chamber. Bassan again thanked his father's former status for their position on the chamber steps and above the crowd. Filled to the brim, the streets of Ktren threatened to burst with residents. They pressed up against the barrier around the steps, the only obstacle between them and the refugees from Ugar. Situated near the entrance and next to his parents, he and Sirella feasted on the view.

I've never seen this many turn out.

Sirella squeezed his hand. *It's a major occasion. Never have so many Kintals entered our cities at once.*

I'm glad First Prefect Ubarce and Prefect Ireth welcomed them. I would've felt horrible if Tgren turned them away.

Her laughter drifted through his mind. *Tgrens turn away valuable skills? Never.*

Bassan smiled, his gaze on the Ugar refugees. *True. They've always taken advantage of any opportunity.*

This is a grand one. Sirella shifted closer and peered up at him. *And you made it all possible.*

A wave of protest rose in his mind. Before it formed a coherent thought, Sirella crushed it. Bassan reeled, still struggling with their new and intimate connection. Unless he shielded tight, his mate heard every emotion.

Do not belittle your part in their escape from Ugar. Your knowledge, skills, and quick wit freed them. If not for you, they would still be stranded on that planet. You made the impossible happen.

A wave of realization hit Bassan. The impossible. He'd accomplished the impossible. Freed hundreds trapped on a planet with no other chance of escape. His actions made it possible. Not a code in his head. His own wits, ability, and power of computation.

Plus a special ability from my parents.

"Former citizens of Jaree on Ugar," First Prefect Ubarce said, projecting his mental voice as well to be heard over the crowd noise. "You have risked your lives and journeyed far to find freedom. We are grateful for the forces that broke you free and brought you to us."

Ubarce paused and glanced in Bassan's direction. Aware of the shift in everyone's focus, Bassan shrank from the attention. A mental push from Sirella and his parents buoyed his confidence though.

"Tgren is an open planet," continued Ubarce. "We know what it's like to be outcasts and on the edge of the world. We welcome diversity and knowledge."

Beside him, Ktren's prefect stepped forward. "And we welcome you as new citizens of the planet Tgren," Ireth said, his joyous voice echoing across the city.

A cheer erupted from the Ugar refugees, followed at once by the Tgren witnesses gathered for the occasion. Bassan cried out in joy, pumping his fist in the air. His gaze locked on Zendar, Bassan shot him a private word of congratulations. His friend, still jumping with excitement, turned to find Bassan.

Thank you. Thank you so much for listening to me even when I made no sense.

You made sense. That's why I followed you down to the planet's surface.

You didn't have to though. And I forced you...

It was my choice, Bassan thought, adding stern reinforcement to his words. *And had I not chosen that path, I wouldn't have discovered I was a jumper.*

Or capable of more than carrying a code in my head.

Gratitude flowed from Zendar, as it did from all the other refugees. No longer refugees, though. They were officially Tgren citizens.

Bassan noticed Liron and her father among those gathered and he sighed. Navent would never experience the freedom her daughter now possessed. At least the girl's future appeared bright. Liron would flourish here.

Our family will flourish as well, Sirella thought.

Bassan gulped and spun her closer. Sirella laughed. *Not now! Eventually.*

The group on the steps began to disperse. A clasp on his shoulder jolted Bassan back to reality.

"Well done, my son."

Bassan turned to see his father. Dark eyes greeted him, along with a myriad of emotions. His father thanked him on many levels. It filled Bassan's chest will joy.

"Thank you, Father, Mother," he said, nodding to his mother who clung tight her mate.

"I think I'm finally done filling out reports on this event," his father said. *And managed to avoid the exact truth of how you kept the probe from firing.*

His shoulders eased and Bassan offered a smile of thanks. *I hope no one ever finds out.*

Someone might crack the code one day. But for right now, everyone wants to know more about your connection with our past. Your position on Mevine's team is secure for a long time.

Maybe one day it will be my team.

His father offered a sly smile. *I suspect it will.*

A hand slapped down on Bassan's shoulder. "There's our adventurer!"

He spun around and discovered Sirella's brother Tarn, with Drent a step behind.

"And I thought I was the reckless one," added Drent, gesturing to the mechanical device wrapped around his leg that allowed him to walk while still healing.

A flicker of guilt escaped from Bassan. Drent shook his head.

I told you to forget about it, Drent thought. *You reacting a few seconds faster wouldn't have saved my broken leg.*

Bassan started to protest but refrained. "How I didn't break every bone in my body during my adventure, I'll never know."

Zendar joined them, a silly grin on his face. Bassan didn't need to read his mind to know what tickled his funny bone. Bassan pointed a finger at his new friend.

"Especially when we jumped from that Narcon garbage ship."

Zendar snickered. "I'm not sure I'd call it jumping." He offered a wink. "Now what you did on our ship, teleporting it like you did, now that was jumping."

"Yes, we still need to test your jumping ability," Bassan's father said. Bassan eyed him anxiously and his father waved his hand. "But not today. Go enjoy the celebrations."

"Yes, there's a feast prepared in the town center," his mother added. "Plus there will be dancing."

"What are we waiting for, then?" Zendar said. "I'm ready for a party."

Bassan turned to Sirella. "Ready to dance with me?"

She closed the distance and her lips pressed against his.

I've been ready to dance with you for years.

The end

About the Author

Alex J. Cavanaugh has a Bachelor of Fine Arts degree and works in web design and graphics. He is experienced in technical editing and worked with an adult literacy program for several years. A fan of all things science fiction, his interests range from books and movies to music and games. Online he is known as Ninja Captain Alex and is the founder of the Insecure Writer's Support Group. His books are Amazon Best Sellers and winners of the Pinnacle Book Achievement Award. Currently the author lives in the Carolinas with his wife.

www.alexjcavanaugh.com
www.insecurewriterssupportgroup.com
www.twitter.com/AlexJCavanaugh

Other great science fiction titles!

Blood Red Sand
By Damien Larkin

"I'm awed by Damien Larkin's imagination... So truly Heinlein."
– Phil Parker, author

Mars will run red with Nazi blood...

Print ISBN 9781939844781
eBook ISBN 9781939844798

Lost Helix
By Scott Coon

"...the ride is an entertaining one."
– SF Reviews - Don D'Ammassa

Lost Helix is the key...

Print ISBN 9781939844682
eBook ISBN 9781939844699

Revolution 2050
By Jay Chalk

"Revolution 2050 has a valuable message behind it."
– Sierra Decker, Andromeda Spaceways

Samuel Moore is living a dystopian lie...

Print ISBN 9781939844439
eBook ISBN 9781939844446

CPSIA information can be obtained
at www.ICGtesting.com
Printed in the USA
LVHW032053020721
691720LV00001B/51